Our Secret Circle

By
Tecia McLaughlin

About the Author

Tecia McLaughlin is a 57-year-old author, business owner, and public speaker. She joined the US Army at the age of 17 and was stationed in Germany as a Counter-Intelligence Agent/German Linguist. Her military experience provided a foundation for her role as a German Exchange Student while earning her BA in Marketing at Troy University.

She has been married to her soulmate for 35 years and has one daughter. At the age of 50, she embarked on a new journey by starting a beach wedding business and becoming a wedding photographer. She enjoys long walks on the beach and spending with her three dogs and family.

DEDICATION	7
OUR SECRET CIRCLE	8
CHAPTER ONE	1
Braydee	1
CHAPTER TWO	14
CHAPTER THREE	26
Duke	26
CHAPTER FOUR	42
CHAPTER FIVE	61
CHAPTER SIX	75
CHAPTER SEVEN	86
(The Girl's Trip)	86
CHAPTER EIGHT	97
CHAPTER NINE	105
CHAPTER TEN	119
Duke	119

CHAPTER ELEVEN	**129**
Duke	129
CHAPTER TWELVE	**138**
CHAPTER THIRTEEN	**153**
Braydee	153
CHAPTER FOURTEEN	**160**
Braydee	160
CHAPTER FIFTEEN	**167**
Braydee	167
CHAPTER SIXTEEN	**179**
CHAPTER SEVENTEEN	**186**
CHAPTER EIGHTEEN	**201**
CHAPTER NINETEEN	**218**
Braydee	218
CHAPTER TWENTY	**229**
CHAPTER TWENTY-ONE	**239**
CHAPTER TWENTY-TWO	**251**

CHAPTER TWENTY-THREE	260
CHAPTER TWENTY-FOUR	273
CHAPTER TWENTY-FIVE	286
CHAPTER TWENTY-SIX	293
CHAPTER TWENTY-SEVEN	304
CHAPTER TWENTY-EIGHT	324
CHAPTER TWENTY-NINE	331
CHAPTER THIRTY	338
SIX MONTHS LATER	346
CHAPTER THIRTY-ONE	348

Copyright © 2023 Tecia McLaughlin

All rights reserved.

No portion of this book may be reproduced in any form without written permission from the publisher or author except as permitted by U.S. copyright law

Dedication

This book is dedicated to anyone who is missing a child today. Maybe they were kidnapped like the children in this story, but maybe they made a choice to leave on their own under difficult circumstances. It's possible that you lost a child to miscarriage, and you grieve daily. Whatever the case is, you are not alone. As you read this book, I hope you'll feel the love I'm sharing with you through the pages.

Our Secret Circle

Chandler Grey arrived at the office at 7:45 and headed to the break room. He lingered there as long as possible, hoping to find Braydee, but she never showed up. The words she had spoken to him yesterday had sent a chill down his spine. The pain in her eyes was instantly recognizable. It was a look he had seen in the eyes of his late wife in the months leading up to her suicide.

"Help me!"

He went to his computer and began to search the employee data list. There was no one working at the company by the name of Braydee Quinn.

He conducted a Google search, hoping to find any clue that would reveal her identity. A multitude of news articles surfaced, sending shivers down his spine. This explained the terror he had seen in her eyes. Braydee Quinn was a missing person, and her whereabouts were being searched for by people all over the world.

When the fingerprints of a local police officer are discovered in the abandoned car of a missing woman, the small town of Orange Beach, Alabama, erupts in rumors. Forced into hiding for his own safety, the officer is confronted with shocking accusations that tear a family apart. As the investigation narrows in on a local judge, a horrifying revelation emerges that no one expected.

Chapter One

Braydee

Sometimes events in our lives are clearly mapped out, and we know exactly which direction we're headed. Other times, we go left when we should've gone right.

This was the year my life was catapulted into darkness. I have asked myself a million times, "Why me?" Surely God knew someone else on this planet who was better equipped to deal with the extreme circumstances I found myself thrust into. On this day, I followed my gut into the danger zone. Still, if I could change anything, I wouldn't.

It was Saturday night, and I was sitting at a little hole-in-the-wall dump called The Undertow in Orange Beach, Alabama. It's the kind of place you go to either disappear from anyone who knows you or to be the star of the show with a couple of seventy-year-old drunks who look like their arms are a part of the bar, dark brown, wrinkled, and crusty from way too many years of fishing.

I took my seat at the far end of the room so that I could watch TV and mind my own business. There were roughly thirty people there, and they all seemed to be regulars intermingling with different groups and joining each other's conversations.

As quickly as I sat down, I found myself wishing I hadn't come in, but I didn't hate it enough to leave. I must admit, I was somewhat amused and entertained by the mannerisms of some of the men and the general vibe of the place.

The volume of noise swelled and subsided, punctuated by roars of laughter like waves from the ocean. I ordered a Bloody Mary from a Jamaican waitress and wondered how in the world she had ended up here.

My drink arrived, and I sat fumbling with the olive and celery, trying to decide which I would eat first while eavesdropping on the characters near me.

As I sat studying my rim salt, dissecting what ingredients had been used, the door opened. In walked a beautiful redhead with milky white skin. She was young and clearly out of place. She sat at the tall bistro table just within earshot of me.

I could see her young face under the ceiling light near the pool table. She stared at her phone, her thumbs flying rapidly across the tiny keyboard. Was she upset, angry, or happy? I couldn't tell.

It was my habit to guess what the emotions of those around me were. I love to people-watch. I studied her closely. Her expression was stoic. I knew she must have felt a bit like me, though, just trying to hide away for the evening and not be bothered by anyone.

As I continued my study of this girl and the other decrepit people in the bar, a man walked up to her table.

"You look too young to be in a place like this." He was extra boisterous and annoying.

"I'm old enough," said the redhead.

"Then let me buy you a drink."

"No, thank you. I'm good."

"You aren't drinking?"

"Not at the moment. I'm waiting on someone." She continued to stare at her phone.

I couldn't be sure, but she seemed to have a Slavic accent. She continued.

"He'll be here soon."

"Well, he's not here now."

He laughed so loud that the other men turned to see what was happening. He leaned down as if to tell her something private. She scowled and turned away.

She looked back at her phone and began to type. He reached down, took her phone, and laid it on the table.

"It's rude to text while someone is talking to you. Everybody knows that. Look at me, girl."

I watched in disgust as he laid her phone on the table. She bit her bottom lip and looked up at the man.

He stood there for a few seconds and continued to talk to her in a low voice that I couldn't make out. She shook her head again. What had he said to her?

I was so very curious. Before I could hear anything else, the band took the stage and began to play. I kept my eye on the girl. Something felt very wrong. The man began to walk away, then suddenly he turned back and picked up her phone and stuck it in his pocket. I could hear him yell back over his shoulder, "If you want your phone back, you'll have to let me buy you a drink."

He laughed loudly as if it were the funniest thing he'd ever done. It was a peculiar laugh, dry and rough. It was like the sound a car makes when you're trying to crank it with a dead battery. It rang out over the music with the most grating sound imaginable. I made mental notes. Weird laugh. A mermaid drinking beer tattooed on his arm.

"Stay in your lane, Braydee." I kept repeating the phrase to myself. This is not your business, your town, or your bar.

The other men laughed along with him as he returned to the bar and took his seat. I imagined the stench of his foul breath and smoky clothes. I nearly gagged just thinking about him being so close to her young face.

As I focused on minding my own business, with one eye on the girl and the other on the men at the bar, another man approached her. This one sat down at her table. He was barely moving his lips, but I knew by the look on her face that he was spewing something she didn't want to hear.

He reached across the table and took her hand. She made no attempt to resist, which was odd. I would have gotten loud and embarrassed him until he got up and left. Instead, she just nodded as he spoke. He walked back to the bar.

I was worried and intrigued. I wanted to just walk over and say, "Hey, don't let these idiots intimidate you." But I didn't. I just sat there, secretly watching, and telling myself it wasn't my business.

She grabbed her purse and headed to the restroom. Two of the men gawked as she walked by. They quickly flagged down the bartender, paid their tabs, and gulped down their drinks.

My heart began to race.

I pulled out a twenty-dollar bill and laid it on the table. My gut said to get up, but I didn't follow my gut right away. Why didn't I just get up and tell her I thought she was in danger?

I watched as she walked outside. I knew I needed to follow her to make sure she made it safely to her car. If only I had known that this one small decision would completely flip my world on its axis and smash my life into a million tiny pieces.

As I moved across the parking lot, I heard a scream and saw a flash of red hair as the girl was being stuffed into the trunk of a black Chrysler 300. I could hear the muffled screams and her beating against the inside of the trunk as I stupidly ran toward them with no weapon or means to help either of us. The two men jumped into the car and sped away.

I quickly jumped into my car to follow them while frantically calling 911.

"911. What's your emergency?"

"I just witnessed a kidnapping outside this bar called The Undertow!" I screeched.

"Where are you now?"

"Following them on Canal Road towards The Wharf."

"Thank you. Are you close enough to get a tag number?"

"No. They know I'm following them, though. Please hurry! They're turning. We just turned next to the big Ferris wheel where the palm trees are."

"You're now on Beach Expressway. You should see a toll booth soon."

"Yes, I see it. I still see the car."

"What kind of car is it? Don't get too close, ma'am."

"It's a black Chrysler 300."

"What are you driving, ma'am?"

"It's a rental car. Ummm. It's a red Ford Fusion." I couldn't think straight. I wondered if the redhead was still screaming and banging inside the trunk. Surely the toll operator would hear her and not raise the gate!

The gate was raised, and the car passed through with a nod from the booth operator.

"Oh, God! They just raised the gate arm and let them through!"

"Officers are en route now. What's your name?"

"Braydee Quinn. They've got to hurry!"

"Where are you from?"

"I'm from Waco, Texas."

"Can you describe the men who took the girl?"

"Mid-forties. Both were heavy-set. Average height. One was wearing a ball cap. Both have brown hair."

"Is there anything you can tell me about either one of them that would distinguish them? Tattoo or scars?"

"I noticed that one had a tattoo on his forearm. It was a mermaid. I saw it clearly when he took the girl's phone from her. He has a weird laugh. Sounded like a dead motor trying to start."

"This is all very good information. Can you still see the car?"

"Yes. How far away are the police? I don't hear any sirens. Oh, God!"

"That's okay, ma'am. We're tracking your phone location. Just stay with me. We'll find them."

I was crying. My heart was pounding so hard.

"Dear God, help her! Help her!" I was praying out loud on the phone to God, but the operator was the one responding.

"We're doing everything we can. Stay on the line. Don't get too close. You could be in serious danger if they see you're still following them."

"I'm sure they realize the same car has been behind them since they pulled out."

"You need to stay back, ma'am."

I had been following them for more than fifteen minutes.

"We're turning."

"Do you see what road it is?"

"It's not showing on my GPS. It's a small road off of this main expressway." There was no response. "Hello? Are you there?" Nothing. I had lost service.

We drove down a very dark, long, and winding road. There were no lights anywhere. Without warning, I ran over something and completely lost control of my car. The car was violently shaking and rumbling, and I went barreling off the road and into the brush, ramming into the ditch before I came to a stop. My head hit the steering wheel, and the window shattered from a tree branch. That's when everything went black.

I woke up to someone slapping me in the face and dragging me out of my car. It was a police officer. I immediately felt safer. I was bleeding from a piece of glass that had cut my forearm.

"Put her in the van," said the man with the funny laugh from the bar.

I was too weak and disoriented to resist. "Stop! Let go!" I screamed. My futile attempts at breaking free only served to cause more pain. I screamed loudly enough for anyone within a football field's radius to hear me.

"There's no one around here, so you can quit screaming."

I swung my arms and landed my hand on the face of one of the men, scratching him as hard as I could on whatever skin I could feel. He twisted my arm behind me like it was Play-Doh. I couldn't move.

I continued to kick and scream with all my might, but it was useless. I was held down with my face against the bottom of the van floor.

"What are you doing?" I screamed. "Why are you doing this?" Fear and adrenaline had me writhing and screaming like a wild animal. I was certain I was about to be raped.

They flipped me over and held my arms together while the police officer zip-tied my hands and feet. I knew then that our chances of being rescued were over. Maybe this was the officer sent by the 911 operator. I was dizzy with crazy thoughts.

"That's a nasty cut you got there," said Officer Duke Davis. "Let me get something for that."

I screamed. An inhuman noise, like nothing I had ever heard, came tearing out of my throat, and the officer jumped.

"That sounded demonic," he said.

"You're all demons!" I continued screaming until one of the men slapped me across the face.

The officer returned to his patrol car, retrieved a first-aid kit, and headed back toward the van but was reprimanded by one of the other men.

"We don't have time for you to play doctor," he said.

"But she's bleeding."

"So?"

"So, if something happens to her while she's in custody, you're responsible."

"Custody?" The funny laugh pierced my soul. If I escaped from this, I would listen for that laugh every day until the day I died. "Whatever, man. Make it quick," he said.

The officer disinfected my cut and placed a large bandage on it. Ironically, I couldn't help but notice his tenderness. I had just been wrangled and hogtied, yet this guy was washing my wound as if he cared.

I noted the number on the side of his police car was 428.

"That's a pretty bad bump she has there. It could be a concussion. She needs to be seen by medical ASAP." He rubbed his hand over my forehead, and I jerked away.

"Right," said the big man. "I'm sure there's a medical team waiting to make sure she's in tip-top shape." He laughed again, and the other guy in the bar laughed with him.

"Just hurry up! We don't have time for all this."

One of the men yelled to someone around the corner. "Get in the van!"

The redheaded girl appeared, stepped into the van, and sat down across from me. They zip-tied her hands and feet without a struggle and closed the door. It was pitch black inside and stunk of urine and something so foul I gagged once the door was shut.

"Are you okay?" I said in the dark.

The redhead didn't answer. I saw she was very young. Maybe seventeen? Maybe younger. "Did you see me earlier at the bar where you were taken?"

Still, she said nothing.

"Are you hurt? Did they hurt you? What's your name?"

No response. Just the low rumbling sound of the van pulling away.

"Why won't you answer me? I'm here to help you," I said in utter frustration.

Tied up and bandaged, I realized I didn't inspire much confidence. I sat praying to God that He would help me remember every detail of this night. The laugh. The tattoos. The van. The officer's face and the number on the side of his police car. The redheaded girl across from me.

There were no sirens. No police chasing us. Why? Where were we headed? How did I go from sitting at my computer in my condo to being tied up in the back of a van just a few hours later?

After several hours of driving the girl finally spoke.

"Lucy Kravchenko is my name."

I could barely hear her over the roaring of the highway. "What did you say?"

"My name is Lucy."

"I'm Braydee. We're going to be okay, Lucy."

"No, we're not." The words were cold and deliberate as if she knew something I didn't.

"I called 911. I followed you from the bar. The police were on their way when I crashed. They have my cell phone pings, and they're looking for us. They'll find us."

"No, they won't." There was something so unusual about her cold, stark words. They cut me so deep that I suddenly believed her instead of what I was saying and began to shake.

"Why do you say that? You've got to speak positively and believe. It's fate that I saw you leave the bar and followed you. You would be alone right now. We have each other."

Lucy lowered her eyes. "Fate? Is that what you want to call it? What was your name again?" Her foreign accent was noticeably strong.

"Braydee. You can call me Bray."

"Okay, Bray. I'm seventeen years old. I didn't go to that bar to get a drink or get a burger. I wasn't waiting on anyone. I was told to go there. I was told where to sit. I was told when to leave by the very men who are holding us in this van. I didn't go into the restaurant to get anything. They made me go in so that they could get you. How old are you, Bray?"

I couldn't speak. I had no words. Panic and utter fear swept through my veins.

"W-wh-what?" was all I managed to mutter.

"I'm sorry. I don't have any choices. I do what they say."

"What are you talking about?"

"I work for these men. I have been working since I was fifteen years old." Her voice was slow and deliberate, quivering with sadness in every word.

"Where are you from? How do you work for them?" I was afraid of the answer, but still, I had to ask.

"I'm from Ukraine. The people come to us at the orphanage and promise to give us work. We have no choices when we leave the orphanage, so we believe them."

"So, you've been in America for two years?"

"Yes."

"Doing what?"

"I'm what they call a recruiter. They use me to lure people like you into dangerous situations so that you will be taken. It never fails. So many good ladies in America are ready to help."

"Random people?"

"Usually, it's random children and teenagers. I'm not sure why you're special, but we have been following you for a very long time."

"What? Where have you been following me?"

"We followed you near your job in Waco, Texas for a few weeks. Then we followed you to Panama City, Florida last week. We could never find time to see you alone. You're usually a very careful person."

"You've been watching me for weeks?"

"That is nothing for a time. We watch some people for months before we know we can catch them. Only one other time I have seen a person close to your age we catch." The more she spoke the more it was clear how broken her English really was. "We normally only take children, no more than thirteen years old."

"Then why me?"

"I don't know exactly. I have heard them speak of you. I pretend not to listen. You have a special job at the university, and I think they need you for something."

"I'm a biomedical research scientist. I'm not sure how that's going to benefit anyone outside of a lab."

"I don't know. It was confusing, and I didn't understand the words many times. I heard them say "you will help make new body parts or organs for people."

My body went limp. All I could do was roll over on my side and cry. I would figure out what questions I needed to ask when I could think more clearly.

We rode for what seemed like twenty-four hours. I dozed in and out of sleep and urinated on myself several times until I was too dehydrated to even pee.

The van stopped, and the doors opened.

"Get out."

I couldn't walk on my own. My knees gave way, and my hungry stomach cramped with pain. I buckled over and was pulled up by one of the men.

"Keep walking."

"I'm trying." The words barely squeaked out of my throat. I looked around and Lucy was gone. I didn't see her leave, nor did I hear her make any sounds. She was just gone.

Chapter Two

They brought me to a house that looked like any other house in a nice neighborhood. We entered through the front door and walked down a long hall. At the end of the hall, there were stairs leading down to a huge metal door with several bolts, locks, and combinations to an underground room.

There was no point in struggling or even asking questions. I had nowhere to go if I were to break free from the massive grasp of the man holding me.

He squeezed my neck as he pushed me forward. I stumbled into a dark room. A light was flipped on, and inside the chamber were seven young faces sitting around on a concrete floor.

Chains and handcuffs bound their arms. They squinted at the sudden light.

There was an awful stench of body fluids and feces mixed with rottenness that I had never smelled before. My stomach wrenched, and I dry heaved. There was nothing in my stomach to throw up.

The horror before my eyes was quickly snuffed out when the light was extinguished. I found myself standing in complete darkness. The door shut behind me. All I could do was feel around for an empty place to sit. I touched the heads of some of the girls as I felt for a free space. I felt someone touch my hand and tug gently for me to sit next to them. I sat.

There were whimpers and cries and someone was muttering something. I cried too. The tears started, and I couldn't stop them. They flowed, and my body shivered. Not because I was cold. I just couldn't stop shaking. In the dark, I felt a touch on my shoulder. The small hand patted me gently, then rubbed my arm. The sweet hand of a child. Soft. There were no words. Only the gentle touch. It made me sob even more.

I don't remember sleeping, but morning came without me knowing, so I must have slept. The light was seeping in around the top of the holding chamber. I could see the girls around me clearly now. If I had to guess, they all ranged between six and thirteen years of age.

A voice boomed out. "Get on your feet. We're moving. Everyone needs to stay behind the person in front of you. If you look anywhere except at the back of the head of the person in front of you, you will be thrown back into the holding chamber. You will not speak. You will not move unless I tell you to move. Now line up and follow the man in the orange shirt."

The voice was harsh and full of hate. We followed the man in orange up the stairs, out the back door, and across a long field to a concrete house. It looked a lot like a bunkhouse I had seen at some of the camps I had attended as a child. It wasn't a nice house, but it wasn't particularly out of place either. I wanted to look around, but I didn't dare. I kept my face straight ahead.

"Stop!"

We all stopped.

"When you enter this house, you will show reverence and humility. You will not speak unless you're spoken to. Do you understand?"

We all nodded our heads. "You will be able to shower, and put on clean clothes, and you will be given a bunk that will be yours for however long you're here. You'll no longer be called by your name. You'll go by a letter of the alphabet." He rattled off letters A-H.

"If I hear any one of you telling anyone your real name, you will spend a week alone with no food in the chamber you just left. Do you understand me?" Again, we all nodded.

"You will find your clothing on your bunk." He pointed at me and said, "G, step forward."

I didn't move. My name was Braydee Quinn.

"I said, G, step forward." I felt a strap hit my back, and I screamed as I fell forward. "You're G. Pick a letter for the rest of 'em. Your duty is to take care of this house and these kids. You'll feed 'em and be sure they're healthy until they're removed from your care. Do you understand?" I nodded. "This house sits in the middle of 142 acres of woods. There are guards and cameras watching every part of this property. We have cameras inside and outside the house. Follow me."

We walked outside.

"Don't cross any further than that wooden post." He pointed. We all nodded. I looked around for the first time.

"Listen carefully. No one knows you're here. No one is coming for you. No one cares that you're missing. As of this moment, you belong to me. You'll do what we tell you to do, or you'll suffer grave consequences. We have cameras and microphones everywhere, inside and outside of this house. You will be monitored 24/7, and you will do as you're told."

We walked back into the house. "Willis, show them how the alarm sounds." He was speaking to someone behind the camera. The siren rang out, and we held our ears until it stopped. He closed the door as he left without another word.

We stood there, dumbfounded. Just completely lost in a tiny house. I felt the eyes of the youngest girls looking at me, and I forced a half smile. I shoved my fear down deep and that's where it was going to stay.

"It's going to be okay. We're going to be okay." I wanted so badly to believe that. "Let's start with those showers. Someone check to see how many showers we have. I'll go see what food is in the kitchen. Let's get cleaned up."

I was moving on autopilot.

There was hot water and soap, fresh towels, and washcloths. Each of us showered and put on the frumpy floral dresses that we had been provided. They were all way too big for all of us, and I knew this was just another way of stripping our identity.

The food in the kitchen was plenty enough to feed us all for weeks, but I wasn't sure how long it needed to last. We all agreed to eat sparingly.

I boiled pasta and added spaghetti sauce. I opened a can of chicken and chopped it up adding it to the mix. Standing at the counter, I could feel a small body next to my leg.

"Hi. What's your name?"

"My name is Katrina."

Her tiny voice was so sweet, but an alarm immediately screeched, and we held our ears to shut out the sound. Just that quickly, I had forgotten. It lasted for more than a minute, and we all stood frozen with fear. Several minutes after the siren stopped, a man walked in that stood a little more than five feet tall. His features were scrunched like a gargoyle, and he was very fat and bald-headed.

"You will not say your names out loud to anyone!! Do you hear me?! You will be known as the letter you are. We have eyes and ears all around this place and DON'T forget it! This is your only warning." As quickly as he entered, he exited.

The realization that we were being watched hit, and I began to shake inside. I bent down and hugged Katrina, who would now be known as B. Another child hugged my back and then another came from the side of the room. We held each other tightly, and I fought back the overwhelming desire to break down and cry. Instead, I began to pray.

"Dear God, I know you see us. I know you love us. I know you can rescue us. Give us the strength we need to survive these monsters!" I said it loudly. I wanted the men to hear me. One small voice said, "Amen."

I hugged the three little girls who were clinging to me. "Someone IS looking for us, someone IS coming for us, and we'll ALL survive this together." I waited for the siren, but nothing happened."

We all gathered around the table, and I served the pasta I had just cooked.

"If you don't mind, please don't start eating until we're all served, and I sit down. I know you're hungry, but please wait." They nodded.

I sat.

"Do any of you ever say the blessing before you eat?"
One child nodded yes.

"Well, would you like to say it today?"

"Okay."

"Your letter will be C. C stands for courageous. I'll call you Courageous." The girl smiled.

"Bless this food, God, and bless all those that are about to eat it. Dig in."

As we ate, I began to study the faces of the children in front of me. Each one, from this day forward, would be called something other than their name.

"I have an idea. Instead of me calling you a letter, I'm going to call you a word that starts with your letter."

"What if we get in trouble?"

"Let's give it a try and see. A is for Adventurous, B is Brave, C for Courageous, D for Daring, E for Exceptional, F for Fearless, G for Grace, that's me, and H is for Helper." No sirens.

There was silence, and then one child spoke. "You're like Snow White, and we're the seven dwarfs." She smiled.

"I guess I am, in a way." I liked that.

I tried hard not to stare at the frightened children around the table, but I wanted to memorize their faces along with their new names. There wasn't any conversation. We just ate very quickly and quietly.

After lunch, everyone was given a job, and we worked together to get the kitchen cleaned.

While drying the dishes, my mind raced back to the years I tried so hard to have children. For more than five years I had taken pregnancy tests and tried so hard to do everything just as the doctor instructed, but nothing worked.

I was married right out of college to the love of my life, Marco. He was from a big Italian family, and we started trying to have children right away. It was just expected that we would have a large family. After five years of marriage and still no kids, we decided to see a doctor. It was then that they found a rare disorder in my fallopian tube; the reason I was unable to carry a pregnancy to term.

I remember the day, the hour, and the minute that the doctor told us the sad news. I was wearing a purple V-neck sweater and black slacks, and my husband was wearing a red and blue plaid button-down shirt. When we came home from the doctor, I put the sweater in a box and put it at the top of my closet. It would forever serve as a memorial; A grave for all the unborn babies I had lost over the years and the ones I could never have.

Something changed between me and Marco that day. When we got home, I went straight to bed. I couldn't face him because I knew his worst fear was coming true. I couldn't give him the family he always wanted.

That night when he climbed into bed, I remember touching his back and saying, "Marco. I'm sorry." I had hoped he would roll over and say, "We'll get through this together," but he didn't even respond.

That night I curled up into the fetal position and just cried. I thought he would at least comfort me, but he didn't. He was broken and lost himself, and I was part of the problem.

After about an hour of us both lying there silently sobbing, Marco got up and put on his clothes. I heard the door open and shut and his car pulled out of the driveway. I wondered then if he would even come back to get his belongings, or would he just pull away and start over somewhere. Just leave and forget the past and start over with a woman who could give him the family he'd always wanted.

It was well after midnight when I heard him come in. I hadn't slept. He eased into bed and slipped in quietly behind me. He wrapped his arms around me and snuggled into me so tightly that I could feel our hearts thumping together.

"I'm so very sorry, Braydee. I'm sorry I've pressured you. I'm sorry my family has made it seem that having a big family is the only way to live a happy life. I'm sad and I'm broken, but if you will forgive me, we can be happy without children. Just me, you, and a couple of dogs. I love you, Braydee."

"Do you really believe we can be happy together without kids, or are you just trying to convince yourself?"

"I do."

"I believe you. I love you with all my heart and you know that, right?"

"Yes," said Marco.

"But your family doesn't love me like you do. I know the pressure they have put on us having a big family."

"As long as we love each other, we'll get through this."

I pulled his face close to mine and we kissed.

"I was so sad when you left tonight, Marco."

"I'm sorry. I just kind of lost it. I didn't know what else to do but to drive around and try to clear my head."

I could feel the heaviness in his words, and I could tell his head wasn't really clear yet.

"We're going to be okay," I whispered.

"Of course, we are," he whispered back.

I knew he wanted to believe what he was saying, but once his family found out, the pressure would be on him to make a choice. I wasn't so sure that choice would be me. Tears continued to puddle on our pillows. Both of us knew the pain of that diagnosis and what it meant for the rest of our lives. Both of us knew that when we woke up, our lives would be on a different trajectory from now on.

The next morning, Marco had the coffee made and was sitting at the table working on his iPad, just as he had done so many mornings before. I kissed him as I passed, just as I did every morning, but it was a sad kiss. Looking back, it was a kiss goodbye. I could feel it, even if he didn't know it yet.

Less than six months later, he asked me for a divorce, and just like that I was single again at twenty-eight years old. I never doubted that Marco loved me. I just wasn't enough for him, not with a barren womb. He needed and wanted more. Society, family, and outside influences had convinced him that having children of his own was very important, and adopting just wasn't the same.

"Braydee, I need to talk to you," said Marco.

"Okay. Let's sit." I already knew what he was about to say. Call it a woman's intuition.

"Do you know how much I love you?"

"Yes, of course. Hold on. Can you give me just a minute? I'll be right back."

I could feel the tears coming, but I wouldn't let him see me cry. I clenched my teeth, breathed in through my nose, and left the room.

I went to my closet and pulled out the purple V-neck sweater I had worn when we got the awful news that I couldn't have a baby. I put it on with the pajama pants I was wearing, and I came back to the table and sat down.

"What were you saying?"

"Why did you put that on? What's going on?"

"What were you about to say, Marco? Just continue. You were saying that you love me."

"I do. With all my heart. I always will, Braydee."

"But?"

"But I want kids of my own."

"How dare you. You know I want the same thing. What if it were you with the problem? Do you think I would leave you? No! Never!"

"You don't know what you would do."

"Yes, I do, and if you loved me, you wouldn't be leaving me right now."

"I do love you. I just..."

"You don't have to explain. I understand completely. Don't expect me to say I love you too and it's fine. I'm going to cry and have tons of regrets, but I promise you, I'll be okay."

I got up and emptied both of our coffee cups. I don't even know if he was done drinking his. It didn't matter. I just needed him to go and go quickly. He followed me to the sink and tried to grab my hand, but I jerked away.

"I don't want you to hate me and think I'm a piece of crap for leaving you."

23

"That's not what I think of you. I think you're a weak man who has decided that having me by your side until 'death do you part' isn't enough. You've made the choice to take another chance on a woman you may not love as much in hopes that she will give you a family. I'll be good though. I promise."

"Braydee."

"Braydee, what? Don't be like this. Do you remember the last time I wore this sweater?"

"No. Why?"

"I didn't think you would, but I'll never forget it. I'll never forget the smell of mint on the doctor's breath, the plaid shirt you were wearing, and this purple sweater! The dying bug that was in the corner barely kicking his legs. The beeping of machines in the hall as you held my hand and said 'It's going to be OK.' Yea, I remember it all, Marco. This moment will forever be etched in my timeline of pain. Just go."

I didn't need to explain why I kept the sweater. I wasn't going to diminish it by expressing it to him.

I left the room, packed a bag, and slipped on the black slacks that I could still fit into from years before.

I ended up at my girlfriend Tate's house and we planned an annual girls' trip to Panama City Beach, Florida. We've been taking the trip every year since.

The purple sweater no longer made me sad. It turned out to be the one thing that reminded me of *the moment I decided to be okay* with exactly who I was and the future I would create for myself without Marco. The color purple would be my color of strength and a reminder that I was enough just as I am. No one would ever make me feel like I wasn't enough again.

Now, standing in the kitchen surrounded by these children who were helping me clean up, I imagined the way it might have been to have a big family. I thought of what it would be like to love them, laugh with them, teach them to cook and clean, and how to become little ladies.

"Grace?"

"Grace?"

She was talking to me. "Yes?"

"Can we play a game while we're washing the dishes?"

"Of course we can. What do you have in mind?"

"I'm going to pretend that we're at a restaurant and someone has ordered a big plate and a little plate. Then you say 'one big plate and one little plate, coming up' and I'll wash it, and she can dry it."

She pointed to the other girl.

"Okay, let's do it." It wasn't much of a game, but to her it was something. To the rest of us, it was something that kept our minds from the obvious, even if it was only for a few moments.

Chapter Three

Duke

Duke Davis had been an officer for the Baldwin County Police Department for three years. Young and gorgeous, he had tried his hand at being a cowboy, real estate agent, bartender, office manager, and more.

His looks had given him so many opportunities, but he was also married to a federal judge's daughter, so that had helped him open doors as well. Judge John Sands wanted to see his son-in-law successful, but only for his daughter's sake. The judge had never cared much for Duke. He never thought Duke had the smarts necessary to make a good living for his daughter.

Three years ago, he applied to the police academy and was accepted. He had excelled as a police officer and was proud of his position on the force, even though it didn't pay much. Charisma and charm were two of Duke's strongest personality traits.

Duke checked his watch periodically. It was almost time. He drove to the outskirts of Foley, Alabama, and down a long, dark road. He parked out of sight as he waited for the call from his point man. Three hours later, he was still waiting. He didn't mind it. He was used to it. He watched Netflix and sipped a Yuengling.

The call came in.

"We just turned down County Road 12. We're ten minutes away from you. Keep your eyes open and get ready."

"I'm ready."

Ten minutes later the black Chrysler 300 passed with a quick honk. Duke ran to the road and threw out the spike strip tire shredder. Within minutes, Braydee's car crossed the strip, and she spun out of control. The car crashed into the ravine, hitting a tree.

Duke retrieved the spike strip and placed it in his trunk. A white van pulled up next to the car. Duke ran over to the car and opened the door. He pulled Braydee out. She was conscious and muttering about a girl and the car she was following. She said something about the girl being kidnapped. Braydee saw the officer and thought he was there to help.

When she realized he was pulling her towards the van, she began to fight him.

"I need help over here! She's like a rabid dog!" Duke yelled.

The two men came and threw Braydee into the van with the other girl, holding her face down. Duke watched her fighting with everything she had in her.

He wasn't sure what the girls had done, but it had been very clear to him that only a few people in the department knew about this operation and that he was not to speak to anyone about what he was doing. This included his wife. He had been warned that he would lose his job and that his family would be put in danger if he mentioned any part of the operation to anyone. He had promised his father-in-law that he wouldn't tell a soul.

He thought about the conversation with his father-in-law.

"Me and you. That's it, Pops. No one else will know. I promise you from the bottom of my heart I won't let you down."

"Don't make me regret that I picked you for this job, Davis. Don't let our family down," the judge had said.

Duke had no idea what he had agreed to do nor that he had just agreed to kidnap two perfectly innocent people.

"I won't let you down, Pop."

The girls didn't look like typical criminals, but whatever they were a part of was big enough to get the judge involved.

"I'm not sure what you two have done, but you're in a heap of trouble."

Lucy responded with her thick Ukrainian accent.

"We haven't done anything, you son of a beech. You have! I hope to God, they put you under the jail when they find out what you're a part of."

Lucy spat as hard as she could in his direction, but it fell short of reaching him.

"Nice try." He turned his head and spit twice as far as Lucy did. "That's how it's done!"

Duke saw the rings on Braydee's hands as he zip-tied her wrist.

"Fancy rings."

One of the guys grabbed her hands and pulled the rings off her fingers.

"Here you go, Bud. Give 'em to your wife. She'll love 'em."

Duke held out his hand instinctively and took the rings.

Braydee screamed. "Those are from my parents!"

"Looks like these two are ready for transport. Where are they headed?" asked Duke.

"None of your business."

"Well, okay then."

The doors were closed.

Lucy yelled from inside the van, "Be sure your wife knows that you are assisting a human trafficking cartel! You're a disgrace!"

"Shut up!" One of the men banged on the door and the girls jumped.

Duke watched as the van pulled off. He was proud to be a part of something so secretive, but he hated that he couldn't share it with anyone.

He was wide awake with adrenaline rushing through his veins, so he decided not to go home yet.

Duke pulled into the parking lot of The Keg. He sat drinking until two a.m. The more he drank the more he thought about what the redhead had said as they were leaving. Everything about what he had just participated in started to feel off, especially stealing the rings from the woman. Even though he had not actually taken them from her, he was now in possession of them, and that was an all-time low for him. He had heard about other officers taking evidence and stealing from victims, but that had always been a line he swore he wouldn't cross.

The secrecy of the operation had been very different from anything he had ever been a part of. He felt connected to the judge in a different way now, and that part he liked. It was the rest of what he had done that he wasn't so sure of.

He fumbled with his drink, thinking about everything that had just happened.

The redhead had yelled something about a human trafficking cartel from inside the van. Sitting at the bar, he couldn't get the faces of the girls out of his mind.

"Hey, Jenn."

The bartender made her way over to him. "Watch need, Duke?"

"Have you ever been a part of something you thought was a good thing, but you weren't really sure about it and regretted it later?"

"I'm sure I have."

"Something that could have hurt someone.

"I don't know. I would have to think about it. What's on your mind?"

"You know we get involved in all kinds of stuff as police officers, and some of it gets weird."

"I'm sure it does. Just trust your instincts. You'll be okay."

"That's what I'm afraid of. My instincts kicked in around midnight, and I can't shake this feeling. Do you know Judge John Sands?"

"Your wife's dad?"

"Yeah."

"I don't know much about him, but I know who he is. Why?"

"Nothing I can really talk about. Something's got me sort of rattled."

"Sounds like you're talkin' 'bout it."

"I guess I am."

"You want another drink? That always shakes off an instinct," she said jokingly.

"That shakes off more than an instinct. Drinking shakes off all my good sense, and I don't have that much sense to shake off."

Jenn laughed. "When you're that good-looking Duke, you don't have to have a ton of good sense." They both chuckled.

"Thanks, Jenn. I better get out of here. Don't mention my father-in-law to anyone."

"Why would I, Duke?"

He paid his tab and headed out. He needed to make a pit stop first.

He pulled into the post office and went inside. He had been given the key to a post office box a few weeks before by his father-in-law, Judge John Sands.

"It's a great place to stash private things you might need to get to quickly but don't want recorded at the bank. Keep it to yourself, though. There's no reason for Melissa to know you've got it. It's kind of like a lockbox in plain sight, but it's easy because you don't need to show an ID to get to it," said John.

Duke wrapped two of the rings in a napkin, placed them inside an envelope, and stuffed them in a folded McDonald's bag that had cash in it. The other ring, he would give to his wife. The cash was his cut for throwing out the tire shredder and keeping his mouth shut. He ran through the conversation about the operation replaying every word the judge had said to him.

"I've never heard of this kind of money for an undercover job," said Duke.

"Well, you've never played with the big dogs, have you?" said John.

"I guess not."

"You guess not?"

"I mean, no. I haven't."

"Right. There are things that need to be done. Things that can't be done if everyone knows and is talking about it. This is your one chance, Duke. You won't get another one if you blow this. It's high stakes, which means high reward."

"I understand. I'll be ready."

He hadn't been on the force long enough to question the judge. He knew there were sting operations, but he didn't know what else was going on behind the scenes.

Instead of driving home, stumbling in drunk, and waking his wife, Duke decided to stop at his best friend Whit's house. The back door was unlocked, as usual. Duke lay down on the couch, pulling the blanket over his head. This was nothing new, His buddy, Whit, wouldn't be surprised in the least to find him there. Whit Thomas was a high school friend and close confidant.

"Good morning, Man." Whit flipped on the TV.

"Hey, Whit."

"You look rough. Late night, I guess?"

"Too late."

"Your wife called. She was upset."

"What did you tell her?"

"That you were on the couch. What else?"

"Did you tell her when I got here?"

"No. I didn't know when you got here. Would have told her if I knew." Whit had been friends with Duke's wife, Melissa, since grade school. They had been a couple during middle school, but when Duke showed up during their freshman year, everyone had fallen in love with him, including Melissa.

"You have a good wife, Man. You better not take her for granted or you're going to end up single like me. Girls like that are hard to find. I don't know how she puts up with your bull."

"She loves me. I put up with crap, too, you know."

"I'm just sayin'. Staying out drunk is a level of disrespect not too many wives would put up with."

"I was working, okay?"

"Working, my butt. You were working your biceps, chugging beer at The Keg. That's about it."

"Not true. I was on an assignment till nearly midnight. I only went to the bar afterward. Just needed to regroup a bit."

"An assignment?"

"That's right."

"Top secret mission, I'm sure."

"As a matter of fact, it was." Duke sat up and took the glass of orange juice from Whit.

"Yeah, right."

"Why didn't you let me sleep a little longer?"

"Cuz my boy is on the way over. I need you to get up and out. We have a big day planned."

Duke drank his orange juice, reluctantly got up off the couch and headed out.

"Take care of your wife, man, or somebody else will."

"Is that a threat?"

"That's a promise." He slapped Duke's back on the way out and laughed.

"I'm taking care of her. I just bought her a ring yesterday. I'm on my way to give it to her now. Gonna take her on a picnic on the pontoon boat this evening."

Duke pulled up in the driveway and sat there for a few minutes staring at the ring. It was a beautiful sapphire and diamond oval. Very unique with ornate gold strips like a rope around the band. Now where could he say he had gotten it and why? He thought about the jewelry stores but knew it was too risky. He would just say it was from a pawn shop if she asked.

He had been warned by his wife not to stay out again without calling. Things had gotten heated and ugly the last time he had stayed out and come home drunk. This time, he had an excuse. He would blame it on her dad if he could, but John had told him not to mention it to Melissa.

He opened the door. Melissa was seated in the recliner watching an Oprah rerun. She was athletic, kind, and beautiful. A triple threat. Her heart radiated kindness, and she never met a stranger. Duke had pulled her heartstrings from the minute she had met him in the ninth grade.

She turned off the TV and stood up to face him.

"Do you know how much it hurts me when you don't call or text me when you aren't coming home? What's so hard about letting your wife know that you won't be coming home so that she doesn't stare at the clock for hours? I called you four times and left two voicemails."

"I'm sorry. I was working on something important. It's something I couldn't talk about."

"You could have at least told me that much."

"I turned my phone off. I saw your calls this morning. I'm sorry, Babe."

"You're sorry? Sorry for what, exactly?"

"I'm sorry you worried all night. I'm sorry I have a job that makes me keep secrets from my wife. I'm sorry I can't tell you everything I do. I'm sorry I haven't been the man you want me to be, but I love you with all my heart." He leaned in and tried to kiss her. She pulled away.

"Duke, you could've told me you were turning your phone off. I don't ask for much, do I?"

"I know. You're the best, and no, you don't ask for much. I should've told you. I'm sorry."

"Again. You're sorry again."

Duke dropped his head. He was truly ashamed of himself.

"I got you something. Something special. It's a peace offering." He pulled the ring from his pocket. "When you wear it, I want you to look at it and know that out of every woman in the world, you're the only woman for me."

Melissa looked at the ring in disbelief. Disbelief at the timing and how beautiful the ring was.

He continued.

"It doesn't matter how drunk I get or how late I stay out, there isn't another woman in this world that could turn me on like you do."

"Duke. This isn't about another woman or jealousy, for God's sake." She was upset, and he continued to apologize. "I've had a wake-up call. I swear. If my job is going to interfere with us, I'll find a new job."

"It's not your job. It's you. You are being irresponsible. You not calling. You making me worry!"

He took her hand and slipped the ring on her ring finger, but it was too loose. She moved it to another finger, and it fit perfectly.

"It's beautiful. Thank you. I wish I could be a little more grateful right now."

"I understand."

"This won't work a second time, Duke. I'm so tired of this."

"I know."

"You have a dangerous job. It worries me when you're out and I don't know if you're dead or alive. It's just that simple."

"I'll call. I promise you. This ring is a symbol that I'm turning over a new leaf! Never again. I swear."

"Where did you get this?"

"At the pawn shop."

She assumed it was from a pawn shop because she knew Duke often looked for guns at the shop nearby.

"It's stunning."

"So are you." He pulled her in for a kiss and this time she didn't resist.

"Do you even know how much I love you, Duke?"

"I think so, because that's how much I love you." They held each other in a warm embrace, swaying back and forth.

"Do you have anything planned this afternoon? Mom has asked us over to cook out. I told 'em yes, assuming you didn't have other plans without me."

"I was hoping we could go out on the pontoon later. Just the two of us. But if that's what you'd rather do, I'm good. I need to sleep a bit first." Duke kissed her on the head and pulled away.

"Go ahead and rest. I may ride over early, and you can join us later."

"Sounds good."

Duke lay in his bed, pondering the words the redhead had said to him. *Human trafficking.* What would make her say something like that to him? So specific. He tried shaking it off. Criminals would say anything to take the blame off themselves. Still, he had heard the chatter about trafficking activity along the coast for years.

Melissa's dad, Judge John Sands, was a huge man. He was around six feet tall and full of lard. His cheeks jiggled when he spoke, and his fingers were as thick as stuffed beef sausages. He had a red face that always seemed to be sweaty, even on a cold day, and a cock eye that he couldn't control. He was good to Duke, but the truth was, he never cared much for him.

Melissa sat at the table visiting with her family and waiting for Duke to join them. When he finally arrived, the mood instantly changed. Judge Sands became stern and less himself. Melissa noticed it and brought it up to her dad once they were alone.

"I don't know why Duke can't see the chatty father that I get to see. You're always so strait-laced when he's around."

"I don't want to let my guard down. I want him to see me the way he sees me, and that's it. We have boundaries."

Duke strolled up and patted John on the back.

"Pops, it's good to see you."

"Likewise. Are you doing okay?"

Duke suddenly felt a special bond with the Judge. "I've been busy taking care of all kinds of things."

The judge whipped his head around and gave Duke a death stare. He wasn't about to try to decipher banter from Duke.

"What kind of things?" He gritted his jaw in displeasure at having to carry on with his daughter's husband of five years now. 'Idiot' he said in his mind and hoped everyone around had not heard it out loud.

"All kinds of stuff happening around Baldwin County. I stay busy."

The news was playing on the TV near the grill, and Melissa, who was paying attention to the news, started commenting on it.

"Oh, my God! Are you guys hearing this? A woman called 911 last night because a girl was being kidnapped from The Undertow. She followed the kidnappers and ended up having a wreck, and now she's missing!"

The 911 call was being aired and there were subtitles marching across the bottom of the TV screen.

Melissa's mom, Rhonda, spoke first. "This town is turning into Miami! There are rumors of a human smuggler ring right along the coast. What's next? The cartel?"

"Seriously, Mom! I know. It's scary."

Duke glanced over at his father-in-law. "What did the girls look like?"

"I'm not sure. They aren't releasing any information yet."

'Dear God! I hope one of the girls wasn't redheaded' he thought to himself.

For Duke, the BBQ had just taken a turn. He felt queasy and ready to leave, but he didn't. He could feel the heaviness between him and the judge.

During dinner, Rhonda noticed the ring on Melissa's finger. "Honey! That is absolutely gorgeous! When did you get that?"

"Oh, my gosh. I completely forgot to show you." She slipped it off her finger and passed it to her mom. "Duke gave it to me today. I just love it. It's so unique!"

"Probably an heirloom piece," said Rhonda.

"Where did you get it, Duke?" Judge Sands didn't blink while he waited for the answer. His temples bulged.

"I got it at the pawn shop near the outlet mall. You know, the one I go to on occasion to look for hunting gear?"

"Yeah, I know the one. You must have paid a pretty penny for that!"

"I've been saving up for something special for our anniversary." He blurted out the words before he even thought.

"Our anniversary was three months ago," said Melissa.

"True." He stuffed his mouth with a large portion of meat and began to chew. "But I didn't have the money then, and I finally saved enough. I thought it was as good a time as any to give my wife something special." He smiled at Melissa hoping he could brush past the gaff of mentioning his anniversary.

"I'm not complaining, but you didn't mention our anniversary earlier." She smirked.

"Oh, sorry. I just forgot," said Duke.

The judge grimaced and there was awkward silence for the next few minutes.

The conversation at dinner was mainly between the two ladies. Duke was becoming more and more uncomfortable in his own skin after hearing the news report. All he wanted to do was leave. He needed to get somewhere and try to find some answers about the missing women.

Melissa decided to hang around a bit longer and visit with her mom, so Duke headed to his car. Judge Sands appeared out of nowhere and put his arm around him.

"I don't need to tell you again to keep your mouth shut about the operation last night, do I?"

"Not a word, Pops."

"Where did the ring come from? Don't lie to me."

"From the woman."

"Do you know what kind of idiot takes something from a person in custody and gives it to their wife?"

"I wasn't thinking," said Duke.

"Clearly, you weren't thinking. You better find a way to make it disappear today."

"Okay, Pops. I'll find a way. I didn't take it, though. One of the men did. He just pulled 'em off and said take 'em. It was all so quick."

"Them? As in more than one ring?"

"There were three."

"Just shut up talking. Get rid of all of 'em."

Duke had never seen his father-in-law this way. He had never been spoken to like this before.

"Don't you see what a predicament you've put us in?"

Duke quipped back. "What the hell?"

"Watch your tone, Boy."

Duke had never before had a reason to stand up to the judge.

"What did you have me do last night?" Duke stepped into the judge's space.

"Careful, Boy. Don't cross a line we can't come back from. Get rid of the rings."

"I'll get rid of them."

"Tell me you didn't have me do something illegal last night." Duke stepped up uncomfortably close to his father-in-law. There was silence as the two men stared each other in the eye. The judge held Duke's stare for a moment and then walked away.

Rhonda and Melissa were watching from the patio as the men conversed. Their conversation grew more and more aggressive.

"What in the world do you think that was about? It looked intense. It looked like they were about to fight."

"Your dad's really been on edge lately. Not sure what's going on at work. He's so private with all that."

John walked back to the patio."

"Is everything okay, John?"

"Mind your business, Rhonda."

"Dad. That looked intense. We're both wondering what the world that was about?"

"I said mind your damn business. That goes for you, too."

Melissa grabbed her mom's hand.

"Let's go for a ride, Mom. I don't want you here with him right now."

She shot her dad a look and they all knew what it meant. There was a side of John only the two of them had ever seen, and it was scary.

Chapter Four

Braydee

There was one bedroom in the house with four bunk beds.

There was no siren waking us up, no clangs of steel bars, or leather straps, only the sound of a distant rooster and birds. Every sound was magnified above the soft breaths of the children around me.

I looked around the room at the precious sight of the sleeping girls and wondered so many things. How could this world be so cruel to a child?

I made my way to the kitchen, started a pot of grits, and buttered some bread for toast and jelly. I longed for a pot of coffee.

One by one, the girls began to wake up and make their way to the kitchen. The sleepy eyes and tousled hair were so beautiful on each of them.

I pictured them waking up and going straight into the arms of their mothers. Mothers who were sitting with their coffee who were so happy to stop everything at the sight of their baby girl walking into the room. Mothers would drop everything and leave work when the school called saying their child was running a fever. I would soon learn that was not the kind of mother these girls had known.

"I'm making grits with butter! Did you sleep well?" I asked. The faces nodded 'yes' but made no sound.

"I have an idea. Let's grab a blanket and go outside and listen to the birds while we eat our breakfast. How does that sound?" Mostly blank faces stared back at me.

There was one smile that was full of rotten teeth, and she quickly covered her mouth so that I wouldn't see. I grabbed a few blankets and before I knew it, everyone was outside.

Gathered around me on an unfamiliar blanket, in the middle of somewhere, were seven young girls who were much more lost than I was. They were so small and fragile.

We stayed outside listening to the birds and the roosters for over an hour. We spoke very softly in hopes that no one would be able to hear us.

"I've never been on a picnic before."

"Really? Well, we'll do this more often if you like it."

"I like it." Another one spoke up.

"Okay, let's vote. Who says we have a picnic every day?"

All the hands went up.

"How many of you have been on a picnic before?" All the hands went down.

"Well, what was your favorite thing to do with your family?" No one spoke.

"Is there something special that you did that was so much fun, you just couldn't wait to do it again? Maybe it was just going to the park and playing with your brother or sister. Let's talk about it. It will be good for us to get to know each other."

No one spoke.

"Ok, then I'll start. One thing I used to love to do with my mom was to dress up in a funny costume and go to the movies. We would spend hours getting ready! We would tease our hair out and put on crazy colorful clothes."

The thought brought me so much comfort and love, but knowing my mom was losing her mind with worry, brought me back to reality. I had to remain focused on staying composed.

"Now you go, Daring." Daring was a mixed-race child. I was remembering her name by saying 'daring dark hair' in my mind when I saw her. She didn't respond. "How old are you?"

"Eight."

"So, you're in the third grade?"

"I'm not in school."

"Well, not now, but before this."

"No, I wasn't. I never went to school."

She looked off at the trees in the distance, and I could see she didn't want to talk anymore. "Fearless, do you want to tell me about your mom? What did she look like?"

"I never met her." I patted her back. I was two for two in asking awkward questions with sad responses.

"Do you have brothers and sisters?"

"Yes, but I haven't seen them in a long time." She bowed her head and bit her bottom lip.

"Does anyone want to talk about their family?" All of the little heads shook 'no.'

"I'm going to ask a question, but I want everyone to close their eyes. No peeking. This is only for me to know, and it's only so that I can help you. I need to know if you have family looking for you. Please, close your eyes. You don't have to answer if you don't want to, of course." Everyone's eyes were closed.

"If you have a mom or a family member who loves you and is looking for you right now, please raise your hand quickly and put it back down. No one is looking but me." No one raised their hands.

"Raise your hand if you live with your mom." No one raised their hands.

"Raise your hand if you live with a foster family or other relative."

All the hands went up. Fear gripped me by the throat. Maybe no one was looking for these kids after all. Maybe they were lost in the system, or even worse, the system was a part of whatever this trafficking scheme was.

"Okay, I want you to open your eyes and look at me. I have always wanted to have a home full of little girls. I was married once to the love of my life. Do you know why he left me?"

The little heads nodded 'no'.

"He and I divorced because I couldn't have children."

"That's sad," said one of the girls.

"It was very sad. I was sad for a long time. But look at me now. I now have a house full of children. I promise I'm going to do everything I can to protect you and let you know how special you are." I knew it was only words to them. Maybe they had never felt loved and taken care of, but I would do everything in my power to make my promise come true.

Two men watched the group on the monitor while eating chicken wings, licking their fingers, and talking with their mouths full. They couldn't hear what was being said, but they didn't care. It was kids in a field. What did it matter?

"I want everyone to sit Indian style in a circle on the blankets. We're going to play a game," I said. Everyone arranged themselves in the circle.

"Now clap like this and then clap your neighbor's hand. We're going to go around the circle, and I want everyone to say their favorite animal. I'll start. Dog," I said.

We went around the circle. Cat. Tiger. Dog. Horse.

"Now this time I want everyone to say their name and their age. Okay? Say it very quietly. I'll start and don't speak until I say next. Braydee is my name and I'm thirty-two years old." There was no siren. She continued to clap. "Next."

"Clara. I'm eight years old."

"Next."

"Katrina. I'm five years old."

Still no sirens. We continued.

"Samantha. I'm six years old."

"Jill. I'm seven."

"Baily. Eleven."

"Lexi. I'm eight."

"Nikki. Thirteen."

"They can't hear us out here." I breathed a long sigh of relief.

"Listen carefully. Remember how the man said they're always listening to us? Well, they can't hear us out here so this will be our secret spot. In the mornings when we want to talk about things that are important, this is where we'll come." Braydee smiled and everyone smiled with her.

"We'll call it *Our Secret Circle.*"

Samantha, with her rotten teeth, grinned and said, "I like the thecret thircle. Will we have a picnic every day?"

"Not every day."

Clara started talking.

"You want to know why I haven't seen my brothers and sisters in a long time?"

"Yes, of course."

"When my little brother was three years old, my mom burned him with a cigarette, because he wouldn't stop crying. He started crying louder, and my stepdad hit him in the head. He said he didn't mean to hurt him, but he died."

"Oh, Clara! Child, I'm so sorry. That's horrible. Can I give you a hug?" I hugged her until she pulled away.

"They took me and my other sister to live with my aunt for a while, but she said she couldn't afford to keep us."

I didn't really have the words to comfort her.

"Can we all hold hands?"

Everyone grabbed the hand of the person next to them, and I began to pray.

"God, only You can bring us peace right now and help us understand why we are here. Comfort us, Father, and help us to see You during this unbearable time. Give us strength and wisdom."

"Why did you say 'Father?'" The youngest of the girls, Katrina, asked.

"God is our heavenly father. He watches over us and helps us when we're sad and lonely. He comforts and gives us peace when we need it."

"If He helps us, then why are we here right now?"

"I know it seems hard to believe, but this may turn out to be the help we have been praying for. Sometimes God sends the answer to our prayers in very strange ways, and we don't see how it's helping until later in our journey through life."

"God hasn't helped me do anything," said Nikki, "Just the opposite. I think maybe He's cursed me."

"You aren't cursed, and you aren't to blame. I know right now everything seems wrong…"

"It IS wrong! Everyone in my life is wrong."

"If everyone in your life was wrong before, maybe you were meant to be away from that life and start over."

"Like this? Being locked up like this? We don't know what is about to happen to us."

"That's true. We don't know, but what we do know is that things were bad for all of you in the life you lived before arriving here. Right now, I care about you, and I'll do everything in my power to make sure you're safe, warm, well-fed, and that you feel loved."

"You don't love me. My own mom don't love me."

"You're right. It's not the kind of love from your mom that you're wanting or needing, but it's the best I've got to give. I love you as a precious girl, and I want to know you better. Can we just start there and try to get to know each other through this ordeal? I promise to do everything in my power to take care of you."

Nikki looked at me with the same broken eyes I looked at Marco with on the day he said he was leaving me.

"I want somebody to love me like a real family loves," she said.

"I understand. That's what we all want. It doesn't matter how old we are or where we come from."

The fat, bald man chewed on his chicken bone. His words were barely understandable as he talked with the other guard.

"What choo think they're doin' out there? I'm keeping my eyes on them. Can't hear anything that far out from the house, but as long as we can see 'em, we're good."

"That big one is about my daughter's age. Maybe fourteen? Do you ever get emotional watching these girls like this? I mean, like, does it ever bother you what we do?" asked the other guard.

"I don't work on emotions. I keep my work life separate from my feelings. Everybody has a purpose and that's it," said Fat Bald.

"Yeah, I understand that."

"Are you leaving now?" asked Fat Bald.

"Yeppers. I'm headed out of town, and I won't be back for a few weeks. You're in charge." A security pass was handed to the fat, bald man along with a set of keys. Take care of things while I'm gone."

"You know I will. I'll be sure they know I'm always watchin'. I'll hit that siren every now and then for the hell of it."

They both laughed.

"Enjoy your trip. Are you bringing any more girls back this time?"

"Naw. This is a family trip. My wife has us on a trip to Darby, Montana. She wants to go out and see where Yellowstone was filmed. We're staying right on the property in a cabin. It's called Chief Joseph Ranch."

"Sounds like a good time. Don't worry about us here. We're good. They have enough food for a month. Can't see any trouble out of a bunch of little girls. When are they coming for the pickup?"

"Not sure. These girls have been sold to an operation out of Russia, but it's not for sex. They're wanting their organs."

"Geez! "

"Yep. Big money for organs on the black market. I'm not sure if that's what they're doing with all of 'em. There's been some sort of delay due to that big bust they did in San Diego last month. I'm not sure how long they'll be here. All depends on a few things that are way over my pay scale."

"Alright, man. Be safe. Tell the family I said 'hello.' Give the wife a hug from me."

"Will do. Rock on, Willis. Keep your eyes on 'em. Remember what happened the last time?"

"Real unexpected turn of events. Never would have thought that girl would have been so crazy. What kind of an idiot would keep trying to run off, knowing we're watching?" said Willis, the fat, bald man.

"Yeah, that was wild. She learned her lesson."

"Alright, see ya."

He remembered the "nanny'" well. Nannies are what they were called because they were brought here to look after all the girls in the house. The last one had taken off running several times, knowing there were cameras everywhere. He had seen her looking straight at him before she took off. He had been ordered to shoot her if she continued.

The last day she decided to run, he shot her multiple times. She lay in the field for hours.

He was told to wrap the body, place it in the transport van, and someone would pick it up, but instead, he dragged the body to the back of the property and burned her. He was sure the girls had seen him, but he didn't care. All those girls were long gone by now and this was a brand-new group.

He had gotten into so much trouble for not following directions, but in the end, the remains were removed from the property, and he kept his job guarding the house.

There was a strength in my gut like I had never felt before. A burden for these kids. There were seven beautiful children in this home, and not one of them had a parent who cared for them. I knew I had to survive whatever this was and get the children to a safe place.

This was my calling in life. My prayers went from "Why God?" to "Thank you, God, for sending me to rescue these girls."

Fat Bald watched. His evil mind was churning.

As evening fell and another meal was served, I made an announcement hoping someone watching the monitor was listening, too.

"I want us to all go outside and find a rock. Walk around the property and look for a beautiful rock. We'll collect one rock every day, and that will tell us how many days we have been together. So far, we have been here two mornings. So, let's all gather two rocks and put them in a special place."

I walked as far away from the house as I could, pretending to be looking for the perfect rock. I wanted to see how far I could go before a siren sounded. I was maybe thirty yards away when the screeching sound of the siren burst through the still air.

I saw everyone grab their ears, and I turned back toward the house, walking intently. I raised my hands and shrugged as if to say "Sorry, I didn't know." But I knew.

We sat around the table and inspected our rocks. These rocks represented one day. Twenty-four hours of life that we would never get back. As we inspected the colors, I asked them questions about places they had been where they had seen big rocks.

"Have any of you ever been to the beach?" Everyone shook their heads no.

"When we get out of here, we're all going to go stay at the beach for a whole week!"

"Where is the beach?"

"There are a lot of beaches, but the one I'm going to take you to is Orange Beach, Alabama!" It was the place I had been taken, but it would forever serve as the place that led me to my destiny. These children were my destiny.

"I know where Alabama is on the map," said one child excitedly.

"You do? Well, you're going to love it there. The beaches are so sandy white, and the water is so beautiful!"

"Do you go there a lot?"

"I've been going to the beach once a year for the past three years. I just left there less than a week ago."

"That's why you have a good suntan!"

"Yes, that's why. I was taking a girls' trip with my best friends. One of the girls I go with has worked with me for a very long time. Her name is Tate, and the other girl started working with us this year."

I was trying hard not to give away information that would make the sirens go off. I knew Fat Bald Guy was watching us.

"Tell us about your trip this year."

"Well, we stayed for almost a week. The three of us rented a car and spent every day eating good food, building sandcastles, and just enjoying each other's company. We laugh a lot when we're together."

"What's your job?" asked Jill.

"I'm a scientist at the University of Baylor."

I expected the siren to sound, but it didn't, so I continued. They girls were interested.

"You're a scientist?"

"I am. Most of my friends are, too. What do you want to be when you grow up?"

One by one, they began to speak. "I want to be the ice cream man."

"I want to be a nurse and help people that get hurt."

"I want to be Miss Texas."

The siren screeched, and everyone screamed. It was such a frightening sound.

That's it! Texas! That was the trigger. Lexi is from Texas. Are we in Texas? Baylor University is in Waco, Texas. That's where Lucy said they first saw me. Maybe we are all from the same area.

"Come here. All of you. Please." They gathered around me, and we held hands. "Look at me. I know that you don't have a reason to trust me, but I need you to. I need you to look at me and say I trust you. Will you do that?" The children nodded and one by one, even the ones that had never spoken said the words, "I trust you, G."

"Call me Grace. Not G. Grace."

We hugged a little tighter. "How about this? After dinner tonight, we'll go outside and play a game. Then I'll tell you a fairy tale. Do you know the story of Hansel and Gretel? Well, you're going to love my version. We'll pretend we have a campfire. Tonight is going to be fun!"

I tried my hardest to have positive energy, and it worked. Everyone was excited, but only for a few minutes.

We were afraid, and it was difficult to hide our fear.

Fat Bald sat listening. He loved watching everyone jump when he hit the siren. It was moments like these that entertained him, but other than that, he faded in and out of paying attention. He was paid to make sure they didn't leave the property. He had no interest in the minutiae of what was really going on in the house.

I can't explain the silence that loomed over us.

There was a child staring out of the window, and another sitting on the lawn. Two little faces watching my every move in the kitchen, others lying on their beds, and one with the covers pulled over her head.

There was no chatter. No little children laughing. No music. No television. There were just solemn minutes that turned into hours. There were occasional sobs from Samantha and Clara, but mostly blank faces.

We were only eating twice a day out of fear that we would run out of food since we had no idea how long the food needed to last.

Days turned into weeks.

I tried my best to find ways to lighten the mood, but often it fell short.

"If I tap you on the head, you'll be cooking with me tonight. If I don't, then you will be setting the table and helping clean up. Does that sound good?"

The girls nodded 'yes'.

As we sat down for dinner, eleven-year-old Baily asked if she could say the blessing.

"Bless this food, Father, and bless our house mother for making it."

Everyone said "Amen."

"That was beautiful. Thank you."

"That's what we always said at the home I lived in when I was six. I lived in a different home last year, though."

"It was very sweet."

Once again no one talked during our meal. Maybe there was nothing to talk about, or maybe everyone was so afraid of saying the wrong thing inside, they just kept silent.

The manipulation was working.

"As soon as we're done eating and we get this kitchen cleaned, we're all going outside. We'll stay until it gets dark if we want to."

"To the Secret Circle?"

The youngest child had said it without thinking.

"Yes, to our singing circle," I emphasized 'singing' as loudly as I could.

I was hoping that if anyone had heard it the first time, they would think it was a mistake. "I can't wait to sing with you guys, so hurry, hurry."

We finished up and all gathered outside in our special spot in the field and sat in a circle where the men couldn't hear us.

"I need to tell you something very important. You can never say the words 'secret circle'. If the men who are watching us hear that, they may forbid us to come out here. Is that clear? It's now our singing circle." Everyone nodded.

"So, let's sing. Do you know the song 'You Are My Sunshine?" Heads nodded. "Then here we go!"

The voices sang softly at first, then they got louder and louder. "Again!" I said.

"You are my sunshine, my only sunshine..." The girls sang so beautifully.

Fat Bald could hear their voices singing. They sounded so happy. Even though he couldn't hear them talking, he didn't care enough to tell them to move closer to the house.

The little souls that had been wrapped up so tightly inside these little bodies, began to unfold, and the music was opening their hearts to something. As bad as things were, we were singing in a field. I wanted to just keep singing because while we were singing, I could think of nothing else except the song.

"Let's stand up. Hold hands. Now this time, let's go in a circle to the right while we sing."

We circled to the right. Then to the left. Then we raised our hands to the middle and back out. We made a train, and I was the engine pulling seven little girls around the yard singing, "You Are My Sunshine." I couldn't remember the last time I had felt so full of love and free.

After quite some time I was ready to sit, all the girls wanted to continue.

"Let's circle up. I want to tell you the story."

I rubbed my hands together like an evil witch.

"Before I do, I need to ask you a few questions. We'll have to move quickly just in case they stop us from talking. I'm not sure how long they are going to allow us to be away from the microphones. I'm going to start with you. Where are you from, and where were you when they took you? Clara, we'll start with you."

"I'm from Hewitt, Texas. I was at the park with my friend."

"How did they take you?"

"There was a lady who told me she had lost her dog and wanted me to help her look for it. We started walking, and then somebody grabbed me and put me in the car."

"Oh God, Clara. Do you remember what the lady looked like?"

"Yes, a little bit. She was about your age I think."

"Do your best not to forget, okay? I need you all to remember every detail about how you were taken and who took you."

"Nikki, where are you from?"

"I'm from Bellemare, Texas. They took me from the gas station. I walked there to get something for my mom."

"Samantha?"

"I'm from Riesel, Texas, I was walking home from school."

"What about you, Lexi?"

"Lorena and I were at Vacation Bible School."

"What? How were you taken from a church?"

"When it was over, I waited at the curb by the flagpole. Everyone was leaving. One of the teachers said someone had called and said they couldn't pick me up, and the teacher was going to bring me home. Now I don't think she was a teacher."

The stories were horrific. So many people working together to take these children in plain sight.

"Baily?" I needed to move quickly.

"Hewitt. I was at the park, too."

"Katrina?"

"Elm Mott, Texas. I was waiting for somebody to pick me up from school."

"Jill?"

"Brockville. They took me when I got off the bus. I was walking home from the bus stop."

Fat Bald stared at the camera. It was getting dark outside, but the automatic spotlights had come on. The girls looked as though they were talking and listening intently. What were they saying?

His finger hit the siren and we all jumped again.

I stood up and walked towards the house. "I'm talking to the girls about their favorite fairy tale. Everyone is describing the part of the story that scared them."

A voice bellowed from the speaker near the kitchen door. "What did you say?"

"I said we were just sharing parts of fairy tales the girls could remember."

"Well, you need to move closer to the house so I can hear you." He paused his Netflix show to move the girls closer to the house.

"OK, girls. You heard him. We need to move closer to the house, but not too close," I whispered.

"CLOSER!" Bellowed the voice.

Now he could hear us.

I told them the story of Hansel and Gretel, again, until it was dark. The stars above us were brighter than I had ever seen.

"The stepmother was pretty mean in that story, just like my stepmother," said Jill.

"Tomorrow I'll tell a happy story. Now, before we go in, I want us all to lie back on the ground and just look at the sky. If you see a shooting star, you get to make a wish!"

"What's a shooting star?"

"Oh, my gosh! It's a space rock that collides with the earth's atmosphere and makes this beautiful fiery glow that shoots across the sky."

We lay there for a while, but we never saw a shooting star. "We'll try again tomorrow night. Let's get some rest. I'm so tired."

"This was the funniest night I've ever had." The little arms of Katrina hugged me so tightly, followed by Samantha.

"I've never done anything like this before," said Jill.

"Me either, and I love it so much," I said, and meant it.

Fat Bald watched on the monitor. It was times like these he wished he didn't know what was going to happen to the girls. He pushed it out of his mind. It's what they were brought here for. He picked up the phone and called his wife.

"Hey, Hon," he said.

"Hey. Are you coming home early tonight?"

"No. Just a few more hours though. My relief gets here around midnight. What are you wearing?"

"Funny. Sweatpants and a t-shirt that stopped fitting me twelve years ago. Does that turn you on?"

"Not a bit, but you're still my honey bunny."

"Good. I'm going to bed. If I'm asleep when you get here, just sleep in the guest room. I have the hardest time going back to sleep when you're working these late-night shifts."

"Okay, I love you," he said.

"I love you. Be careful Bye."

He looked at Nikki on the monitor. Tonight, he was going to use her for his own pleasure.

Chapter Five

I did everything I could to fall asleep. I counted sheep. I prayed. I stared at the girls until my eyes hurt. Exasperated, I got up. Quickly moving across the edge of the wall, I went into the bathroom. The tiny window at the top of the room was only meant for air, not for a body. I wouldn't fit through that window. I needed to figure out how to explore the property while everyone was asleep.

I heard keys rattling, and I froze. Someone was coming through the door. I heard the heavy footsteps and the bumping of someone against the wall getting close. I moved quickly from the bathroom and back to my bed. Pulling the covers up to my eyes, I pretended to be asleep.

I could see the extremely large belly and bald silhouette moving toward Nikki's bed. I recognized Fat Bald. In an instant, his hand was over her mouth, and her scream was muffled. She struggled to get free, to no avail. Tonight, she would be forced to do as he pleased.

"Don't scream. There's no use. It won't help you..."

He pulled her violently from her bed while I watched. My body was numb with fear. Why couldn't I move? I had promised to protect them. There were gasps and whimpers from a few of the girls that had woken up, but no screams. I lay frozen in horror at what was about to happen to this thirteen-year-old child, but I was AFRAID to fight for her. What could I do except bring more trouble on the rest of us? I felt powerless. Everything was happening so fast.

Nikki screamed despite his warnings, and everyone woke up. There was crying in the dark, and Nikki grabbed one of the bunk beds as he pulled her towards the door. The bed slid with the girls lying on it, and Fat Bald yanked her arm so hard, he thought he had yanked it out of the socket.

"Stop fighting me!" he yelled.

Nikki was screaming and kicking with all her might. From out of nowhere, eight-year-old Clara appeared with an iron skillet and swung with all her strength. The fact that he was short was to her advantage, and she landed a blow square on the back of his head. He slumped to the ground, and Nikki broke free.

"Did I kill him?" Clara stood three-and-a-half feet tall. She wielded the heavy skillet like a six-foot-tall warrior. My mind was blown away by the strength and bravery of this child. I had sat frozen in my bunk while she stepped in to help without hesitation. I rushed to her side.

"I doubt it," I said, as I flipped on the light. "You just stunned him."

He began groaning and moving.

"We're going to be in a lot of trouble." I ran to the kitchen and grabbed a sharp knife.

"What are you doing with the knife?" asked Nikki.

"He's going to remember this night for the rest of his life, and I want everyone who sees him to ask what happened." It was crazy how the bravery of a child awakened a sleeping giant in me.

I leaned down and sliced his face from the top of his cheek to his chin. Blood poured out from the gash.

He screamed and sat up. Holding his face with one hand, he ran from the house. I could hear him talking to someone on his radio outside the door. It never occurred to me that I could have sliced his throat and maybe we could have all run away. I was too afraid, and killing someone just wasn't in my blood. Yet.

He radioed for help. "I need back up at the farm, now!" said Fat Bald.

"Roger that. What's happening?"

"I was attacked by one of the girls."

"Are the girls secure?"

"Yes, but I'm cut pretty bad. Hurry."

"Are you kidding me right now? Who did it?"

"One of the girls."

"How did a little girl attack you?"

"I'd rather not say."

"I don't care if you'd rather not say. I need to write a report, and I need the details. How did they get to you?"

"There was a disturbance in the house, and I couldn't see what was happening in the dark, so I went to the house."

"And?"

"Just send backup, alright?"

"I've already done that. Now, tell me what happened."

"One of the girls sneaked up behind me and hit me with an iron skillet."

"You need backup because a kid hit you with a frying pan?"

"No, she nearly knocked me out, and the woman slashed my face! I'm headed to the emergency room. I'm going to need stitches, for sure! I'm pouring blood everywhere. Just now got in my car, so nobody is watching the girls."

"Don't leave that house unattended. You leave, you risk your life. The boss will have your entire face sliced off if those girls disappear."

"I'll just sit here and bleed out tile backup arrives."

"So dramatic! Just stay put until someone arrives. Do not leave those girls unattended."

"I said I was staying."

Fat Bald made it to the hospital and called his wife from the emergency room.

"Hey, Hon. I got attacked tonight by one of the prisoners. He sliced my face pretty bad. I'm okay, but I'm here at the hospital getting stitches."

"Attacked again? Your face? Dear God!"

"I'm fine. It's going to give me some character."

"Seriously? I don't see why you keep this job. It's too dangerous, and one day one of those beasts is going to kill you. It's not worth it."

"Well, its kind of IS worth it. Where am I going to make this kind of money somewhere else?"

"I don't care. We need to rethink our lives and get on the same schedule. I'm headed your way."

"No. There's no need. You stay put. I'll see you in the morning. They're pretty backed up here. They stopped the bleeding, and I could be waiting for hours. I'm good."

"Okay. I love you. I'll see you soon."

"Love you."

We didn't sleep the rest of the night.

"I'm scared." Katrina, the youngest, was shaking.

"Me, too. Do you want to come over here and get in my bed?"

"Yes."

Her small, malnourished body climbed into bed with me.

"Can I come too? I'm scared," asked Baily.

"Of course, you can. We're all scared." I wished so much that it was a larger bed that we could all fit in. It was so crowded with three people in the small twin bunk bed. I didn't care. I would've piled every one of them on top of me if they had wanted to join us. I felt the little bodies shivering with fear, not from the cold. I would find a way out and get these girls to safety or die trying.

When morning came, no one wanted to get out of bed. My prayers seemed to be bouncing off the ceiling. How could children be living in this kind of fear while our government was doing so little? These people were monsters. Terrorists. They, and their evil network, need to be destroyed!

Through the small window, I could see that the sun was rising higher in the sky. The longer I lay there, the more I was giving the appearance that I was defeated. But I wasn't defeated, I felt stronger than ever.

"Is everyone awake?" I asked.

All the little voices said "Yes."

Nikki sat up in her bed. "Y'all fought for me last night. No one has ever fought for me."

"You're worth fighting for, and we'll continue to fight for each other." I was ashamed that I didn't have the courage that Clara had to step up first.

"I can't believe you hit him with a frying pan!"

"I can't believe it, either. I just wanted to help." Clara smiled so proudly.

"Well, it helped but he's going to come back again," said Nikki.

I knew she was right. If not him, someone even worse. "Well, we'll deal with that when it happens. For now, we're okay. I want to say something right now, and I hope you will remember it always. Being afraid can make you sit quietly and not fight back." I looked at Clara. "When I said your letter was C and that you would be called courageous, I had no idea just how much courage you had inside of you."

"I wasn't even afraid. I just got up and did it," said Clara.

"You saved Nikki from being taken last night. That takes courage for sure."

Nikki's tears started to flow. "I've been raped so many times, I quit fighting a long time ago. Last night I realized that if I fight back, I might get hurt, but at least I fought."

"That's right. That's how I feel. We may be hurt along the way, but at least we'll stand together and fight for each other."

Jill's raspy little voice said, "Just like a real family does."

"Yes. Just like a real family."

We ate, gathered a rock, and put it in our special place like we had done the day before. Each of us had our own special place to put the rocks. Mine was on the windowsill nearest my bed. Our pile of rocks was growing.

As evening came, I struggled to think of things to keep us occupied.

"Let's take the table outside and make a fort. Have you ever made a fort before? "I asked. No one knew what a fort was.

We pulled the table into the backyard along with five of the chairs. We grabbed some blankets from the bed and began covering everything, leaving a small hole so that we could climb in and out.

Fat bald undoubtedly was watching, but he didn't tell us to stop. We were close enough to the house, but the blankets would be enough to buffer our voices. Everyone loved being in the fort.

"I need you to listen carefully. You're going to start to smell something cooking later tonight, then a burning smell. There will be smoke. Whatever you do, don't mention it. Pretend you don't notice it. Don't ask 'what's that smell' at all, okay?" Everyone nodded in confusion.

We stayed in the fort until it was dark, then decided to look for the shooting stars. While the girls looked for shooting stars, I went inside, put five pieces of bread on a cookie sheet, and placed it in the oven at three hundred degrees. A smoky kitchen would be my excuse for leaving the door open tonight. It would be my chance to sneak out into the tree line and see what was beyond this field. I wanted to see if this property was as big as it seemed, or if perhaps the trees obscured something just on the other side.

After cleaning up the fort we gathered on my bed. We held hands and prayed. "I'll start and if anyone else wants to join in, please do."

"Well, here we are, Father. Still asking for Your help. Still needing Your strength and wisdom to endure what we're going through. We ask that you bind us together as a strong unit, fill us with your Holy Spirit so that we may be comforted, and forgive us of our sins and help us to forgive others. Protect us and keep us safe."

"Amen," said all the little voices.

"Why didn't God protect Nikki last night?"

"He protected her through us. We are the vessels God uses."

"But why did He let the bad man come in the first place?"

"If the bad man had not come, then Nikki would never have known that we love her enough to fight for her."

"That's true," said Nikki.

"Because the bad man came, we all became strong together as a real family, and today, we all feel connected instead of distant. We bonded through our awful circumstances."

"That makes sense."

"The Bible says that God's strength is made perfect in our weakness. To me, that means that when we're experiencing sad or bad things, we can become the strongest by trusting God."

"I want to trust God." Lexi was always so quiet, but these words would be the loudest and most heartfelt words of her young life.

"If you want to trust God right now, you can. Do you know the scripture of John 3:16?"

"I do. I learned it at Vacation Bible School the day I was taken." Clara started to recite the verse.

"For God so loved the world, that He gave his only son, and whoever believes in him will not perish, but have life forever."

"Life forever? I don't understand?"

"It means that if you believe Jesus came to save the world, and you trust Him to be your heavenly father and ask Him to come live inside your heart. He'll never leave you."

"I want to do that!"

"Me, too."

The excitement of asking Jesus into their hearts was palpable. I led them in the prayer, and everyone said "Amen."

"Now what do we do?"

"Now we are truly the family of God, and no one can ever take that from us! Come in for a hug."

That group hug was truly heavenly.

The lights were turned off. We could already smell the burning bread. The smell filled the kitchen and permeated our bedroom. Everyone was tucked into bed when I jumped up doing my best performance of panic.

"Everybody up! Something is on fire!" I hustled the girls out of the house and into the yard. I removed the burnt black bread from the oven, coughing and hacking for whoever was watching. The girls immediately followed my lead and began coughing and stumbling out of the kitchen door.

Fat Bald's replacement looked up from his phone, seeing but not hearing the commotion. He had turned the audio down to watch his YouTube videos. He could see the smoke in the kitchen.

"That dumb bitch," he said out loud watching Braydee remove the bread from the oven. "How do you burn bread?" He disabled the alarm that would scream if the door was opened after dark.

I looked straight at the camera and spoke. "Whoever is listening. I have to leave the windows and doors open tonight because we can't breathe in here. We're choking."

He saw her mouth moving but didn't care what she was saying. He saw the door open and knew the reason why. He could see the smoke. His video was more important than a smoky room full of kids.

The sleepy-eyed girls watched my every move as I removed the pan and ran the smoking bread outside. I'm sure no one had a clue why I had done this.

We opened the windows and doors, and after an hour, everyone went back to bed. I waited until everyone was asleep, and then I slipped out of bed and through the door. I ran as fast as I could to the tree line. I didn't know if someone had seen me leave or if the sirens were about to sound, or if there would be a sniper in the distance. The only thing going through my mind was to RUN for my life.

I reached the tree line much faster than I anticipated. The adrenaline catapulted me headlong toward the trees. I stopped and waited for signs that anyone had seen me. Nothing. I started walking straight through the woods. They weren't thick woods like you would find in a forest. These trees had been purposefully left, and I could tell that the underbrush had been somewhat manicured. Viewed from the house, it had seemed much bigger. Deeper. Deeper I went. I didn't have much time. Far through the trees, I could see lights. Possible streetlights or house lights? Could we be this close to other people? It certainly wasn't a hundred and forty-two acres of forest like we had been told.

It was enough for one night. The lights were much too far away for me to investigate. If I had known for certain that there were people I could trust near those lights, I would run straight to them! But I didn't know if this might be an extension of the property; the property of the monsters that were holding us against our will.

I had to get back immediately. I didn't want one of the girls missing me. The last thing I needed was for little Katrina to wake up and start calling my name throughout the house!

Coming out of the trees, the house seemed so close. But from the house, the trees seemed like a lifetime away. I began to run as hard as I could to the house and straight to bed.

Fat Bald walked into the house ready to replace the man who sat sleeping with his head resting on his neck. Drool dribbled from the side of his mouth as he snored loudly.

"Wake up. The girls are gone!" He pushed the man on the side of the shoulder.

"What?"

"Naw, just kidding."

"Dang, that's a gnarly scar you're going to have there."

"Yep. Twenty-eight stitches."

"I'm still trying to figure out how you got attacked by a five-year-old and got your face sliced."

"She wasn't five, and don't worry about it. Go. I've got it from here."

When morning came, I felt a new sense of urgency to get everyone up. Today, we would learn a new hand game in our secret circle.

"We're going to do something very fun today!" I announced at the breakfast table.

We gathered in our secret circle. I passed out sixteen pieces of silverware. One utensil for each hand. "This is called "Ma Koo-ay Ko Tay-o." I learned the Native American Indian stick song when I was a Girl Scout. We used Lummi sticks in Girl Scouts, which are simply wooden sticks that are roughly eight inches long.

"Everyone get a partner, and face each other," I said.

As I taught the girls the words and hand movements, love began to swell inside me. A new sense of protection filled my heart, and my chest tightened at the thought of Fat Bald coming back for Nikki. I smiled as we sang, but behind my eyes were tears just waiting to pour out. Tonight, I would go farther than last night. I would go until I could see where the lights in the trees were coming from. Then, we'd all go!

Night fell. I lay motionless. Everyone was sleeping. I eased out of the door quickly and began to run.

"WEEEE oooo! WEEEE oooo!" the siren blasted. I stopped in my tracks and ran back to the house, through the door, and straight to my bed. The siren was still blasting, and everyone was holding their hands over their ears.

"What's happening?" asked Jill. I couldn't answer her. I just shook my head no.

After two more minutes of the blaring siren, Fat Bald walked in with a leather strap. He looked more like Frankenstein with the long stripe of stitches down his face. He flipped on the light. He was ready for revenge.

"Who opened the door?" He looked around the room. "Who opened the door?" he screamed. He was on full alert and watching every move we made this time. "Line up over there!" He shouted and pointed to the wall.

"It was me! I didn't know we weren't allowed outside after dark. I just went out for air. I'm sorry."

"Air, huh? Then why did the perimeter alarm sound?"

I didn't know there was a perimeter alarm so someone must have forgotten to set it last night when I went out.

"I just went too far. It was dark. I was restless and went for a walk to regroup. I just lost track of where I was. That's all."

"Sure, you did." He slapped at my legs as hard as he could, and a stabbing pain ran through them. I jumped to my feet. "You're the one that cut my face?"

He beat my legs until I fell to the ground, then he beat my back. The girls didn't move this time. I writhed in pain as his strap repeatedly struck my body, but I didn't scream.

"You're lucky they won't let me do worse to yam right now! Who hit me in the head?"

"It was me," Clara said.

He pointed at Clara. "Get up!"

Clara stood. He slapped her with the belt across her shoulder, and she doubled over. He hit her across her back, and she screamed.

"Now both of you, walk to the tree."

We knew the tree. There was only one tree close to the house. It was a large oak tree.

He placed us facing the tree. Me on one side and Clara on the other. Our hands were zip-tied together so that we were both hugging the tree. The zip-tie was tight. It hurt so badly. Then, with the leather strap, he beat us some more. There was no way to fight it. I wrenched my body and tried to twist around, scraping the side of my face. I screamed. The girls screamed.

"Stop! Stop! Please!" I could hear the girls screaming "Noooo!" Clara's piercing scream was a sound I would never forget. This hell had to come to an end.

"Why God? Why?" I whispered the words out loud.

Fat Bald looked at Nikki and winked as he walked by her. She began to shake. He kept walking.

Hour after hour passed as we hung against the tree. Strapped on like animals and beaten with a leather strap. The pain was excruciating.

Clara sobbed for hours. Then she stopped.

"Clara?" There was no answer. "We'll survive this. Please don't give up on me."

"I'm trying."

Morning came, and the girls came to check on us. We had been standing all night because of the way we were tied to the tree. They brought a couple of chairs out, and we were able to turn our bodies enough to sit on them.

Suddenly there was a voice over the intercom.

"Get a knife and cut them loose."

Nikki retrieved a knife and set us free.

We leaned on each other as we hobbled into the house. Katrina held my hand and Lexi held my arm. Nikki held Clara's hand. Clara and I slept while the rest of the girls prepared breakfast...and lunch.

Chapter Six

We were learning to work together and somehow not cause the siren to go off. We cooked and cleaned, played outside, and continued to build forts. We made regular trips out to the secret circle. It had taken a few days to slowly move our circle away from a listening intercom, but we had managed to do it discreetly. Slowly the girls began to open up more and more.

Katrina, the youngest, was just five years old. She had two brothers who were older and one baby sister. Her mom had left them with an aunt and disappeared. She didn't know how long ago that had been, but at some point, a social worker took them away from the aunt and placed them in foster care. She was separated from the other kids and had not seen them or her aunt in a very long time.

I asked her if she would share more with us about how she was taken. She nodded.

"I was playing at the park by my house. I played there a lot. I was talking to a lady about her dog. She said she was sad because it had been hit by a car."

"So, what did she want you to do?"

"The lady had the dog for a long time. She said her name was Sadie. She wanted to show me a picture of her. She said she had one in the car. I just wanted to see the picture. When I got to the car, she opened the door, and this man grabbed me and pulled me in. We drove away."

There was a long silence, and Nikki breathed heavily.

"Some men used to come to my house, and my mom would give me to them. She would just say, "Go, Nikki".

She made me do stuff before with her on the streets. She's on drugs. People have told me she can't help what she does. I hate her, though." She stared at the blades of grass she was breaking into tiny pieces.

"I'm so sorry, Nikki. I'm truly so sorry." I couldn't think of anything else to say. Giving your child away was something I just couldn't process. I had spent five years trying to have a child. Hearing this was ripping my heart out.

Lexi whispered, "I wish you were my mom. I feel different when I'm with you." The others nodded.

Hearing these words, my heart was full of so much emotion. Happiness, sadness, pain, regrets, and anger! Everything was boiling up at once. Anger at the man who had divorced me because I couldn't give him a big family. Sadness that I couldn't erase all the bad things that had happened to these girls. Happiness at the thought that maybe I could one day provide them with a home and a better life.

"I'm trying hard to think of a plan to get us out of here. I just haven't thought of one yet."

It had been more than a week since we had seen or heard from Fat Bald. As night fell on our little home, everyone said their prayers, and we were about to sing some bedtime songs when the door opened.

"Let's go." The man stood holding a gun at me. He motioned for me to move.

I couldn't move. I was terrified. I didn't want to leave the girls alone with no one to protect them. I had no idea where I was going, or how long they would be without me. There were cries and screams for me not to go. The man stepped outside the door and shot the gun into the air. The sound rang out, and everyone screamed louder.

"Shut up. Let's go. Now!"

I moved as slowly as I could. "I'll be back. I promise you!" I didn't know if I would be back. Were they going to rape me? I would do anything to get back to the girls.

Before they loaded me into the car, they placed something like a pillowcase over my head. We drove for only a few minutes. The house we arrived at was beautiful. Well-manicured and large. I was led to the back of the house where an older man and woman were sitting next to a swimming pool. The man looked to be in his seventies, and the lady was probably in her late fifties. There was a security guard standing behind them.

"Sit," said the man.

I sat.

"I'll get straight to the point. We've chosen you for a very important project. We're working to provide a service for those who can afford it. We'll be growing clones to supply duplicate organs and replace body parts. Our clones will be genetically matched to clients. They will then be used in transplants, to prevent rejection by the client's immune system."

I knew it was possible. I had even worked on some of the research involved in replicating organs, but this was illegal and unethical.

He continued, "The client's clones will be grown as headless embryos, without a brain or a central nervous system."

I gasped. Skirting the unethical part of the scenario by leaving off the brain and central nervous system was smart.

"So why am I here? What do you want from me? And what makes you think I'll do anything for you?"

The woman began to speak softly and slowly. I couldn't determine her accent. German? Swedish?

"You're our new recruiter, scientist, and caretaker. The previous caretaker did not last more than a month. She tried to escape, and she was laid to rest in a shallow grave. You will be responsible for finding children of all ages. You will help us recruit them for our research. You will help care for them in the morning and evening. During the day, you will work at our lab."

"I won't! I won't bring children here for you to harvest their organs. Are you people insane?"

"We're doing what it takes to save people's lives. It is a necessary part of the process to have plenty of organs. You, of all people, should understand that sometimes you must sacrifice the idea that something is evil, in order to make progress with science." She paused long enough to see if I would respond, then she continued.

"We will be using the organs of the children in your care. Should you choose not to cooperate, you will die, but only after you watch the children die. We'll harvest their organs with very little anesthesia, and you will watch. Then, we will harvest your organs without any anesthesia. Now tell me. Do you wish to help with the research and continue caring for the children?"

I nodded yes. "I'll help. How soon will this begin?"

"We've put together an extraordinary team of scientists. Everyone is ready to go. We're just waiting for a few important details to work themselves out. We should be ready next week."

"And what day is today?"

"Thursday," said the man. "The lab isn't ready yet. However, you'll begin recruiting for us tomorrow. Someone will come for you after lunch and take you to a city park. You will find a lonely child and befriend them with kind words. You will develop a relationship with them by telling them about your very beloved dog. You will offer to show them a picture that is in your car. Someone will be waiting in the car to take the child."

He spoke without emotion. It was as if he were telling me how to fix a leaky faucet. I nodded. I didn't have a choice.

When I returned to the house, everyone was still awake. Worried and afraid, they couldn't sleep. They jumped out of bed and ran to hug me. I had only been gone a few hours.

"I'm okay. I haven't been hurt in any way. Let's go sit at the table. I need to tell you some things."

We gathered around the table.

"As you already know, there are some really bad people holding us here. They have bad plans and bad ideas. They have threatened to kill us if I don't do exactly what they tell me to do."

"What do they want you to do?" asked Clara.

I couldn't bring myself to tell them what it was that was about to happen to them, but I had to tell them I was going to be bringing more children in. "They want me to kidnap children for them. Just like you were taken, they want me to go to the park and be the woman who tells the story about the unique dog that died." I couldn't look up at their faces. "If I don't do it, they are going to torture and kill us."

"It's okay, Grace. We know you don't want to do it. You're protecting us."

Nikki touched me on the hand, and I reached for hers instinctively. "You don't have a choice, just like we don't have a choice."

"I'm leaving tomorrow. I'm not sure when I'll be back, but you guys have got to take care of each other while I'm gone." Everyone agreed that they would look out for each other.

We drove less than thirty minutes and arrived at a park. I didn't recognize the area, but I made mental notes of where I was. There weren't very many people there. A couple of moms with strollers and boys throwing a football. There were some kids playing chase. We pulled up near a dumpster.

"Boss said get a black kid this time."

I exited the car and walked toward the swings. There was a little girl there, maybe seven years old. She was digging in the dirt next to a broken seesaw. I walked past her smiling. She didn't look up. I walked to the swings and sat watching her.

Someone's little girl was sitting in the dirt playing at this very moment, and later today she would be locked away, terrified. She would never see her family again. I became physically sick and stood up just in time to throw up my breakfast a few steps from the swings. The little girl looked up.

"Are you okay?"

"No, not really."

"What's wrong?"

I hesitated. I took a deep breath and said, "My dog died today."

The little girl stood up and walked toward me, leaving her spoon and plastic bowl in the dirt. That bowl would be what her family would show the police. The plastic bowl she had taken from the cabinet so that she could play chef in the park. I wondered if her mom had told her not to talk to strangers. I was that stranger every child should fear.

"How did your dog die?"

"She was very old. I never had any little children like you, so she was my baby. She was such a beautiful dog. She had long brown hair. I would let her hair grow so long that I was able to braid it, just like yours."

"Just like mine? Your dog had little ponytails?"

"Yes, would you like to see a picture of her?" My heart was so tight, and I knew I was about to throw up. I turned quickly away from the child as I dry-heaved. We walked toward the car. A little girl slid down the slide as we were walking off. She had been watching us from the top of the slide, but I had not seen her.

"Where are you going?" she said.

Startled, I jerked around to see the small frame.

"We're going to see a picture of her dog. It has pigtails just like mine."

"Can I come see, too?"

"That's my little sister, Marlea. Can she come? I'm helping Mom babysit today. She's cleaning our house for a birthday party. My other sister is going to be sixteen years old tomorrow."

"Umm. Yes. She can come."

"You're really sad, aren't you?"

"Yes, sadder than you will ever know."

"Well, I really want to see the picture. What was her name?"

"Luna."

I could see her mouth moving, chattering to herself about Luna, but I couldn't hear her. My ears were ringing, and I felt faint. I knew what was about to happen.

We went around to the back side of the car. The dumpster blocked the view of the car. I opened the door, and as quickly as a rattlesnake, two arms grabbed the girls and yanked them inside. They fought hard. The two of them couldn't be managed by the man holding them, and before I could get the door closed, the oldest one had gotten away.

"Get in you damn fool! Drive!"

I jumped into the front seat, and the driver sped away. I cried all the way home.

"I'm so sorry. They made me do it. I'm so sorry," I sobbed.

"Shut up. Nobody cares," said the driver.

"I care!" I yelled. "I care!"

"Never bring two children to the car. How did you think I was supposed to contain two children?" The little girl screamed until she was smacked in the face. After that, she just sobbed.

The older sister ran with all her might, screaming at the top of her lungs.

"They took my sister! They took my sister! Help me!"

Someone in the park called 911, and a police officer was there within a few minutes. The officer took the little girl to her house. She jumped out of the car and flung open the front door, screaming.

"Momma! They took Marlea. This woman took Marlea!"

The officer stood in the doorway watching as the mother tried to make sense of what her daughter was saying.

"Where's your sister?" Replied the mom with panic in her voice.

"She's gone. We got pulled into a car, but I got away. She couldn't get away, momma." The girl cried.

She grabbed her phone and called her husband. "Come now," she said. "I can't talk right now. I just need you to stop whatever you're doing and come now."

"Where's my daughter?" The mother asked the officer.

"I'm sorry, ma'am. We're just getting the news as you are. Your daughter, Shyla, told us what happened."

"What happened?"

The officer explained the story as it had been told to him and the woman's knees buckled, and she fell to the ground screaming. The officer could do nothing to console her. It wasn't until the husband arrived that she was able to finally speak to the officers.

A description was given of the light blue romper the little girl was wearing and the matching blue hair ties that were wrapped around her braids.

A description of me was given to the police as well.

"She was a beautiful white lady. She had blond hair and no makeup. Her hair was in a long ponytail. She was wearing a big dress with flowers on it. That's all I really know."

"What kind of car was she driving?"

"She wasn't driving. There was a man driving, and another man was in the back seat. He's the one that grabbed Marlea."

The officers took notes. This was an organized kidnapping. There had been so many recent kidnappings in the area. It was becoming more and more important for children to never be without an adult.

"Do you remember what color the car was?"

"Yes, it looked just like the car my sister is getting for her birthday."

"Same color, or also the same style?"

"Everything looked the same."

"Okay, what kind of car is your daughter getting for her birthday?"

The dad spoke. "It's a silver KIA Telluride."

The officer made notes, and a search party was organized. The family began candlelight vigils, and they hung signs with photos of Marlea everywhere they could. The birthday party for the older sister was canceled, and lives would be forever changed.

I walked into the house with Marlea. The girls all gathered around us and began introducing themselves as if she were a new kid at school. I knelt down so that I could speak to the little girl.

"I know you're scared. We all are. Everyone you see here was kidnapped. I didn't take these children, though. Some very bad people did. They forced me to take you and your sister today." I hoped she could feel my sincerity and pain.

"Why did you do this? You're a bad person!" she said.
"They are the bad people. Not me. That's all I can say right now. I don't expect you to understand, but I hope one day you can forgive me."

Chapter Seven

(The Girl's Trip)

"Hey, Mom!"

"Hey, Braydee. Are you all packed and ready to head out?"

"I have a few more things to do before I meet Tate and Britney, then we're Panama City Beach bound!"

"How many trips to PCB does this make?"

Braydee recounted when they had first started their annual girls' trip.

"Marco and I divorced when I was almost twenty-eight, so this will be the fourth trip."

"You girls need to be extra cautious this year. I've been seeing so much crime in that area on the news."

"Well, Mom, we aren't spring breakers, this isn't spring, and we're in our thirties! I do love that you still call us girls, though."

"Okay. How long are you 'ladies' staying this time?"

"Britney is staying until Friday. Tate's going to see some friends in Pensacola before she heads out on Saturday."

"And what about you?"

"I don't want you to worry, but I'm going to rent a car and drive home. I'm going to stop off in Orange Beach, AL, then take my time and drive back to Waco."

I certainly didn't want to tell her that I had met a guy online who was from Alabama, and this was the closest I would get to meeting him in person. That would have stressed her out to no end.

"You know I don't like you driving that far by yourself. That's so dangerous!"

"I know you don't. That's why I didn't want to tell you."

"Thank God, you did tell me. I'm not going to say I'll be worried sick while you're on the road. Instead, I'm going to say 'Y'all have fun!'"

"We will. What's daddy doing?"

"He's sitting on the couch waiting to talk to you."

I always loved the way both my parents dropped everything just to talk to me on the phone. I can't remember a time when I needed something, and they weren't there to step in before I even had a chance to work it out on my own.

"Hey, Daddy."

"Hey, Bug."

"What have you and Mom done lately that I can brag about to my friends?"

"Well, your mom just rescued a litter of Boston Terrier pups. She's turned the basement into an all-out kennel, and the backyard looks like we have ten grandkids. There are dog toys everywhere!" He laughed, but it quickly reminded him that they would never have grandkids.

"Oh my gosh, seriously? I want to see! How old are they?"

"They are all around three months old. There are six of them. It's like a circus when those pups go outside. I've never seen such whooping and hollering in my life."

"I hear they're hilarious."

"We're enjoying it. Not sure it's much to brag about."

"Sounds fun. I hope they're still there when I get back. I'll come see you guys and tell you all about the trip."

"We can't wait. Are you good on money?" Dad still asked me this question as if I were 19 and in college.

"I'm good Dad. Very good. No worries there. I love y'all. I need to finish up and head out. I just wanted to hear your voice before things get crazy and I forget to call home."

"Y'all be careful, hon. You're the only Braydee we got."

"I love you, Dad."

"I love you. Your mom is reaching for the phone, even though you're on the speaker."

"Send us lots of pictures! I love you. Be sure to check in with us when you're driving by yourself."

"Oh, I will. Love you, momma!"

Britney picked me and Tate up, and we all headed to the airport.

"Can you believe a year has gone by since our last trip? Gosh, it seems like it's only been a couple of months," said Britney.

Britney was from Boston. A gorgeous twenty-nine-year-old who always drew stares from everyone. This was just her second trip with us. She had started working with us at Baylor University just a few months before our last girls' trip. We quickly gravitated to her wit and charm and invited her to join us. We boarded the plane and settled into our seats. As quickly as the seatbelt light was turned off, we all asked for wine.

"It feels like more than a year for me," said Tate. "This trip could not come soon enough."

"Well, I just found out on Facebook that my ex-husband's wife is pregnant with their second child."

"Oh God, I'm so sorry."

"I'm ok now. I'm just exhausted and so ready to get away. According to Facebook, the baby girl will be born around Thanksgiving."

It was just before Thanksgiving that he had told me he was leaving me. For two years after that, Thanksgiving was awful. Now, at thirty-two years old, I was finally at a place where I could eat Turkey and dressing and celebrate the holiday without being depressed. Hearing that he would be having another baby sent me into a little bit of a tailspin again.

"Well, guess what? You can't change what has happened. You can only do something about the future. So, tell us about this guy you've met online!" said Britney.

Work didn't leave me much time for mingling in the world, so sitting up at midnight online seemed like the perfect way to meet a man. Yes, I knew all the pitfalls of potentially being catfished or worse killed by a maniac sitting at his computer.

"Yes! Tell us all about him!" Tate was rubbing her hands together with great anticipation.

"Oh, gosh. His name is Grant. He's forty years old and I'm a tiny bit smitten."

"Look at you grinnin' like a possum eatin' briars," said Tate.

"Um, not sure I like that expression, but ok?" I grinned even bigger.

The girls all laughed as the drinks began to dissolve all thoughts of anything but the fun ahead of them.

"What does he do?"

"He's a full-time photographer. He said he travels all over the world. He sent me lots of pictures of his work. He's so good."

"What kind of photography does he do?" asked Tate.

"Everything from high-end weddings to artistic scenery for office buildings."

"What's his website?"

"Um, you know, I didn't even think to ask."

"Well, you would think a professional photographer would've said 'Oh here's my website.' Hmmm," said Tate.

"What's that 'hmmm' about?"

"What else do you know about him? How tall is he?"

"It was hard to tell from his pictures, and I didn't ask."

"What? You didn't find out how tall he was? That's a big deal."

"I know, but I was trying to think outside the box and just focus on the chemistry in our conversation. Besides, successful relationships can happen with a short man. You know height doesn't matter when you're lying down."

Everyone got a good laugh at that.

"Tate said you're meeting him in Orange Beach, Alabama," said Britney.

"Yep. He's doing some work in Birmingham for a few weeks and said he could come to spend a few days with me."

"But you're going to meet in a public place and blah, blah, blah," said Tate.

"Yes! I'm going to be extra careful."

"Can't wait to hear the details! What happens if you get to Orange Beach and fall in love with him? Have you thought about what the relationship would look like with your work and his?" asked Britney.

"Yes. We've talked about it. One night he mentioned how being a photographer gave him the flexibility to be anywhere and travel a lot. We think it would be the perfect profession for a fledgling relationship."

"This could be serious."

"Right now, I love everything about him. We have the best conversations, we have so much in common, and he already has two children and doesn't want anymore. That's perfect."

"Wow. You guys have really discussed it all in a few short months," said Britney.

"We've been talking every night for three months. That's a lot of conversation."

"Did you ever FaceTime?"

"Of course! I may have fallen off a turnip truck, but it wasn't yesterday."

Again, the girls laughed at the dumb expressions that kept jumping out of their mouths.

We arrived at the airport in Pensacola, retrieved our rental car, and headed to Panama City Beach, Florida.

I couldn't help but notice the missing persons posters on the board as we stood in line to get our car.

"Did you guys see all the missing kids on the board at Enterprise?"

"Yes. I was thinking the same thing. Like is there some kind of satanic sacrifice cult in the area or what? It was scary."

"There must have been thirty kids on that board. Not all from this area, but pretty close."

"Remember when we were kids and they used to have the missing person on the milk carton?" I asked.

"Not really," said Tate.

"You don't remember that?"

"My mom must have bought a different kind of milk than your mom."

"I can't imagine anything worse than a child going missing. Tim and Lea would lose their minds if I disappeared. I'm their whole world," I said. "When I miscarried, I felt like a part of me died, and it wasn't even a baby yet."

"Geez, it's vacation y'all. Let's reign in the sad talk!" said Britney.

One of the reasons we had grown to love Britney so much was that she would speak her mind and tell the truth, even when the truth hurt.

We arrived, and our beach condo was perfect. A three-bedroom with giant sliding glass doors that faced the ocean.

I flung open the sliding door on the balcony.

"This view! Come see!" I yelled.

"Let's drink! I'm starting to sober up," said Britney.

We made Bloody Mary's, and I toasted. "Here's to friends who do things together and love each other through all the ups and the downs."

"Cheers."

The days passed quickly and before we knew it, four days had flown by.

"It's our last day," said Britney with a gloomy look, as if we were headed to the gas chamber.

"I know. I don't want to think about it. Especially if you take that other job in San Diego, Braydee," said Tate.

"I'm not sure if I'm going to take it. You two are the main reason that I've dragged my feet in responding to them. It's such a great opportunity for my career, but what's life without your friends?"

"Awwwww. My vote is for you to stay in Waco. We need you, and the research needs you, too."

"I'm leaning that way, for sure. But tonight, we have more important things to discuss."

"What?"

"Where are we going to go to karaoke?"

"Hold on." Tate googled top karaoke spots. "I've got it. We're going to Whiskey's Saloon!"

"Yay! Let's do it!"

The only thing we knew about Whiskey's Saloon was that the pictures online looked good, and we could sing karaoke. That was enough for us.

When we arrived, I was so pleasantly surprised. The bar was lit with blue and purple mood lights, and there was an absolutely amazing stage. The sign over the stage read "Keep Calm and Karaoke!" We were ready. I signed up first and strutted confidently onto the stage. It was another one of my happy places.

The bar was pretty full, and my friends cheered so loud it forced others to join in the clapping and yelling,

As I started to sing "You're So Vain" by Carly Simon, I noticed a heavy man in a ball cap in the back corner. He was sitting alone. There was something eerily familiar about this man. So eerie, in fact, that he almost rattled my performance. Had I not done this same song a hundred times in my life, I would have been distracted. He clapped with the others when I finished my performance.

"See that guy in the corner? The heavy guy with the ball cap?"

"Yes." They both responded.

"Does he look at all familiar to you guys?"

"He looks like one of those men who were sitting in the parking lot for weeks at Baylor," Tate responded.

"Oh, my gosh! Yes! That's it! He looks so much like him."

"What were those guys doing there, anyway?"

"Who knows? I asked a few people. No one seemed to know or care enough to find out."

We stayed until the bar closed and then headed back to the condo in an Uber.

Tate asked the Uber driver to play Shania Twain's song "Man, I Feel Like a Woman" and he cranked it up for us.

We hung our heads out of the window and sang as loud as we could to anyone who would listen at 2:00 a.m.

"I love you two so much. I truly mean it," said Britney.

"I love you both so much, too. I can't imagine life without you guys." Tate laughed, and we all squeezed each other's hands.

"I'm so thankful for our friendship. There's just nothing that can replace girl time."

We hugged in the back seat as the driver tried not to watch us in his rearview mirror.

Morning came and we all had the grumpies. I told them what my dad always told me. "All good things must come to an end so that better things can begin!"

We loaded up and dropped Britney off at the airport. I grabbed a rental car, and Tate used the rental car we already had to go visit friends in Pensacola before her flight back to Texas later that evening.

I headed to Orange Beach, Alabama, to meet Grant, my new online love interest.

I called him as I was leaving Panama City Beach, but he didn't answer. He later texted me and said he couldn't talk but he would see me soon. We planned to touch base at 6:30 and then meet at seven p.m. at the Flora-Bama Lounge. I had never been there before and was looking forward to seeing all the bras hanging from ropes tied to the ceiling.

I checked into my room at Sugar Beach Condos around 4:30 p.m. and quickly showered. I texted Grant to let him know I was dressed and ready by 6:30. I kept my phone close by, checking every now and then to make sure I hadn't missed a text.

I checked my phone often and texted random people just to make sure my texts were going through. My heart was sinking by the hour.

By nine o'clock I realized I had been stood up. Whoever Grant was online, had quickly taken a turn. He wasn't coming. The Grant I knew would have messaged me over and over to explain what was happening on his end.

As my heart sunk deep and my thoughts began to run to Marco and his new wife and kids, I decided to find a place where I could duck away, people-watch, and just hide from reality.

My heart had opened up the last few months, and for the first time in three years, it felt like I might actually be able to fall in love with someone. We laughed together, shared our heartbreak, and found a way to comfort each other online, all in a very short time. I just couldn't understand why he didn't show up.

My mind went through every scenario. Maybe he's married. Maybe he wasn't in Alabama. Maybe he was in an awful accident. Maybe he lost his phone. That had to be it.

I made my way down Canal Road, not seeing anywhere I wanted to stop. Pulling into The Wharf, everything was so bright and cheery. There were families and people laughing and enjoying themselves, and that was definitely not the place I wanted to be. There were palm trees lit with colorful lights! I just wanted to be in a dark corner.

I turned around and headed back in the direction I had come. That's when I stumbled upon a little bar, tucked away in a group of shops, called The Undertow.

Chapter Eight

Braydee's sixty-year-old mom, Lea Quinn, sat in her recliner with her phone in her lap. She was exhausted from lack of sleep. It had been three days since she had last spoken to her daughter. Rarely had more than a day passed, that the two of them didn't talk on the phone. When Sunday came and went without so much as a text, she knew something was wrong.

She reached out to Britney and Tate, but only one responded.

"Hey, Britney. Thank you for calling me back. When did you last see Braydee?"

"She dropped me off at the airport and then she headed to Alabama for a few nights."

"Why Alabama?"

"She was meeting up with a guy named Grant."

"Who is Grant?"

"It's the guy she met online about three months ago."

"Oh God, no! No! That doesn't sound like Braydee. She never mentioned it to me."

"She didn't want you to know. She said you would worry about her too much."

"Oh, God! Why didn't you call me right away?"

"I don't have your contact information. I'm so sorry. I've been trying to find you on social media, but I couldn't find anything on you guys."

"Do you know if she met the guy?"

"She sent us a group text around 9:30. It said he was a no-show, but now I don't know if he sent it from her phone or if she sent it. She was definitely in Orange

Beach when she texted us though. She said she was headed to a bar to chill out for a while."

"Thank you. I'm going to call the Orange Beach police now," said Lea.

"I'm so glad you called me," said Britney, "I've been worried sick. There's another thing. Tate didn't come to work, and I haven't been able to get in touch with her. No one has. Her parents called me this morning, and they haven't heard from her either. She's been reported missing, too," said Britney.

"When did you see Tate last?"

"She and Braydee dropped me off at the airport three days ago, then they went their separate ways."

"Okay, is there anything else you can tell me? Will you text me Tate's mom's number?"

"Sure. The guy Braydee was meeting is Grant Wilson, and he's a professional photographer. I'm not sure if that's his real name, though. I would tell that to the police when you call them."

"For sure. That's the first thing I'll tell them. Thank you."

Lea Quinn called the Baldwin County police and was transferred to Gary Marshall.

"Hi, Mrs. Quinn. This is Captain Gary Marshall. I understand your daughter is missing. What's her name?"

"Hi, sir. My daughter is Braydee Quinn. I just spoke to a friend of hers, and she said Braydee came through Orange Beach on Friday evening, most likely. She was supposed to be meeting a guy she met online. Grant Wilson is his name."

"We actually had a 911 call late Saturday evening from your daughter."

"What??"

"Yes. She said she was leaving a local bar and had witnessed a young girl being kidnapped. She was following the car as she was speaking to the operator."

"Following the car?"

"Yes. The operator explained the danger of following them, but she wouldn't stop. We told her we had officers in route to the expressway, and we would put up roadblocks to all the possible exit areas, but she continued to pursue them. She made a few turns down some pretty remote roads, and we lost contact. We found her vehicle yesterday."

"Her rental car?"

"Yes. All the tires were flat. They were obviously flattened with what we call a spike strip. It's used to stop criminals in a high-speed chase. There was blood inside. Not a whole lot, but she was gone. The car was empty. There was no luggage, but her phone was there. We have been making every effort to reach her kin, but it takes a little while to get these phones unlocked. We can't just go through people's personal stuff. We have to adhere to certain protocols."

"I understand. When did you find her car?"

"Less than twenty-four hours ago. The car was in a ditch down a remote county road about thirty minutes from here. Officers were responding to the 911 call, and when they found it, it matched the description your daughter gave of the vehicle she was driving."

Lea was shaking all over. Her jaw had tightened with fear, and it was difficult for her to speak.

"Okay, so what do we do from here?"

"We're running a forensics exam of the vehicle. We're looking for fingerprints, hair, and any foreign matter that could provide us with vital information."

His southern accent had a way of calming her a little. He made her feel like he was invested in finding Braydee.

"What can I do from this end?"

"Contact anyone who knows her. Find out when they last spoke. Take notes and call me with any additional information you uncover."

"I tried reaching out to the other ladies she traveled with. All three ladies are scientists at Baylor University. One of the other girls, Tate, is missing, as well. No one has heard from her, either."

"Hmmm. Not good. Where is Tate from?"

"She's from New Orleans. That's where all her family lives. She's been living in Waco for nearly ten years, though. She's thirty-three years old and very responsible. She was supposed to be at work on Monday morning and didn't show up."

"Interesting. Definitely not a coincidence. Did they travel to Orange Beach together?"

"No. According to the other friend, Braydee left in a rental car and headed your way. She was supposed to be meeting up with a guy she met online. She had never met him in person, as far as we know. This would have been their first face-to-face visit. Tate took their rental car and drove to Pensacola to visit friends."

"Do you know the name of the guy she was meeting?"

"Grant Wilson. As far as I know this is the first time, she's ever done something like this."

"Online dating has never been more dangerous. I'll see what I can find on the guy. Has anyone talked to the friends Tate was going to see? Did she ever make it to see them?"

"I'm not sure. We don't even know who they were. Maybe her parents know."

"Okay. Give me any names and numbers of people I can talk to concerning Tate. I'll check the manifest and see if she ever boarded the plane in Pensacola. I'll need the name and phone number of the other friend they were there with, as well."

Lea gave the officer as much information as she could. She described both of the girls and passed along phone numbers and contact information. He reassured her that they would be doing everything possible to find her daughter.

"Is there any reason for me to come there? Any reason at all?" asked Lea.

"No, ma'am. The city is unfamiliar to you, and there is nothing you can do here. We've issued a missing person's report and put-up posters around the neighboring towns, as well as here."

"Thank you, sir. I know you'll call us as soon as you hear anything."

Lea called the science department at Baylor. After several transfers, she spoke to the head of the department where Braydee worked.

"Hi. This is Lea Quinn. I'm Braydee Quinn's mother. I'm just checking in to see if there's anything you can tell me about the last time you saw Braydee at work."

"Hi, Mrs. Quinn. We're all so worried. Braydee and Tate are favorites of ours. As I told the police here in

Waco, there was a gray SUV sitting in the parking lot for days. Two men. They were mostly working on their computers and phones. Several of us saw them. We discussed it amongst ourselves, but no one cared enough to approach the car and to what they were doing here."

"Is it possible they were stalking the place or watching the girls?"

"Yes, maybe."

Lea's mind was racing. "It's possible they had planned to take Braydee from the school, but when she left on vacation, they decided to take her from the beach instead."

"Yes, I guess anything is possible."

"Did you give the police a description of the men?"

"Yes. I was able to describe them distinctly because they just didn't fit in with the surroundings. Both were heavy men. Well over 250 pounds, I would say. Both had beards. One was bald and extremely sunburnt. The other one wore a ball cap. I would say they were at least mid-fifties. One wore a t-shirt and the other one had on a short-sleeved button-up shirt. Both days when I saw them, they were wearing similar clothes. I saw one standing outside the SUV one day. He was smoking, and he had a big tattoo on his forearm, but I couldn't make out what it was."

"Thank you. I'll get that reported to the officer in Alabama. If anything else comes to mind, will you give me a call?"

"Absolutely."

Capt. Marshall called the forensic lab.

"Do we have any prints or information on the Braydee Quinn car yet?"

The officer on the other end of the line looked at the report. "We just got it in. It took a little while because there were numerous sets of prints that had been lifted from inside the car. None of them were in the database."

"It was a rental car, right?"

"Yes, that's right. However, there is something very odd. There were several prints on the outside of the car and on the door handle. The prints match a Baldwin County police officer. The problem is that he wasn't the officer who found the car, so his prints shouldn't be there."

"Who is the officer?"

"Duke Davis."

"Duke Davis, the son-in-law of Judge John Sands?"

"Yep. That Duke. This sounds beyond messy."

"My thoughts exactly. The responding officer's handprint was on the outside of the car door. It was a flat palm print where he'd shut the door after he'd looked inside the vehicle. Duke's prints were on the outside handle and inside of the car. His prints are even on the seatbelt. This means that Ofc. Davis arrived before the responding officers and opened the door and removed the seatbelt from the woman. It doesn't make a lot of sense."

"Can you email me the report? Whatever you have, send it to me. Keep this to yourself for now. We can't have this leaking out to the press. They will have a feeding frenzy."

"You got it."

Capt. Marshall took out his cell phone and called Judge John Sands.

Chapter Nine

"Hey, John. This is Gary Marshall. We have a big problem. I wanted you to hear it before anything goes any further."

"Hey, Gary. What is it?"

"Duke Davis's prints were found on the handle of a car we brought in. The driver went missing three days ago."

"What does this mean?" John spoke through gritted teeth.

"We aren't sure yet. He wasn't the responding officer. The woman in the car was following a kidnapping victim. She spotted the girl being harassed at The Undertow, followed her outside, and saw her being shoved into a car. She was following them while she was on the 911 call."

"So how in the world are his prints there? This doesn't make sense." John squeezed his fist as if he were about to punch something.

"I'm not sure, but this doesn't look good at all. The caller ended up with four flat tires from a spike strip. Looks like the same type of strips we use. Officers were given her location when the 911 caller lost contact. After searching the area, they found the car in a ditch and the caller was gone. Her name was Braydee Quinn. We got pictures, and forensics stepped into the dust for fingerprints. Davis wasn't one of the officers we sent out that night, so his prints have no reason to be there from our perspective."

"There's got to be an explanation for it."

"I hope so."

"Do you have any details on the missing woman? Where is she from?" asked the judge. The judge knew exactly where they were from. He had masterminded the entire operation.

"The woman driving the car was thirty-two years old, and she's from Waco, Texas. We think the other girl that was kidnapped from the bar is around seventeen years old, according to the caller. No one at the bar had ever seen either one of them before."

"Thanks for the heads-up, Captain. I'm not sure how to even respond to this. I'm at a loss. I mean, the kid is an idiot sometimes, but he's a good kid. Just don't see him being involved in something like this." John squeezed the phone until his knuckles were white.

"I don't know. I've seen it all in my line of work. I'm sure you have, too. People can fool you. You can be sleeping with a viper and not even know it sometimes."

"Aren't that the truth? It's hard to trust anyone these days."

"I'm going to have to bring Duke in for questioning."

"Yeah, I understand that. Keep me posted. Thanks for the heads-up."

"Will do."

Capt. Marshall had known the judge for nearly twenty years. They weren't friends, just acquaintances, but he thought the judge deserved to hear it from him instead of the news. Things had a way of making the headlines pretty quickly around a small town.

Judge Sands called his son-in-law.
"You stupid son-of-a-bitch!"
"Hold up. What?"

"Your prints are on the woman's door handle; you dumb sack of potatoes!"

There was no response from Duke.

"Do you know what you've done? Do you know what kind of trouble you're in?"

"Forgive me for being lost here. I saw an injured woman, and I jumped in to help her."

"This was a very clandestine operation. I made that clear. I just got a call from the station! Your stupidity has now got me involved."

"I'm sorry, I don't know what I was thinking."

"You weren't. That's the problem. I should have never trusted you with something so important as this."

"What exactly did you get me involved in, sir?"

"Shut up with the questions. You haven't earned the right to ask me any questions."

Duke was shocked. "I haven't earned the right, sir? With all due respect, I just helped stick a girl in the back of a van, and I didn't ask you a single question about it. Questions like: What did she do? Where is she going?"

"Because that's not your business, boy."

"Don't 'boy' me. I'm not your little boy blue. I've never disrespected you and..."

"And you won't start now." The judge interrupted.

"And neither will you. I'm telling you that if I'm in some trouble, I need to know exactly what it is. Maybe if I had asked the questions before, I wouldn't be in this situation."

"No, if you had followed the directions I gave you, you wouldn't be in this situation. Taking the ring ... well, that was just pure stupid. This could open up so many questions that could eventually lead back to people you don't want to piss off. I told you not to leave one single piece of evidence that you were at the scene. Don't you think fingerprints are the one thing you wouldn't want to leave at a crime scene?"

"Are you serious right now? A crime scene? Let me ask you this. Who were the good guys, and who were the bad guys last night?" asked Duke.

"How dare you insinuate that I would do anything improper! I've served this community longer than you've been wiping your own ass."

Duke sat quietly. He didn't know the facts about what he had done, and he certainly didn't want to make assumptions about his father-in-law."

"Now, how are you going to explain those fingerprints at what was supposed to be a very top-secret operation? Go ahead. Give it your best shot." The judge was getting louder.

Still no response from Duke as he processed the magnitude of what was happening.

"Did any of the other officers see you there?" asked John.

"No, but tell me now. Did I do something illegal, or was it a secret mission? Why does it matter if my fingerprints are on the door? You asked me to be there. I thought I was helping."

"You thought. There you go again. When's the last time thinking got you anything good?"

"When I married your daughter."

"Don't be coy with me. Those girls are now missing, and you were at the scene. You're in a world of trouble, Son. You just kicked a fire ant mound that you can't possibly control."

"And why are they missing persons?"

"How am I supposed to know? Maybe the men in the van didn't take them where they were supposed to go! I can't talk right now. I'll have to see what I can do. This is out of my control now. You know how this goes. Keep your mouth shut."

"You got me into this."

"What did you say? No. I didn't get you into anything. You were told to hide and lay spike strips in order to catch a person of interest who has eluded authority for a long time. It was a secret mission. Instead, you dragged a woman out of her car and threw her in a van you knew nothing about. Now, tell me, what part of my instructions did you misunderstand?" He had the gift of gab and for confusing Duke.

Duke thought about what he had been told to do, and the judge was right. There had been no mention of grabbing a girl or putting her in the van.

"Oh God. I really screwed up. I'll figure it out. I'll keep my mouth shut. I especially wouldn't say anything that would implicate you, Pops. I think I need a lawyer."

The judge cringed. He hated being called 'Pops' by Duke. He was an idiot. His daughter had married an idiot. He was just thankful his daughter had not been stupid enough to get pregnant.

"I'll see what I can do. I need you to meet me at the boat slip in Perdido Key. I have someone that may help you. Meet me at three p.m. Turn off your phone and take it to the post office box, like last time. Are you confused by any of this?"

"No sir. I mean ... yes sir. I'll be there. No, sir, I'm not confused. I'll see you soon." He was willing to do whatever he needed to do at this point. He knew he was in way over his head.

The judge made a phone call to Bob Seagrave.

"We have a serious problem. I need you to take care of it. Be at the town square at 2:30."

"You got it."

The "town square" was a code word for the secluded meeting spot between Orange Beach and Perdido Key. There was a boat slip that sat on twenty-two acres of unoccupied private land. Whoever he was meeting there would be disposed of as fish food deep into the ocean.

Bob had worked for the judge for twelve years after strings had been pulled and backs scratched to get him out of prison. He'd made a deal with the devil, and that kind of deal couldn't be broken without a serious price. He didn't mind doing the dirty work for John. It paid well and beat being in prison.

Capt. Marshall called Ofc. Davis. He looked at his watch. It was nearly lunchtime.

"Hey, Davis. I know this is going to be inconvenient and a little alarming, but I need you to come in this afternoon and answer some questions regarding a missing lady."

"Can it wait till tomorrow? I have plans this afternoon." He blurted it out without thinking.

"No. It can't wait. I'm going to need you to cancel those plans. We found your prints at what's now considered a crime scene. You're in some deep trouble unless you have an explanation as to why your prints are there."

"I really can't cancel my plans. Kinda important meeting with my father-in-law this afternoon. Also, it's my day off and you know I've had a few beers. I'm not in any shape to answer questions." He hadn't had any beer but needed time to figure out how he would explain what he'd done.

"I understand that. I like you, Duke. I'm going to cut you some slack, but you need to be here first thing in the morning."

"Will do. I'll see you by 8:30 a.m. Is there any reason I might need a lawyer present?"

"I don't know. You tell me. Is there? Strange question from a kid who had no idea why he's being called in."

Duke bit on his lip and shook his head. Why couldn't he just shut up?

"Alright, then. I'll see you in the morning," said Duke.

Bob pulled up to The Wharf Marina. He parked his car and casually walked down the dock to the slip that housed Judge Sand's boat. He unhooked the ropes and stepped on board.

"Hey, are you the captain of this boat today?" A voice yelled down the dock.

"I am today. Why?"

"Just bein' nosy. It's a beauty. I keep an eye on things around here."

The boat was custom-made with crimson, gray, and white paint. On the side of it was painted 'The Lollygagger'.

"No time to chat, buddy. Sorry, I'm in a bit of a hurry." Bob had not wanted to make any contact, of course, but sometimes it just couldn't be avoided.

Bradley, who worked at the Marina, made a note of the time the boat pulled out at 1:05 p.m. The boat was driven by a man with gray hair. He was wearing a straw hat and work boots. Older fella. He committed the details to his memory and watched as the boat pulled away.

Bob arrived at the secluded boat slip around 1:45 and parked the boat. He made his way into the brush and hid until Duke arrived.

Duke pulled in around 2:45. He didn't expect to see the boat sitting there. He stepped out of the truck and called out to John on the boat, but there was no answer. He got back in the truck and called Melissa. The call went straight to voicemail. He really wanted to explain everything to her.

He hung up the phone and remembered the judge telling him to leave his phone at the post office. He knew why. It was obvious he didn't want the phone pinged in their secret meeting area. It was too late. He had forgotten to drop it off.

He had met the judge here one other time and was instructed the last time not to bring his phone as well. Before today, he felt so privileged to know about this private location used for undercover meetings, but now he wasn't so sure about this place. He felt uneasy and stepped out of the truck to get some air, leaving his phone inside on the truck seat.

Sitting on a rickety bench on the dock watching the waves slap the shore, his pulse raced. His God-given instinct for survival kicked in. He could feel someone near him. His body went on full alert mode.

Scrunched down in the brush, Bob recognized him immediately. The son-in-law? He said to himself. Good grief.

He began creeping from the brush line and across the sand holding a syringe filled with a powerful sedative. Duke could sense the movement behind him but didn't move. He sat very still, barely breathing, until he felt the perpetrator upon him. With a single swing, he knocked the man to the ground and pounded him with his fists. They fought ferociously until Duke managed to grab the syringe and stab Bob in the neck with it. Within seconds, Bob went limp. He dug a hole with his shoe heel, dropped the syringe in it, and covered it with sand.

He dragged Bob across the dock and put him in the boat. Within an hour, they were far from shore and safely at sea. Bob's hands and feet were tied securely with zip-ties he'd found on the boat. Most likely zip-ties that were meant to be used on Duke.

An hour passed by, and Bob began to wake up.

"You decided to wake up and enjoy the view?" asked Duke.

Bob said nothing.

"I know my father-in-law sent you."

No answer.

"I'm just not sure how he could be so cruel as to kill his daughter's husband."

Still nothing from Bob but a groggy expression.

"So, if you're interested in living, you can tell me what's going on. I'm a fair and honest man. I promise."

"They'll kill me if I tell you anything."

"So, what do you think I should do? I mean if you were in my shoes. My father-in-law sends a guy who's attempting to tranquilize and tie me up. Now here we are, with the tables turned. You're all bound up with the ties I found that were most certainly meant for me."

No response.

"Should I let you live or throw you to the sharks?"

"I'm a dead man either way."

"Not at the moment. You have a chance to live. You can literally choose life right now."

"That easy, huh? My job is to kill. If I don't do that, then I won't have a job. You understand? They will always come for me. This is bigger than you can imagine."

"What's bigger?"

He didn't answer.

"Why did the judge want me dead?"

"Do you really not know?"

"No."

"Those rings you took and the fingerprints you left on that girl's car put you right in the middle of the kidnapping. Once they begin questioning you, it won't take long for things to lead to John."

"Kidnapping? I had no idea it wasn't a legit operation. I did what John asked me to do, but I would never get involved in a kidnapping! I didn't take the rings, either. They were handed to me."

"Seriously? And that makes it okay?"

"I swear I didn't know what was happening. Has he done this before?"

Bob sat slouched on the chair. He was so tired and broken. All his years of loyalty and hard work had come to this - being zip-tied in a boat in the middle of the ocean.

"We're all in over our heads," said Bob.

"Who?"

"Everyone involved with the judge."

"Tell me what he's doing?"

"I'm a dead man either way right now. What's it going to hurt if I tell the truth?" he said under his breath. "He's kidnapping children and women."

Duke stared stone-faced, even though he was shocked.

"You mean he's part of a human trafficking ring?"

"No, he IS the human trafficking ring. Everyone follows his orders."

Duke breathed slowly. That's what the girl in the van had said. It was true. His heart pounded in his chest.

"And he wants me dead," said Duke. It was a statement, not a question.

"That's right."

"And if I don't kill you, you're going to kill me?"

"Yes."

"And if I untie you when we get back to the shore, you can't just walk away?"

"No. Not a chance. I know too much. He'll hunt me down for the rest of my life."

"Why can't you just stop and do the right thing? Testify against the judge and start a new life?"

"It wouldn't matter. If the judge gets locked up, there are ten more men ready to step in and take over. This is a global crisis. They won't stop until they find me."

"I don't want to kill you, man. What's your name?"

"Robert Seagrave." It had been so many years since someone had asked his name. "They call me Bob."

"Listen, Bob, we don't have long. The judge will be waiting for you to check-in. When you don't, he'll start looking for you, me, and the boat. It won't be too hard to find this boat, especially if he has GPS on it."

"True."

"I'm going to be hiding out for a while, it seems. I'm asking you one more time. Can you give me your word you will just walk away and disappear. I'll let you go when we get back to the shore. I promise."

"Not happening."

"So, you're saying it's either me or you? No chance you're coming over to the good side?"

"The good side? Really? Listen, I've faced death around every corner and every job I've done. I'm not afraid and I'm ready to die."

Duke could feel the despair in his voice. He couldn't imagine what had happened in Bob's life that had led him to this place.

"You've got five minutes to make your peace with this world and God. If there's anything you want to say, say it. This is it. It's down to me or you, Bud."

Bob dropped his head. "There's a little girl living in Tyro, Kansas. I need you to find her. She's going by the name of Kasey Walton."

"Okay. How can I find her?" It was the most unexpected thing Bob could have said.

"Tyro is two hours south of Wichita. It's one of the smallest towns in Kansas. Only a few hundred people live there. Go to West Olive Street. There's only one house on the street. Just knock on the door and tell them Bob sent you, and that you're here for the girl. They've always known someone was going to come for her."

"Who is it? Why would I just go get a child in Kansas for you?" He was so confused.

"It's that kid, Kasey Kendall, who disappeared from Orange Beach several years ago."

"Dear God! Seriously?"

"Yep. One of your officer buddies took her."

"I remember." Duke was suddenly nauseated and filled with utter disgust. "He wasn't my buddy. Is this your way of redeeming yourself?"

"You could say that."

"Go downstairs and move that small green dresser. Behind it there is a panel that's a little loose. You will find her shoes and an officer's badge. It belongs to an officer who once worked for John. You know, the one who disappeared."

"Woody Thomas?!"

"Yes."

"Woody was working for John?"

"Yep. He took the girl. John told me to bring the girl out here and dump her. But when that little girl looked me in the eyes and asked me where her mommy was, I just couldn't do it. I could never hurt a kid like that. That's not part of my job."

"Damn. What about the badge?"

"Four months after Woody took the girl, John started seeing signs that he was too big of a liability for this kind of work. He told me to get rid of him. I dumped him at sea, and I took his badge. I even used it to get women sometimes."

"Seriously?"

"Yep, and it worked."

Duke headed down the stairs to look behind the green dresser.

Bob stood up. His hands and ankles were still tied up, but he inched his way to the side of the boat. He leaned over as far as he could until his weight pulled him overboard. Duke heard the splash and ran back up the stairs holding the two little Disney princess tennis shoes. Bob was gone. He looked over the side and saw the last of him sinking just below the surface of the water. He shook his head. This was bad. Now he would be blamed for the murder of Bob Seagrave.

He needed a plan fast.

He looked around the boat at all the food and supplies onboard. It would have been so easy to just stay on the boat, but he knew there was no way he could take a chance on staying for even one night. He grabbed a rucksack and filled it with blankets and as many supplies as he could. He placed the shoes and the badge back in the hidden compartment behind the green dresser.

He rummaged through the drawers and looked under the seats. Jackpot! It was just like the judge to have a wad of cash stashed on board. In the box was thirty-nine thousand dollars neatly stacked. He placed the box in his bag.

He drove the boat to Pelican's Perch Marina in Pensacola and parked it. He would go by foot and pay with cash from this point forward. That wasn't too hard in a place like Pensacola. It's full of transients and beach bums. He could sleep on the beach, for that matter. He would lay low for as long as it took to expose the judge. Meanwhile, he had to get word to someone that Kasey Kendall was alive!

Chapter Ten

Duke

Capt. Marshall sat with the other investigative team, waiting for Duke, but he never came.

At 8:45, Marshall called Judge Sands.

"We're here at the precinct waiting on Davis. He was supposed to meet us at 8:30 this morning. He hasn't shown up. Said he had plans with you yesterday afternoon."

The judge held back his urge to let out a string of cuss words. "No, we didn't have plans. Not sure why he said that. We had plans on Sunday. We had a barbecue at my house for the family. Yesterday I had cases until late in the evening. I left here at seven p.m. and met my wife for supper at 7:45."

"That's a strange thing for him to say. He never struck me as being very quick on his feet with an excuse. Always seems to blurt out the truth when he's pressed."

"I agree with that."

"Did you talk to him yesterday?"

"Yeah, I called to tell him that he better have a damn good excuse for leaving his fingerprints on the car."

"What time was that?" asked Marshall.

"Maybe 1:00 p.m. He said he'd met a woman at The Keg. They talked for a while, and he walked her to her car. He opened the door for her, and that was it. It had to be the same woman." Its too bad Duke couldn't have thought of such a simple story. He would have been all over the place trying to recreate his encounter with the woman. He was such a loose cannon.

"Ah, that makes sense."

The judge half-smiled at his own wit. He had always been able to talk circles around everybody until they believed what he was saying. He always considered himself the smartest man in the room.

"If you hear from him, be sure to let him know it's crucial that he come in today. If he doesn't show up, I'm issuing a warrant."

The judge smiled again. He was finally done with Duke Davis for good. No more fake smiles or back pats. He doodled a happy face on the document in front of him. "I'll be sure to tell him."

The captain called Melissa.

"Hi, Mrs. Davis. This is Capt. Marshall down at the precinct. I need to ask you a few questions. It's about your husband."

"Is he okay?"

"I'm not sure. He was supposed to meet me this morning at 8:30 a.m., and he hasn't shown up. I was just wondering when you last saw him?"

"I saw him yesterday when I left for work. I talked to him at lunchtime."

"Was he ok?"

"Yes. He just called to say he loved me. He left me a voicemail around 2:45 yesterday. He didn't say where he was, just that he needed to talk to me about something. Said he may be in some trouble. I didn't hear the message until after I got off work. By then, he wasn't answering his phone. So no, I haven't seen him since yesterday."

"Really? And is that normal?"

"I don't know his schedule. Couple that with his irresponsible night binges every so often. I haven't seen or talked to him since that last phone call, though. He made me a promise on Sunday after he'd had an all-night bender, that he wouldn't stay out without letting me know where he was. He gave me this outlandish ring as a token of his sincerity." She held up her hand and looked at the ring. "I haven't bothered checking on him because I'm just so angry. He did the same thing to me on Saturday night."

"What did he do Saturday night?"

"Stayed out all night. He said he was working late. Sunday morning, I called our friend, Whit and found out he was sleeping on his couch. Been there drunk all night and his phone was dead."

Someone was calling. She looked at her phone, hoping to see that it was Duke. "I'll have to call you back. That's my dad calling."

"Okay. I need to hear the voicemail he left you when you get time."

"Sure thing."

"Hey, Hon. Have you heard from Duke?"

"No, I was just on the line with Capt. Marshall. I'm a little worried. Capt. Marshall said he didn't show up for work today. They had a meeting scheduled at 8:30. That's not like Duke."

"Don't worry yet. He was off work yesterday. We know how he can get on his day off. A bit sloppy."

"He's never missed work because he drank too much on his off day. Come on now, Dad. I'll let you know when he calls."

"Call me if you hear anything at all. I'm so sorry he keeps putting you through this. I'd call him a piece of shit if he wasn't your husband."

"You've called him that many times. I don't know why now would be different. I'll call you later, Daddy. Love you."

It had been three days since Duke had officially gone missing. Det. Cory Knotts had been assigned to the case.

Rumors were swirling about Duke's fingerprints on a missing girl's car door. The story was beginning to grow and spread. It was getting out of hand. There were whispers in the local Walmart. A number of people thought they had seen the two of them together.

"I heard the two of them ran off together," one lady was heard telling another lady at the supermarket. "Apparently, she was some wealthy businesswoman from out of town who'd been setting up rendezvous with the officer. Seems they both just disappeared into thin air," said the cashier.

Melissa didn't know what to believe anymore. She would never have dreamed that Duke would cheat on her. She searched the house for any clue she could possibly find. As she pilfered through her husband's drawers and pockets, she found a small piece of paper with four sets of numbers on it.

She called the phone number she had been given for Det. Knotts.

"Hi, it's me. Melissa Davis. I found something this morning. It's just a little piece of paper with some numbers on it, but it looks like a lock combination. We don't have any locks with combinations that I know of."

"Can you take a picture of it and send it to me?"

"Sure." She took the picture and sent it.

"Thank you. Every little thing matters when it comes to finding someone. I'm looking at it now. The first number is most likely a locker number. The other three are definitely numbers to a combination."

"I'm not aware of any lockers he would have."

"Let me do some research. I'll get back to you soon."

"Okay. Please do."

After asking around, someone recognized it as a post office box.

Det. Knotts made a phone call. "I need to get a forensics guy to go with me to the post office. I'm going to open a box, and whatever is in it will be taken as evidence. How soon can someone meet me there?"

"I can have someone there in less than an hour."

"Great. That will give me time to call his wife and get her to meet us there. She'll give us the okay to open it up without a warrant."

"Roger that. I'll be sending Richard. You guys have worked together before."

"Yes. I'll be looking for him."

Melissa arrived at the post office within twenty minutes. She and Capt. Marshall waited inside the lobby for the forensics expert and the detective.

"I'm so nervous to see what's in this box. I don't think my heart can handle any more bad news. Do you think he was having an affair? Could he have been getting mail from a woman?"

Marshall laid his big hand on her back. "I just don't know what's going on. My instincts tell me he didn't disappear on his own. Everyone we've talked to has told us how much he loved you, and that Duke had never been seen with another woman. Even on his drunkest nights."

She wanted to believe that.

Richard and Det. Knotts arrived, and the four of them walked to the mailbox number listed on the scrap of paper. It was a larger mailbox. The detective turned the small knob and opened it up.

With rubber gloves on, the forensic expert removed the contents slowly placing them in a box. Melissa gasped.

Inside the mailbox was an envelope containing five thousand dollars stuffed in a McDonald's bag along with two rings. The detective pulled them out and carefully examined them. Inside one of the rings was an engraving. "We love you".

Melissa felt the ring on her finger. "This isn't good. I think I'm going to throw up." Her stomach churned, and she felt weak.

Capt. Marshall took her by the arm to steady her.

"Let's step outside." Capt. Marshall walked outside with her. "Sit down right here, and just relax for a few minutes."

Melissa sat with her head in her hand fighting the urge to puke.

"I'm so sorry, ma'am. I know you want answers, and we're going to do everything we can to get those answers for you."

She stared at her hands. "I want you to take this ring." She slipped it off her hand and handed it to the Capt.

"Why?" he asked.

"Something tells me it belonged to the same person who owned those other two rings. If it turns out I'm wrong, you can give it back to me."

"Oh no. I'm so very sorry. Where did you get it?"

"Duke gave it to me Sunday."

"Oh God. This is bad."

Her phone rang, and she jumped. "It's my dad. I need to answer it." She put it on speaker.

"Hi, Dad. I'm at the post office." She began to cry hysterically. "Duke had a post office box! I found the combination in our drawer. We're here. They just found a ton of cash in it. He also had a couple of rings in the..." The judge interrupted.

"Stop. Who's with you?"

"The Captain, Det. Cory Knotts and some other forensics guy."

"Don't let them take anything. Do you hear me? They can't just go through his stuff without a search warrant. It's illegal." His words were sharp and angry.

"Dad! What are you talking about? They don't need a search warrant. I asked them to come over and go through it. I'm trying to find out what happened to my husband!" She took him off of the speaker. The detective could still hear every word as he sat next to her.

"I understand. But anything they find will be used against him, and we just don't know what he's up to."

"He's missing, Dad! He could be anywhere at this point. Maybe even dead. No one has heard anything from him. It's not like they're going to charge a dead man with something. I'm concerned about where he is and what he was involved in. Why would he have thousands of dollars stuffed in a post office box instead of in the bank? I don't give a rat's ass about what incriminates him at this point. I want to find him!"

"Listen to me. Get them out of there now. I'm telling you. It could incriminate you, as well."

"Me? How?"

"Things that could look suspicious. When they go through his phone, it could involve you inadvertently. I'll help you figure this out. We'll get a lawyer."

"His phone?"

"Yes."

"I didn't say they had his phone, Dad. Calm down."

"His phone isn't there?"

"No. Why would his phone be at the post office?"

Marshall listened and made a note of the bizarre assumption that his phone would be at the post office.

"Why would anything be at the post office other than mail? Just stop them now." He growled angrily.

He had told Duke to put the phone in the box. The plan was for Bob to pick it up and destroy it. If it wasn't there, that meant that Duke had done something stupid and most likely had taken it to the meeting place.

"Dad, you're scaring me. Now if you don't mind, I need to regroup and finish up here."

"Melissa!"

She hung up and sat there thinking, confused at her dad's response. He should have been as confused and curious as she was. John called back but she didn't answer this time. The judge pounded his desk with his fists.

Det. Knotts and Richard joined them outside the post office.

"Thank you, Mrs. Davis. This has proven to be extremely helpful in so many ways. We'll fill you in on anything we discover about these rings."

"Thank you." She barely squeaked out the words.

"You don't have any idea where Duke could have gotten all this cash?"

"No clue. I'm as shocked as you are."

"I'm sorry, ma'am. We'll get you some answers soon."

The detective placed the ring Melissa had handed him inside the box. "We'll be in touch as soon as we know something. Are you ok to drive?"

"I am."

Melissa called her mom as she sat in the car and cried like a baby as she explained what they had just found. Rhonda Sands was a strong woman who had been through so much pain in her own life, but hearing her daughter in this kind of anguish was unbearable. She silently prayed for peace as her daughter broke down on the other end of the line.

Back at the station, everything was processed into evidence. Capt. Marshall made a phone call to Mrs. Lea Quinn.

"Hi, Mrs. Quinn. It's Capt. Marshall from Orange Beach."

"Yes, hello. I've been expecting you."

"There have been some developments."

"Thank God!" said Lea.

"We found fingerprints from one of our officers on the handle of the car your daughter was driving. He was called in for questioning but never made it to the meeting. He disappeared, and no one had seen him in three days. We located a post office box from a piece of paper his wife found. We also found some rings. One of the rings has an inscription inside."

"We love you," she interrupted. "It was from me and her dad when she graduated college." She began to cry.

"You found that in the officer's post office box?"

"Yes. Obviously, this means he knows something. Since no one has seen or heard from him we're beginning to worry. He could have left the state or worse, he could have been killed, or committed suicide.

"Hopefully, he's still alive. We need answers."

"Yes, we do."

"We have search parties looking for him. I'll be in touch as soon as we find him. Call me if you can think of anything at all that could help us."

"You know I will. Goodbye, Capt. Marshall. Thank you," said Lea.

Chapter Eleven

Duke

Judge Sands called Bob for the fifth time. Still no answer. Something was terribly wrong. Bob had never failed to check in after a job, and it had been way too long. His body was clammy with sweat as he anticipated what problems Duke had continued to create for them.

Meanwhile, in Pensacola, Duke pulled his hat down over his eyebrows and checked in at a local dump under a fake name.

"Hello, sir, what can we do for you?" The old-timer sat behind the rundown desk and put aside the book he was reading.

"I just need to get a room for a few weeks. Do you have one available?"

"You're vacationing?"

"Just going through some hard times and need a place to lay low and relax a bit."

"Well, you came to the right place. Pensacola Beach has everything you need to recuperate. Women, booze, and beaches. I recommend them in that order." He chuckled. "Just need you to fill this out."

He shoved a piece of paper across the counter, and Duke filled in the information with a fake name Don Watrous.

"So, your name is Don Watrous?"

"Yes, sir," he lied.

"I used to know some Watrouses. Are you any kin to Charles and Kayla Watrous?"

"No, sir. We aren't from around here. My family's from up north."

"You sound like a southern boy."

"I am. We moved here when I was in middle school."

The old man handed Duke the key and directed him to the room. "If you need anything, come on down or give me a call. My name's Kenneth. I'm the owner."

"Will do, Mr. Kenneth."

Duke found his room and unpacked his belongings. The first thing he wanted to do was call the judge and let him know that he had outsmarted him, but he knew he had to wait. He needed to gather every bit of information and evidence in order to begin his investigation into the judge's activities. He knew it wouldn't be easy, but he was hoping his survival skills would somehow kick in. In truth, he didn't even know where to start.

It had been several days since Duke had checked into the hotel and now it was time to get busy. He needed a computer and the internet. He walked down to the front desk.

"Hey, Mr. Kenneth. Where could I find the nearest library?"

"You need a good book?"

"No, sir. I need access to the internet and a computer."

"Most people your age has all that on their phone these days."

"I'm a little old-fashioned, I guess. I don't have all that fancy phone stuff."

"Good for you. The library is about ten miles away. You have to go over the big bridge to get to it. I have a laptop here that I don't use. It needs charging. You're welcome to it."

"Seriously?"

"Yeah, just bring it back when you're done. Let me see where that paper is that has the instructions to sign on."

"Oh, man! You're a lifesaver."

"Here it is. The username is trapper Kenneth, and the password is Kenneth trapper. That's me. I keep it simple. You can keep it for as long as needed. You look like an honest guy."

Duke laughed at the irony of being on the run at the moment. "I appreciate that."

"Sure. I don't care anything about it. My kids got it for me. Said it was going to help me get smart. All it did was make me feel dumb."

"I can't even tell you how helpful this is. I don't have a car here. I'm just kind of winging it."

"Sure thing. Glad I could help."

Duke went to his room and began his research. He had never cared to learn any details about his father-in-law, but he was about to learn everything there was to know about him.

The first headline that popped up was "Judge John Sands Son-in-law Linked to Missing Woman." He cringed at the sight. His wife must be going crazy by now. The second headline was "Warrant Issued For Baldwin county Missing Police Officer".

He couldn't find anything negative about the judge. Quite the opposite. There were numerous articles praising him for his benevolence and community achievements over the years.

He thought of the one person he could trust enough to call for help. Whit, his best friend. He waited until late in the evening and then walked to the nearest gas station.

"Any chance I can use your phone?" he asked the cashier. "I'll pay you twenty bucks. I'm in a jam and just need to call my buddy."

She was young and happy to take the twenty dollars. She handed Duke the cell phone. He only knew a few numbers by heart and Whit's was one of them.

He called the number, and the call went straight to voicemail.

He called again and Whit picked up.

"Hello?"

"Don't say a word, Whit, just let me talk."

Shocked at hearing his buddy's voice, he just sat there.

"Are you by yourself?"

"Yes."

"At home?"

"Yes. Where are you?"

"Listen, you're the only person I could think of to call. You're the only person I truly trust."

"Thanks, man, but what the hell?"

"I know. What are you hearing?"

"How about I start with the questions? Where are you, and what are you doing?"

"I know it seems pretty messed up right now. You're hearing all kinds of crap, I know, Whit. It's not true. I swear it."

"Even the part where you gave a stolen ring to Melissa?"

"Well, yes, that's the only part that's true. How did you know?"

"Everyone around here is talking about it, and about how you took the rings off of one of those missing women. They found your post office box, Duke. Where did you get all that cash? It's all over the news."

"Whit, let me explain."

"You had better talk fast because I don't want any part of this. What if I'm being watched?"

"I understand."

"No, I don't think you really do. Melissa told me that the detective on the case is going to talk to me about the night you came by. The night the girls were taken. Do you know how this makes me look?"

"Listen, my father-in-law called me and said we needed to meet, so I did. He told me he had a special assignment for me that very few people in the department knew about. It was something involving a federal case, and he couldn't give me any details. He told me that I was supposed to go wait for this car to come down a certain road and throw out a tire shredder."

"So, you did?"

"Yes. I couldn't tell anyone because he said it was a secret mission."

"And you believed him?"

"Why wouldn't I? He's a federal judge, and he's my father-in-law. Anyway, after shredding the tires, I jumped out of my car and ran to help apprehend the suspects. It was a woman. I zip-tied her, and helped put her in the van, but this other girl in the van was yelling at me saying that I was part of a human trafficking ring.

133

I swear I didn't know what I was doing. I thought it was a legit operation. I swear."

"Why did you take the rings?"

"I didn't take the rings. The fat dude that was there took 'em. He handed them to me, and I just instinctively held out my hand. It happened so fast. It was stupid. I've never stolen from a suspect."

"It was dang stupid, Duke."

"But you believe me?"

"Of course, I believe you. I've known you for twelve years. You're my best friend."

"So, will you help me?"

"Yes. Where are you, and what are you planning?"

"I'm in Pensacola. But there's more. The judge called me the day I disappeared and told me he wanted to meet me. I agreed. When I got there, he had sent a hitman."

"No way!"

"Yes! He ambushed me with a syringe. I flipped it on him and stabbed him with it."

"Where is he?"

"He's dead."

"Oh God, Duke."

"I didn't kill him!"

"You're in way over your head."

"That's what the hitman told me. He said anyone involved with the judge is in over their head."

"Did you kill him?"

"No. I was trying to give him every reason to just testify against the judge and live, but in the end, he threw himself overboard."

"This is insane! And you don't have any proof of any of it, do you?"

"No! I know this is a lot. This guy Bob had the judge's boat. He planned to sedate me, take me out into the ocean, and throw me over. Thank God I was able to take him down."

"Geez. Everyone is saying you're a part of something bigger than just these two girls being kidnapped."

"No! It's not me, it's the judge. He's the one involved in a human trafficking operation, and I've got to prove it. I can't show my face until I have enough evidence. But listen, this is huge! Before the guy threw himself overboard, he told me that the kid who went missing back in 2019 is still alive."

"What kid? Wait. I remember the kid."

"Yes! Kasey Kendall. He told me where she was. It was his last act of redemption. Remember that obnoxious cop who used to start trouble at The Keg?"

"Woody? Yeah, I remember."

"He's the one who took her. Her shoes are on John's boat, along with his badge."

"God Almighty! My head is spinning."

"I know, right? I've got to find a way to get this information to the police without being caught, though."

"Definitely. You need evidence linking John with all this. What about your phone? Are there any text messages or voicemails from him?"

"I left my phone in the truck when I was supposed to be meeting John. I'm not sure there's really anything incriminating, though. He never sent texts. He almost always communicated through a private phone. He said only a few people had the number. Not even his wife or Melissa knew the number. It always came up as a blocked call. I doubt they'll be able to trace it back to him."

"Well, let's hope there's some shred of evidence in your phone. There's a search party looking everywhere for you. They should find your truck pretty soon. It's the real deal - helicopters are looking everywhere. Your picture has been on the news every night since you went missing."

"I could tell you where the truck is but that information links you to me, and we don't need that."

"No, we don't Just lay low, and I'll see what I can do from here."

"Thanks, man."

"Whose phone is this?"

"A cashier at the gas station."

"How will I get in touch with you? I really don't think you should be calling this phone," said Whit.

"I won't call again. I knew it was risky. I'm at a gas station near my hotel. Can you go by Best Buy, get us a couple of burner phoncs, and bring one to me Saturday?"

"Yes. Just tell me where to bring it."

"I'm staying near the Pensacola Dog Beach."

"Been there plenty of times."

"Yep. I'll just be hanging out on the beach near the boardwalk, off to the right."

"Our usual area then? I'll be there at three. I've got to go see my son play in a soccer match on Saturday morning, but after that, I'll head over.

"Okay, sounds good. Thank you, Whit. I can't even begin to tell you what you mean to me."

"I know, man. You'd do the same for me."

"That's right. Hey, don't say a word to Melissa. She would never believe this about her dad. I've got to have proof first."

"I wouldn't dare."

"I would love for you to leave a message with the judge though. Say whatever you want to say, but let him know I'm alive, and I'm coming for him."

"Okay. You got it."

Whit hung up and sat there in disbelief. He googled Judge John Sands and found the phone number and address of the office where he worked. He drove to Best Buy and bought three prepaid phones. The first call he made was to the judge's office. His secretary picked up.

"Judge Sands office, how may I direct your call?"

"Is Judge Sands available?"

"No, he's not. Do you want to leave him a message?"

"Yes, tell him that Bob is at the bottom of the ocean."

"Excuse me? Who is this?"

Whit hung up and smiled. His pulse was racing. He would have given anything to see the look on John's face when the secretary delivered the message.

Chapter Twelve

John walked into his office. It had been a long day in court, and he was mentally exhausted waiting to hear from Bob.

"Hi, Judge. You look rough," said his secretary.

"Thanks, Milly."

"Someone called with a strange message. I left it for you on your desk."

"Thanks." His heart raced at the thought of bad news.

On his desk was a stack of papers he needed to review, along with his messages from the day. He read one after another and stopped abruptly as he read the message Whit had left.

"Bob is at the bottom of the ocean."

He looked around the room as if someone were watching him. Bob had never made a mistake, but if he was dead and Duke was alive, things were about to fall apart. He knew that he'd covered his tracks every time he had spoken to Duke about the assignment. Nothing could trace him to the girls, but this was something he had never anticipated.

He picked up the phone and rang the secretary.

"Did you recognize anything about the person that called earlier with the bizarre Bob message?"

"No, I didn't. Sorry, sir. The voice was a bit muffled. It sounded like a white man if that helps."

"Okay, thanks."

He took his leave through the front office and said goodbye to everyone he passed. "See ya tomorrow."

"Glad to see you leaving early, sir," said Milly.

Driving home, he tried to call Bob one more time. He drove straight from work to the docks where his boat should have been docked.

He walked towards the empty boat slip and stopped. "Hey, Bradley!" He yelled toward the end of the dock.

"Yes, sir?" The young man had been taking care of boats there for some time. He knew the judge well.

"Did you see anyone take my boat out in the past week?"

"Yes, sir. I saw a guy a few days ago. He was wearing some pretty cool work boots, so I noticed him. I asked him if he was the captain for the day. Said he was in a rush and couldn't talk. Kinda brushed me off."

"You mean the boat's been gone for days?" His voice became frantic.

"Yes, sir. It left and never came back. You mean you didn't authorize it?" asked Bradley.

"No, I didn't," lied the judge.

"Sorry, sir. Well, I think I could describe the guy to the police."

"Okay, I'm going to call the police. Just hang tight."

The judge called the captain.

"Hello, Capt. Marshall. There's been a development," said John.

"Go ahead."

"My boat was stolen from the marina. I'm pretty sure it was the day Duke went missing. I think he may have been working with someone who took it. We have a witness here that saw a guy take the boat."

"Okay. I'll send someone over to take a statement from him. In the meantime, do you have a GPS tracker on it?"

"No. I've been meaning to get one for years, just never did. It never goes far, and I haven't needed one. I do have good insurance on it, though," he chuckled.

"Okay, well I'm sending someone over there now. I'll call this in, and we'll find it. It's not easy to hide a custom-painted stolen boat."

An alert was called in, and it went out to all the marinas. "We're looking for a stolen boat with registration number AL-2137-QX. It belongs to John Sands."

Within forty minutes, someone from the Pensacola Marina called to report on the boat. "We have it here at our docks. Young guy docked and paid cash for the slip for the week."

"What did he look like?"

The guy described Duke in detail.

"Yes, that's the guy we've been looking for. I'm sure he didn't give you any details about where he was headed?"

"Not at all. Just paid and left like every other person around here."

"Thanks. Someone will be there soon to pick it up."

The captain called John.

"We found it. It's docked in Pensacola."

"Really? That's great. I'm going to send someone over to pick it up."

"Hold on. We need to send a team over first. We're going to have to hold the boat as evidence for a few days."

"You'll need a search warrant for that, and I'm going to get my boat. I need to see what Duke's done to it." He blurted it out before he could stop himself.

He wasn't used to someone else giving the orders.

"No, sir. You're not. I'm telling you now, don't move this boat. It could be part of a crime scene. You know as well as I do that probable cause of a crime will allow us to search the boat. I'll have a search warrant issued when we hang up."

The judge fumed at the thought of Duke putting him in this position. There were things on the boat that would bring up questions, like why was so much cash being stashed there? He would say it wasn't his, but then it would be confiscated.

"Okay. Well, call me when you're done."

"Of course."

The judge took out his burner phone and punched in a number.

"Duke is alive. He's most likely in Pensacola. He's either paying cash with money he found on the boat, or with his own money. I don't know for certain, so it's going to be hard to find him."

"I'll find him, sir."

"Hey, and Bob's dead. I don't know how this happened, but make sure you take care of Duke. Everything is dependent on him disappearing."

"I will."

The judge's personal phone rang.

"Hey, it's Capt. Marshall. You aren't going to believe this. Someone just called with a tip on Duke's truck. It's down a side road in Perdido Key. I'm headed there now."

"You've got to be kidding!"

"Nope. Will you call your daughter for me?"

"Sure will, thanks."

Melissa answered the phone "Hey, Dad."

"Hey, honey. They found Duke's truck in Perdido Key."

"What? Just his truck? Not him?"

"That's right. That's all I know about it right now. There's something else, though. He stole my boat the day he went missing. He's still alive."

Melissa gasped. "He's alive? Thank God!"

"Did you hear the rest? He stole my boat?"

"Yes. Can it get any worse?"

"He had help from someone. Bradley, down at the marina, saw a guy in jeans and work boots. Kinda wiry guy. Older, with a gray beard. Do you know anyone who looks like that?"

"No, sir."

"Well, they're guessing that he's the one who brought the boat to Duke at a boat slip in Perdido Key. Picked him up there because that's where they found his truck."

"Where's your boat now?"

"They found it in Pensacola. The guy at the marina said Duke showed his ID and paid cash for the boat slip."

"God, help him. What's he thinking? I mean if you're trying to disappear do you go pay for a boat slip? Why not just park it and leave?"

"Probably because they would've looked up the boat registration immediately to see who was parked illegally and called me as the owner to let me know it needed to be moved. Duke needed a head start, so it might be the first smart thing I've seen him do. Risky, but smart."

"Dad. Not now. I'm hurting enough without you making snide comments about my husband. You have no idea how smart, kind, and witty he is."

"I'm sorry, hon. He's still your husband, but I won't claim him as a son-in-law any longer."

"That's understandable. It's like I was married to a complete stranger. I just don't get it at all."

"I know. He fooled all of us. There are evil people all around us. You'd be surprised. You'll let me know if he makes contact with you, right?"

"Of course, I would. He's got to know that there's no way out of this. Everything he's doing is just digging a deeper hole that he can't crawl out of," said Melissa.

"This is Duke we're talking about. He doesn't think past the nose on his face."

"Dad, stop!"

"Sorry, there I go again."

Melissa hated the way her dad always talked about Duke. He'd never been able to see the smart, loving, and kind man she had always known. Duke was more intelligent and calculating than most of the people they hung out with.

"Okay, Dad. I need to go. I'll talk with you soon."

"Wait. They told me they found Duke's phone. I just hope they don't find out more nonsense."

"You never know, do you?"

"No. Hang in there. This will all be over soon."

"I'm trying."

Melissa called Whit. Sobs wracked her voice as she cried into the phone.

"They found his truck just now. No sign of Duke because he stole my daddy's boat and went to Pensacola in it!" Her voice was shaking.

"Listen to me."

"Okay."

"I don't believe Duke is capable of any of the things we're hearing."

Melissa interrupted. "Yes, he is. We found cash and the rings in a secret mailbox, Whit!"

"Just listen to me, please. You and I know Duke better than anyone in this world, right?"

"Yes."

"Does your gut tell you Duke has done something so horrible?"

"No, but everything around me says he did."

"I need you to do something. Just trust me on this."

"What is it?"

"I want you to assume for a moment that someone asked Duke to help them catch a suspect and that it was a secret mission. Do you think he would do it?"

"Yes. He would."

"Right. And what if this person paid him a lot of money to do it, because it was such an important job, and they wanted him to keep his mouth closed about it."

"Go on."

"Where would he be able to deposit that money?"

"Nowhere, and if he brought it home, I would ask questions."

"That's right. I believe it's just possible that someone with a lot of authority orchestrated the kidnapping and needed help from Duke. They paid him and told him to hide it at the post office."

"What about the rings? How can you explain that?"

"How many cops do you know who have taken something at a crime scene? It's wrong, but it doesn't make you a monster."

"That turns my stomach."

"Can you think of anyone that Duke would trust so much that he would have acted without asking any questions? Would he have kept it a secret, even from you?"

"My dad." She said the words without even considering what she was saying. There was silence.

"Your dad?"

"I'm just saying he fits that description. Not that he would ever do anything so bizarre."

"I know what you're saying. I want to help Duke get to the bottom of this, though."

"How?"

"I just need you to replay everything you can from the weeks before this happened. Were there more phone calls or meetings with anyone? Were there any clues that would suggest Duke thought he was involved in a secret mission of some sort?"

Melissa's mind raced back to those days. "I'm way to upset right now to think."

"I know you are, but could you come by tomorrow after work? And please, whatever you do, don't mention a word of this to anyone. Not even your family."

"Okay, I'll come by tomorrow."

Duke's truck and John's boat were taken to the auto pound, where they were being searched by forensics for evidence. So far, no clues were found in the truck. Duke's phone was taken and would be combed through meticulously.

John Sand's man was searching Pensacola and flashing a picture of Duke to every hotel clerk. It wouldn't take long for someone to recognize him.

Det. Knotts was working on possible sightings. With the phone being unlocked and Melissa giving permission to go through it, it saved a lot of time.

He searched through the phone, making notes and looking for details. Capt. Marshall stuck his head inside the door. "Anything so far?"

"One of the last phone calls was with his father-in-law. He has him listed in his phone as Pops. They talked for a little over four minutes. Then he called his wife at 2:45. Nothing after that. No texts. No other calls. Phone pings went from Foley out to Perdido Key."

"Hmm. He told me he had plans with his father-in-law. When I spoke to John, he said he didn't have any plans with him and that he had been in court all day. What time was that call?"

"The call came in from John's number at 11:02 a.m.," said the detective.

"John told me he called him that morning so that lines up. I'll check the log to see if he was in court on the day Duke went missing. What about phone activity on the day the girl first went missing? Anything between them?"

"There were five calls from an unknown number. His phone pinged near the location where we found the girl's car. Records show he was there for hours before the 911 call was even placed. He was there waiting for her, possibly. Lines up with what we already know."

"Davis was working with someone who took the girl from the restaurant. He likely threw out the tire shredder, and we know he opened the door to retrieve Miss Braydee. I'm not sure who he was working with and what he knew at this point, but he was definitely involved."

"I don't know Duke that well," said the detective, "but he sure has a big following in this community. Most people I've talked to think he's a great guy. How much he was involved in this is still to be determined."

"I've known him for a few years. I just don't see Duke involved in a human trafficking ring. That's kind of unheard of in these parts."

"Actually, sir, human trafficking is quite common in Alabama. We think it's only happening in the big cities like New York and Atlanta, but it happens everywhere. According to the Human Trafficking Hotline."

"Seriously?"

"Yes. Some of the young people you see from Ukraine and Moldova working in the restaurants around here were survivors of human trafficking."

"I had no idea."

"Most people don't know. The Mafia takes orphans when they leave the orphanage at the age of fifteen. They offer them jobs around the world at resorts or resort communities like Gulf Shores and Orange Beach. They get them and then they turn them into prostitutes."

"Geez. I had no idea."

"Most people don't know. Sixty percent of all orphan girls in Ukraine and Moldova will become victims of trafficking? Sixty percent! When an orphan girl becomes a victim of trafficking, it's projected that she'll be prostituted around six thousand times and be dead within an average of seven years."

"I had no idea."

"Yeah, I get that a lot. I've worked on some inhumane trafficking cases in the last three years. It's an international travesty. It's getting worse lately with kids having so much unsupervised access to the internet. Not to mention the effect that war and poverty have on their lives."

The captain shook his head in disgust.

"I'm going to do some digging. There was a missing person case a few years back. The situation was quite similar to this case. The officer's prints were found on the car door," said Marshall.

"Whose prints, were they?"

"The judge sealed everything on the case. I can't remember the details other than it was odd. Of course, I do remember the officer said he had met the girl's mother at a bar, and he had opened the car door for her. Same story John gave me about Davis. The mother denied it. She was married at the time, and we believed the officer. It all seemed plausible."

"Hmmm. Yes, we need to find out what we can about the old case and see what other similarities there are, if any."

Detective Knotts pulled up all the old case files from previous years. The missing girl was five-year-old Kasey Kendall. She was taken from a Walmart parking lot. She had been left in the car while her mother ran inside. Prints were found on the door. They were identified as those of a police officer, but it was suggested that they were old prints from a previous meeting. He dialed Mrs. Kendall's phone number, and she answered.

"Mrs. Kendall, this is Det. Knotts with the Baldwin County Police Department. I wanted to talk to you about your missing daughter, Kasey."

"What about her? Have you found something?"

"No, ma'am. But we have a missing persons case ongoing, and there is a similarity in the case."

"What is it?"

"We found the fingerprints of one of our officers on the car door of the missing woman, and he was not the responding officer."

"Was it the same son-of-a-bitch that left his fingerprints on my car?"

"No.

"That officer swore he met you in a bar."

"And that was a lie that you all believed. I swore I had never seen him before and that he had something to do with my daughter going missing. No one believed me."

"I'm sorry, ma'am."

"You're sorry?! Do you know how many years I faced, and still face, the stares of people who think I had something to do with her disappearance? People thought I was cheating on my husband. We divorced, by the way."

"I don't know what to say."

"Then why did you call?"

"I need to know if you had ever seen the officer."

"I told them then, and I'm telling you now: NO! If you want answers to where Kasey is and where this other missing girl is, then go find Ofc. Woody. If this is all you called for, I'll be going now." She hung up before the officer could finish speaking.

His heart ached for the woman. Woody disappeared shortly after Kasey went missing, but it didn't sound like MS Kendall knew that.

He stared at the papers in front of him. There was no new evidence. He reviewed who was on the case at the time. There were no connections to Davis in any way. He was at a dead end.

He turned back to his current case. There were no emails, no pictures, no incriminating texts, or anything else unusual.

Melissa called Whit.

"I'm on my way."

"Okay, be careful. See you soon."

Melissa arrived at Whit's house just before sunset. There was spaghetti cooking and wine chilling.

"Come in, friend." He gave her a big hug.

"This is a nightmare, Whit."

"I know it is."

They sat and chatted about old times as if Duke had passed away.

"Remember our senior year when that stray dog kept hanging around the football field and wouldn't leave? It was because Duke took part of his lunch out to feed him before the lunch wave was over and give him a snack before football practice."

"I remember. That was something I loved about him. He was good like that. I've never questioned his character."

"Same. He was always such a great person and a true friend," said Whit.

"To be such a big guy, he was always so tenderhearted and compassionate."

"Melissa, don't say *was*. I believe Duke is okay."

"I want to believe that. I want to believe there's a perfectly great explanation for why two women would go missing and why he would have the rings of one of the women in a secret post office box with a ton of cash that I knew nothing about. But right now, he's dead to me."

"You don't mean that."

"I do mean it. If he were to walk right through that door tonight, I can't say I wouldn't spit in his face."

"I understand. I really do. Let's hope they find something on his phone that will help him."

"I wish I had your faith."

"I do, too, because it's going to take a lot of prayer and hope for us to get Duke out of this," said Whit.

"For US to get Duke out of this?"

"I'm sorry. I'm just so used to referring to us as a team. It just came out. I meant that it's going to take a lot of faith, hope, and prayers for Duke to get himself out of this."

"Right, and I'm not the one to be praying for him right now," said Melissa.

"Sure you are. Do you still love him?"

"With all my heart."

"Then start praying that you can forgive him and that everything will be revealed so we can find who's really guilty."

"Whit, are you serious right now? You really don't think he had something to do with taking the girls?"

"I'm dead serious. He played a part in them getting kidnapped, yes. But I one hundred percent believe that someone put him up to it and that he had no idea what he was doing. Yes, he messed up and took the rings. Tons of officers have done far worse at crime scenes. Try to move past that part and focus on who could have convinced him to do something like this."

"Okay. I'll try," she said tearfully.

Melissa gave Whit a hug as she left. Driving home, she thought about everything he had said, and she began to pray.

"God, I'm so mad. Please give me peace and clarity. Help me forgive Duke. If he's innocent in taking those girls, please, God, give me answers and help them find the monster who did this. Amen."

Her thoughts became less jumbled as she focused on the last time she had been with Duke. It was a cookout at her parents' house. She had seen her dad and Duke whispering at times, and it was clearly an intense exchange. It was more than intense. It was downright aggressive. Now, thinking back on it, something was going on between them. But what?

Chapter Thirteen

Braydee

"Guess what? As soon as we finish lunch, we're going to spend the rest of the afternoon doing as many fun things as I can possibly think of!" I only had a few more days left with the girls before I started to work at the lab. I wanted every hour to count.

"What are we going to do?" The cries of excitement from the girls took me by surprise.

Marlea stood at the window, unresponsive.

Suddenly her nose began to bleed, and she bent over, covering it with her hand. Blood dripped onto the floor and down her baggy dress. I jumped to my feet, grabbed a towel, and handed it to her.

"Hold it tightly and lean your head back just a bit." I stood next to her as she began to cry.

"It's your fault. Why are you doing this to us?" She whispered.

"I didn't want to go to the park. Those evil men said that they would kill me if I didn't go. They were going to do some very bad things to the girls around you. I didn't have a choice. I hope you'll believe me." She pulled away from my help and sat down with her back against the wall.

"I'm sick," she said.

"You don't feel well?"

"No, I have a disease called leukemia."

I held my breath.

"Who told you that you have leukemia?" I whispered.

"The doctors told my mom."

I whispered into her ear. "Please don't say that you're sick. The bad men will take you away from us, and you will never see your family again. Do you understand me?" I tried to be firm and stern. "They'll kill you if you say you're sick."

Marlea nodded 'yes', and I could see the terror in her eyes.

After several minutes, the bleeding finally stopped, and we all went outside. No one asked any questions, and I was so thankful not to draw attention to the nosebleed.

"Have any of you ever played *Simon Says*?"

Nikki and Clara nodded yes, but none of the others had ever heard of the game.

"Okay. Everyone lines up here. I'm going to stand over there. When I say do something, you can only do it if I say, 'Simon says'. If I don't add the word 'Simon says,' then you can't move. Let's give it a try."

We practiced a few times and then began. The girls laughed as if we were all on the school playground, enjoying the afternoon.

"I have a game we can play." Marlea had not joined us for *Simon Says*, but now she was ready. Her little body moved toward the circle as she spoke. "It's called Duck Goose."

"Does everyone know how to play?"

"Yes!" They all screamed.

"Marlea, you can start."

Marlea walked around carefully tapping each head saying duck until she reached mine. "Goose!" She yelled and was halfway around the circle before I could get up.

Everyone laughed hysterically.

"Duck, duck, goose!" I tapped Nikki and she caught me quickly.

"Now you have to sit in the middle of the circle, G."

The longer we played, the sillier the girls became.

Samantha ran, stiff-legged, hopping, falling down on purpose, and rolling in the grass.

"Let's stand up and hold hands. We're going to circle to the right, and you have to repeat after me."

I really didn't know what I was going to say as we circled, but I was hoping God was going to give me encouraging words that we could hold in our hearts during the awful months to come.

"I'm going to give each one of you a phrase. You will have to remember your phrase."

"Sort of like a part in the school play?" Katrina spoke excitedly. "I always wanted a part in the school play!"

"Yes! Exactly like that." I began giving everyone a phrase to remember. They repeated everything I said.

"The Lord is my shepherd. He sees me on earth.

He knows when I'm hurting. He knows what I'm worth.

He's guiding my footsteps. He knows that I'm here.

He wants me to know that He sees every tear.

When life is unfair and all hope is lost,

I'll look to my Savior, who died on the cross.

This circle reminds us that we are all strong,

and when we feel weak, we'll think of this song.

I love you!" The words flowed from my heart. "Now, let's see if we can do it from the beginning."

One by one, the girls repeated their parts, and it was beautiful.

"Now, let's do it again. This time, when you say your part, you have to step into the middle of the circle and do something. It can be anything! You can do a cartwheel or a backbend, your favorite dance move, or even walk on your hands."

One by one, the girls stepped into the circle. I couldn't remember when I had so much fun. My heart and soul were finally mending. After the divorce, I really didn't think I had any love left in my heart for anything. Being stood up in Orange Beach had knocked me back to feeling betrayed and unable to love. But now, I felt like I had finally found my purpose on this earth beyond science. I had found children who needed me.

After showers, we gathered in the den as usual.

"This area is going to be our pretend lake." I pointed to the side nearest to the door. "Tomorrow we're going to get some branches off of the bushes and make some fishing poles."

"What are we fishing for?" asked Baily.

"Fish, of course, but we can catch anything that will be in our lake! We'll use our imaginations. We can put things in the pretend lake like rags, socks, other branches, and plastic bags. Then we'll catch 'em, build a fire right here in the middle of the room, and we'll cook 'em!"

"Really?"

"Just a pretend fire. But we'll have to watch out for lions and tigers and bears! Oh my!"

"Just like Dorothy," said Lexi.

Nikki smiled at the little one's enthusiasm.

Marlea stood staring out of the window as she had done every day. "I see a man coming."

Everyone froze. A man coming could only mean terror.

The door opened. "Pick a girl." The expressionless face spoke to me, and I didn't respond. "Pick a girl," he said again.

"Nooo!" I screamed. The girls were motionless as if to say don't pick me.

"Then she will do." He grabbed the closest child by the arm and pulled her across our pretend lake and out through the door.

Everyone began screaming in unison. "Samantha! No! Don't take her! Stop!" It all happened within seconds.

I jumped to my feet and rushed to Samantha but stumbled over the children in my haste to reach her. Falling to the floor I grabbed her around her waist and held on with all my might. A quick blow to the head with a wooden baton nearly cracked my skull and left me limp on the floor. The girls gathered around me in horror screaming words I couldn't even make out. It was complete chaos.

Samantha screamed with every ounce of energy her little body could give. She screamed all the way to the car. Some of the screams were muffled, and we knew her mouth was being covered by that large, filthy hand.

Nikki opened the door and yelled at the man. "Please stop. Take me instead. Please." She ran halfway down the path towards the car.

"Get back in the house, or I'll take both of you."

He threw Samantha's tiny body into the car, and they sped away as Nikki watched.

She walked slowly back to the house, and I saw the panic and pain in her eyes as she stood in the doorway. I was still lying on the floor.

"She's gone. Samantha's gone."

The whimpers and sobs reminded me of that first night when I was thrust into the dark chamber with the girls.

"Oh God, why?" It was all I could mutter. I couldn't believe Nikki had just offered herself up as a sacrifice for Samantha. It was like a movie playing out in front of my eyes. I had never seen such bravery in my life. It was inspiring, and it lit a fire inside me.

For the next few hours, we all lay on the floor close together.

"Nikki, I can't believe you would do something so selfless for someone you barely know."

"I feel like I've known her a long time, though. She reminds me of my little sister. My stepdad molested my little sister for a while until I told him to take me instead. I wanted to protect her, but I couldn't. It worked for a while, but then I found out he was molesting both of us."

I grabbed her hand and squeezed it. "You're truly an amazing young girl. I want you to know, I have never in my life seen anything like what you just did. We're on a crazy journey together right now, and nothing makes sense, but you have truly inspired and amazed me with what you just did."

Nikki didn't respond. Nothing about it seemed inspiring to her.

Morning came as morning always does. It doesn't matter if you have had the most amazing night or the worst night of your life, either way, a new day comes. We can either move forward and participate in life, or we can stay in the past. I needed to move forward.

Judging by the rocks in the window, we had been here for twenty-nine days. We didn't play games on day twenty-nine, but we did recite the poem I taught them in the circle. I said Samantha's part. I didn't understand why God didn't just strike these evil bastards dead, or curse them with an awful disease, but that would forever be a part of my new prayer.
"Kill them, God. Burn them alive if You have to." It didn't matter if it was right or wrong to pray. It's what I wanted to pray. It was honest. Unfiltered.
Just after breakfast, an announcement came over the speaker system.
"G, you'll begin work today. There are others who will be helping you. Everything is in place, and we're ahead of schedule. Be prepared to leave within the next hour. You will not be back until well after dark."
"Am I working in this dress?"
"You'll be processed at the facility, and they'll give you scrubs, a lab coat, and shoes," said the man.
"You heard him, girls. I'm going to work. I need you to be strong and take care of each other. Encourage each other. Try not to worry, but instead, focus on using your imagination by mentally putting yourself somewhere else. Can you do that for me?"
The girls nodded.
It was time for me to go.

Chapter Fourteen

Braydee

    I was driven to a facility about thirty minutes from the house. My eyes weren't covered, and I recognized one area of our route. I knew I wasn't too far from Waco. I had been here before, but I wasn't sure what side of town we were on. I tried to remember the road signs so that I could eventually report everything I knew to the authorities once I escaped.

    We turned down an unmarked street. It was long. I'm not sure how many miles down the road we drove, but when we arrived at the facility, I was in shock at the magnitude of the operation. I was expecting some sort of generic black market, metal building with dim lighting and outdated microscopes.

    Instead, the building was state of the art. A magnificent structure that was gigantic. To the right of the building was a barn with sheep clumped together at the edge of the gate. We drove to the back of the building and got out of the car. We walked up to a side door where we entered. I was led down several long hallways. We stopped, and my escort knocked on a green door.

    "Enter," came the voice from behind the door.

    Sitting across the desk was a man in his mid-fifties. Salt and pepper hair, and fairly attractive. He smiled as I entered and stood to shake my hand.

    "Hello, Ms. Quinn. I'm Gavin Pateo. It's my honor to meet you and have you working here at Braxton Therapeutics. I've heard so many great things about your research and your time at Baylor University. Congratulations on your recent job offer in San Diego, by the way."

"How do you know so much about me?"

"I work with some of the people at Fisher Scientific in San Diego. They were the ones who recommended you for the job here."

"Have you people lost your minds? You think you can just kidnap me and force me to work for you?" My voice was elevated and angry.

"We don't think so; we know so. You will work, or there will be consequences beyond anything you have ever imagined. Am I clear on that, or should I rephrase it? Should you decide not to work here at the facility, we'll bind your arms and feet, tape your eyelids open, and force you to watch as we harvest the organs of the children you're living with for the next scientist. Am I a little clearer?"

"Yes."

"Yes, what?"

"Yes, sir."

"Now that we have that out of the way, we can discuss Braxton Therapeutics. We're working hard to become a world-renowned organ distributor, saving the lives of hundreds of thousands by cloning organs. That is where you and your partner come in."

"What partner?"

"I know that you have been working with Tate for many years, and the two of you have become extremely proficient at teamwork. That is why we've brought her here to work with you."

"Tate is here?" My soul leaped with joy and sadness all at once.

"Yes."

"Where is she?"

"She's being held in a different capacity than you. She's in a holding chamber here on campus, as we like to call it. You're being held off-campus."

"When will I see her?"

"Today. I need to make a few things clear before you begin. We're listening, and we're watching. As long as you do your job, the children are safe, and your family is safe. Should you do anything we deem as threatening to our operation, everyone will suffer from your actions."

I nodded. He stood up and made a motion for a woman dressed in scrubs to approach me.

She handed me a white lab coat and a bag and instructed me to follow her. I did.

"This is your workstation. Please ring this bell if you need any assistance. Welcome to Braxton Therapeutics. We're happy to have you onboard. I know you rejoice in the idea of saving lives within these walls." She pointed to my lab room.

She smiled as she stuck out her hand to shake mine, but I couldn't bring myself to touch her. How dare she even think that I would? She handed me a bag.

"There are three pairs of scrubs, two lab coats, and a pair of size seven-and-a-half shoes. Keep them clean and always present yourself as a professional here. There is a laundry service drop-off and pick-up once a week. If your uniforms need laundering, you will place them in this bag, and set it outside your door on Thursday evening before you leave work."

I zoned out on everything she said after that. My mind was trying to figure out how I could get a 'HELP' message to someone through the laundry service. I came back to my senses just in time to hear her say "Good luck" as she exited.

I was overwhelmed with the magnitude of money that had gone into creating such a facility. There were doorways to various rooms and stations along the walls. There were new machines there that we had only just become familiar with at Baylor. So much technology the rest of the world had never seen. I was amazed and impressed.

There were men and women in white coats, walking around with clipboards wearing scrubs and lab coats.

As I familiarized myself with my lab, Tate opened the door, and we ran into each other's arms.

"Tate! I'm so glad to see you!"

We held each other.

"I'm so scared, Braydee," whispered Tate.

"Me, too. Don't let them see your fear. They need us. That much is clear. Are you being held by yourself?"

"Yes. I've been in a little room on the back side of this place. I haven't even been outside the room until today. What about you? Are you by yourself?"

"No. I have eight children staying with me in a house about an hour away from here." My heart sank. "Well, seven now. They took one of the girls yesterday."

"This is a living nightmare."

"I know."

Someone stuck their head in the room, and it startled us. "You have 24 hours before the first donor organs arrive. Get busy. No more talking."

We stared at each other with wide eyes and open mouths.

"Let's go to work."

It was nearly seven p.m. when we were told we were leaving.

"Be strong, Tate. Don't be afraid. There are a lot of people looking for us, and they will find us. I love you."

"I love you. I'm trying to be strong, but it's hard. I can't do this. I'm scared."

"You can do it. You're stronger than you think. Dig deep. I'll see you tomorrow." We hugged; not really sure what tomorrow would bring. Tate was led down the hall and out of sight.

I was escorted outside.

"Wait here until your ride gets here. We're watching you," said the guard.

A car eventually arrived and motioned for me to get in. We drove back to the house. I tried to ease in quietly, but everyone was awake. One by one they sat up in their beds and began asking questions.

"Is everyone okay? Did you miss me?'

There was simultaneous talking and muttering. "One at a time, so I can hear you."

"Did you see Samantha today?" asked Lexi.

"No, I didn't, but I did see a very good friend of mine. Her name is Tate. I can't wait for you all to meet her!"

"How will we meet her?" Nikki's eyes squinted as if she knew it was a stupid thing for me to say.

"I believe that we will all be out of here soon. This isn't forever."

"How do you have a friend at the bad place?"

"They kidnapped her when they took me. They've been holding her in a room by herself at the facility." I whispered the name of the facility as quietly as I could. "It's called Braxton Therapeutics. Don't forget the name. You'll need to tell someone about it one day when we escape."

"Are you hungry?"

"I'm starving," I said.

"Nikki and Clara made supper. We saved you some," said Baily.

"What is it?"

"Chicken casserole. It was delicious, even though it was canned chicken," said Lexi.

"I'll bet it's going to be the best casserole I've ever eaten."

I sat in bed and ate my supper while the girls told me about the games they had played and the songs they had sung while I was gone.

Back at the facility, Samantha sat in a small room. She had been treated with kindness and given a cheeseburger and fries for supper. She sat at a table playing with a plastic jigsaw puzzle that had been placed in the room.

"Hello, sweetheart. What's your name?"

"Samantha."

"Well, Samantha, I need you to put on this bathrobe for me."

The robe was handed to the small child. Reluctantly, the baggy floral dress dropped to the floor, and Samantha put on the robe. The lady reached out her hand. "I need you to come with me."

Samantha took her hand and began to walk down a long corridor and into a room full of machines, strange noises, and unfamiliar faces.

"Can you sit up here, darlin'?" Samantha climbed up on the table. "Do you want a strawberry lollipop?"

"Yes," She stuck out her tiny hand and took the lollipop from the man in the white coat.

"Go ahead and lean back on the table for me."

She leaned back.

"I just need you to put this over your nose and breathe in for a few minutes. You can finish your lollipop in just a bit."

He placed the mask over her mouth and nose, and she quietly slipped into a deep sleep. The sucker in her hand dropped to the floor and one of the nurses threw it in the garbage. A needle was placed in her vein.

"Bless this child as she offers up herself as a living sacrifice so that others will be blessed by her organs."

Her eyes and organs were harvested and placed in containers.

If I thought everything was a bad dream before, I now realized that the nightmare had only just begun.

Chapter Fifteen

Braydee

I don't regret chasing after Lucy. It led me to the children. I now understood how Lucy felt. She had been forced to participate in my capture, just as I had been forced to participate in Marlea's.

Where was Lucy right now? Was she being used over and over for kidnappings? Was she out looking for young children? My mind raced. I shuddered to think of the things she may have been forced to see or do.

I woke up early on this day. I needed some time to be alone before the children woke up. I walked outside, sat underneath the big oak, and watched the sunrise. It was as beautiful as any I had ever seen. There were a few clouds to give it all sorts of dimensions. I was in awe of the handiwork of God. I tried to be thankful. I began naming my blessings, one by one, as the old gospel song from so long ago said to do.

"One: I have seven children who need me. Two: My family and friends are searching for me. Three: I'm a child of God, and I will get out of this."

I watched the door slowly open. Nikki walked over and sat down next to me.

"I couldn't sleep. I heard you come outside, so I wondered if you wanted some company?"

"Of course, Nikki. Have a seat."

"So, what did you do at work yesterday?"

"Well, as you know, I'm a scientist. They want me to do some research for them. I'm not quite sure what that entails yet." I didn't want to say too much and freak her out.

"I wanted to tell you about something that happened yesterday. We were all out here singing, and suddenly there was a drone that flew over us. It came from over the trees in that direction." She pointed toward the sunrise.

"Are you sure it came from that direction?"

"Yes. We all heard it. We stood there and just watched it for a while."

"How close did it get?"

"It hovered around for a while. I mean, it was close enough."

"Hmmm. This gives me an idea. If this drone is from someone in the neighborhood looking around, they could help us. If it's not ... well, at least it's worth a try."

"What are you thinking?"

"I want to get all the clothes that we were wearing when we arrived and spell out the words 'Help Us' with them. We can roll them up to form the letters. We can put them out here behind the house and just leave them there. The camera can't see the area close to the house. It's focused more out there in that direction." I pointed.

"That's a really good idea. Do you think it will work?"

"I have no idea, but it's worth a shot."

As the girls slept, we gathered the clothes and took them outside. I expected the intercom to ring out with questions, but there were none. On the back side of the house, very close to the wall, we formed the words 'Help Us' with blue jeans, t-shirts, and blouses in hopes that whoever had flown the drone over would fly it again, see the words, and send help.

"Can you discreetly tell the girls not to say anything about this? I'll be leaving for work soon, and I won't be able to talk to them about it."

"I'll take care of it," said Nikki. "We really miss you when you're gone."

"I miss you guys more than you know."

Fat Bald rarely glanced at the monitor, and he had the sound muted. He was engrossed in his Netflix show or Tik Tok videos.

Saying my goodbyes to the girls on day two of me leaving for work seemed even harder than the day before. I now knew what I was heading into, and I knew why the girls were being taken.

Again, there was no secrecy in getting to the facility. I was dropped off at the front door and was met by someone who escorted me to my lab room.

"Wait here."

I waited.

Tate joined me within a few minutes, and we just stood together holding hands.

"Are you okay?" I asked.

"Yes. Are you?"

Before I could answer, an iced metal circulation chamber arrived with several bags of solution and small organs.

"You have one hour to get what you need from these organs. Remember, your job is to produce clones. Don't forget that. There's no time to waste. As soon as you're finished with the organs, ring the bell, and place the box outside your door. They are already sold and will be delivered when you're done," said the lady with a thick Slavic accent.

I was a scientist, first and foremost. There were very few things that rattled my psyche, but this rattled me. I couldn't control my muscles. I began to shake. In that box were the organs of Samantha. My legs gave way, and I fell to the floor. I don't remember being transported to a bed, but when I woke up, I was in a small room, only big enough for a single bed. There was an oxygen mask on my face. I wondered if this was where they had been holding Samantha. I was suffocating with intense claustrophobia. There was a button on the side of the bed. I pressed it.

"Yes?"

"Can you tell me what time it is?"

"It's 10:40."

"A.M.?"

"Yes, a.m."

I was glad to hear I had only been in the room for less than thirty minutes.

"Can someone come get me? I'm okay, and I'm ready to work."

"Yes, we'll send someone immediately."

They led me back to my research area. Tate was there, and I fell into her arms. "The organs belong to one of my girls," I told her. Tears rolled down both of our cheeks. "She was one of the youngest girls. She had so many missing teeth," I sobbed. "I wanted to take care of her when we got out of here. I promised her I would take care of her."

My words were barely audible, but Tate knew exactly what I had said. She rubbed my back and stroked my hair.

"There's nothing you could've done, Braydee. Absolutely nothing."

We stood there for as long as we could, just holding each other. When we broke loose, Tate took the thick metal box containing Samantha's organs. She reached inside the box and pulled out the bag containing the solution and the small kidney. We began quickly extracting the stem cells from the blastocyst and gathering what we needed to begin the DNA sequencing.

There were no guarantees that anything we were doing would clone the organ, but it was definitely worth giving it our best shot. If losing Samantha in this awful way could save others, I had to make it happen somehow.

We placed the kidneys back inside the solution and temperature-controlled box and then retrieved the small liver. We pulled our samples and then placed the box outside the door and rang the bell. I wondered where her heart and other valuable organs had gone.

"Goodbye, Samantha. I'm sorry I couldn't do more to protect you," I whispered, as they carried her away. "Your death will not be in vain. I promise."

Weeks passed. I kept my head low and did everything I was supposed to do. Seeing Samantha's tiny organs had zapped my spirit, and it would take me a while to gather my strength to fight back. I was scared, so I moved like a zombie from the farm to the facility everyday like a good employee. The girls knew something had changed, and they tried to comfort me in the evenings.

Tate and I worked tirelessly everyday cutting target plasmid and pasting it into genes. There were so many steps to complete, but our goal was to create little "factories" to create the protein needed to clone the DNA of the organs we were continually handed. It was very tedious and difficult. I cried silently for the children who had given up their lives for the organs in our hands. I wondered when they would come for my girls.

On one particular evening, it was five o'clock when Tate and I said our goodbyes. I was always the only one waiting for a ride. Everyone else had transportation. I was accustomed to waiting for up to thirty or forty minutes for someone to pick me up, but when I exited the building, I saw a car already sitting there.

I wasn't sure the car was for me because I didn't recognize it. The gentleman rolled down his window and kindly greeted me.

"I'm pretty sure I'm here to pick you up," he said with a friendly smile. I walked instinctively toward the car.

I would ask where you're headed, but I've already been given the address," he chuckled.

"Have you worked for this company very long? I never even knew it was back here," said the strange man.

"Not long," I said. This guy was different. I was curious. "Where are you from? Have you never been this far down the road?" I asked.

Suddenly, my mind was so full of questions. How did he not know it was here? Was he just an Uber driver who'd been called to take me to an address?

"I've never really been in this area of town. I'm only filling in for my cousin. His name is Willis Barber. You probably know him. I think maybe he's the one who normally picks you up. I'm not sure. I'm supposed to be guarding someone's house or something."

"Hmm. Willis. Where is he today?" I had no idea who Willis was.

"His wife was in an accident. She's not doing too well. He said she punctured a lung and has some internal bleeding. He's been at the hospital with her. He texted me a little while ago and asked me to pick you up. I was happy to help."

"What's your name?"

"I'm Robert Barber. I'm the good-looking cousin." He laughed. "Willis lost his hair when he was in his early twenties. He couldn't help that, but he sure as hell could've helped that weight he's carrying."

"I haven't noticed him being too heavy." I was just rolling with the conversation.

"How could you not notice how fat he is? Fat and bald. That's a deadly combination."

Fat and bald. Fat and bald. The words were ringing in my ears. He wasn't talking about the other driver. He was talking about fat and bald. The same Fat Bald I had sliced in the face.

"Oh, that doesn't describe the other driver. He's a rather small man."

"Really? Well, I don't trust half the things my cousin tells me. He's got a huge imagination. His face got sliced in the face and he said an inmate did it, but he refuses to say what happened. He works part time at the jail, I think."

"That's awful! Is he okay?"

"I guess so. He has a four-inch scar and something like thirty stitches. Not good. He was already ugly. Didn't need one more thing added on." He laughed. "He's so full of crap most of the time. All I know is that something happened. I guess he was supposed to pick you up, but then his wife had an accident. It didn't make a lot of sense to me. He told me to guard a house and texted me the address. I need the extra money, so I said okay."

"Why are you guarding a house?"

"I asked the same thing. He didn't say. He just said my life depended on making sure this woman was dropped off. I asked who it was and where the woman was coming from, and he said Braxton Therapeutics, but didn't give me a name. I googled the place and saw you waiting out front. I sure hope I picked up the right woman. You must be mighty important." He laughed again.

"Well, I just appreciate you stepping in. Let me ask you something. Before you drop me off, can you run me by a store for a few personal items?"

"No detours. I'm sorry. My brother said his job depended on you being brought to the house."

"Oh, I see."

"Sorry, ma'am. I sure wish I could accommodate you."

"It's okay. I'll survive."

We were getting closer to the house.

"I'm pretty new to this neighborhood. Just visiting for a while. Do you know if there are any good restaurants or places to shop close by?"

"Tons of stuff just a few blocks over. Just depends on what you're looking for."

"Do you think I could walk there from here? I mean, I could Uber, but I'm just curious. Someone said there were over a hundred acres of woods behind the house where you're dropping me off."

He laughed. "Not hardly. There are barely eight acres between this house and the next. I mean this is Lubbock. We don't have a whole ton of forests around here."

"Makes sense."

"Well, here we are. I'm not really sure where to let you out."

"This is fine right here." I could see the house where I had been staying with the girls off in the distance, but I was more interested in the house right in front of me. If I was caught, it was an honest mistake made by the driver. I was sure Fat Bald wasn't inside. My only hope was that he had left the place unattended.

"Thank you. Maybe I'll see you again."

"I sure hope so. Look me up on Facebook. My name is Robert Barber. My profile picture is a pit bull."

"I sure will."

I waved as I slowly headed towards the front door. I wanted him to pull away before I got there, and he did.

Twenty minutes later Robert called his brother.

"Hey, Willis. I dropped the girl off at the house."

"What are you talking about? YOU dropped her off."

"You said make sure the girl got to the house from Braxton. I picked her up, and I dropped her off."

"You did what? No! I said guard the house. I wanted you to sit at the address I gave you and make sure she got dropped off at that concrete block house out back like always."

"You said pick her up."

"No, I didn't! I said make sure she got there, as in *watch the place*. There was another driver picking her up."

"Well, you should have said that."

"How did you know where to pick her up?"

"I asked you who she was and where she was coming from. You said she was at Braxton Therapeutics. It's all good. You said my life depended on her getting there, and your job depended on it. Well, I made sure."

"Where are you now?"

"I'm meeting some guys for poker night."

"Go back!"

"I'm not going back. I have plans. It's all good. She's a nice lady. What's the issue?"

"What time did you drop her off?"

"Twenty minutes ago."

"Bye."

Willis hung up, knowing he was on borrowed time. He needed to get back quickly, but he didn't want to leave his wife.

This was my chance to save us.

I wiggled the front doorknob. It was locked. I felt for a key around the edges of the plants and door mats until my fingers felt the cold metal key underneath the mat. I quickly unlocked the door and returned the key to its hiding place. I walked inside.

My nose was assaulted by the horrendous stench. The place reeked of decay and body odor. There were air fresheners trying to disguise the smell. How could anyone work in this environment every day?

I moved quickly down the hallway. There were no alarms so far. No voices telling me to stop. So, I kept moving. Near the back of the house was a room with a large metal door. I knew I was taking a chance and putting us all in danger.

I placed my ear against the door. I could hear the children talking. It was very clear. I grabbed a lamp from a side room and prepared to hit someone as hard as I could. I turned the knob and swung the door open. There was no one there.

In front of me were six large TV screens. The cameras focused on the front of the house, the back door of the house, the den, our bedroom, the field near the oak tree, and the shower entrance. Thank God there wasn't a camera in the bathroom. There was no sign of the words we had formed with the clothes.

I could see and hear the girls all very clearly. I wanted to just sit and watch them for a second, but I knew I only had seconds. I began pulling wires and disconnecting the cameras and microphones. I knew I had to do everything possible to disrupt this communication surveillance system. I moved as quickly as I could.

I ran down the hall and found the kitchen. Grabbing a knife, I went back to the room and cut as many cables and power sources as I could.

My heart was pounding as I exited the front door. I ran quickly and silently across the field and down the driveway to the children.

Marlea stood at the window in her usual spot. "I see Grace coming down the driveway. She's running."

Everyone came out of the house to meet me.

"What are you doing? Why are you running?" asked Baily.

I was so out of breath I could barely speak. "I need everyone to listen to me. Move quickly! Everyone needs to put on their shoes. Go to the kitchen and grab a bottle of water. Meet me outside at the secret circle."

I grabbed a pillowcase and stuffed as much food inside as I could.

Within one minute, the entire group was gathered outside.

"Where are we going? You're scaring me," said Clara.

"We're leaving."

"What if they see us leaving? They're going to hurt us again!" Clara had a right to ask questions. She had been whipped and tied to a tree because I had left the house. She was terrified.

"I destroyed the cameras. They can't see us."

"How?"

"It doesn't matter right now. Everyone stay together, and run as fast as you can. This is our chance to get away. Let's go!"

We ran as hard as we could. I looked around at the frumpy dresses flopping up and down as the tiny legs did everything they could to keep up with me. We reached the tree line and eased into the woods undetected. I had done it! I had gotten us out of the wretched house. Now, I needed to focus on what to do next, and I had no idea what that was.

Chapter Sixteen

A notifying alert was sent to the communication station, the main research campus, and directly to Judge John Sands. Alarms were sounding as men scrambled to figure out why communications were down at the "farm."

Judge Sands was sitting in court when the alert came through on a private phone reserved only for emergency communications with the Braxton facility.

He interrupted the prosecutor who was speaking. "I'm sorry. I'm going to need to call a recess. Be back here in fifteen minutes."

He stepped into his chambers and made a phone call.

"Why am I getting a code red?"

"Sorry, sir. We have an emergency situation. There's no audio or visual on the girls at the farm here in Lubbock. We have absolutely no communication with them at all. I'm headed over there now. I'm only ten minutes away."

"That's ten minutes where anything could be happening! Move it! Who's in charge of monitoring the house?"

"His name is Willis Barber. I tried calling, but he's not answering."

"Keep trying! Let me know as soon as it's all clear."

"Roger that."

"Do we know if he's at the house?"

"No, sir. He should be. He's on the schedule, and he didn't tell anyone he was leaving."

"He better have the excuse of his life for why communications are down. Don't we have backup generators in case the power goes off?"

"Yes, sir, we do. They didn't kick on, so that tells me the power is still on in the rest of the house," said the officer.

"There's no excuse at all for monitors being down. We have backup plans for backup plans around there," said John.

"Yes, sir, we do. My gut says this isn't good, though."

"Handle the situation, then handle Willis."

"Will do." He dialed Willis's number again, and this time he calmly answered the phone.

"Hey, man."

"What the hell is going on?"

"What do you mean?"

"What do I mean? I mean we've lost all communications with the girls. No visual and no audio! What's going on there?"

Willis was stunned. He had no response that would make sense. "What do you mean you've lost communications?"

"We got an alert five minutes ago. All systems are down. Red alert."

"Code Red?" asked Willis.

"Yes! The boss was notified."

"You called the judge?"

"I didn't have a choice. It's protocol. Now, what's going on where you are? I'm five minutes away."

Willis was silent. There was no excuse he could give. He had left the house unattended to see about his wife. There would be no way out of this. There was no telling what they would find when they got there, but he knew he was in deep trouble.

"My wife was in an accident. I left to see about her. I was going to come right back once she was safe in a room."

"You're kidding me, right? You left the girls unattended?"

"I asked my cousin to go to the house and make sure the woman arrived."

"Are you serious? You're telling me you left the house and didn't tell a soul you were leaving?"

"It was only for a few hours. I don't see how anything could have happened with the girls. They didn't know I wasn't there. No one knows."

"You don't have a clue what they know, and we don't have a clue what they are doing right now because the surveillance system is out. It could have been destroyed, for all we know!"

"By whom?"

"We have no idea."

"What did the judge say?"

"What do you think he said? He said take care of it and to take care of you, too. I don't need to explain to you what that means, do I?"

Willis hung up the phone. He dropped his phone in the pitcher of water that was sitting next to his wife's bed. He stared at his wife. They would be coming for him soon. His life was over. He loved his wife, but he couldn't risk them finding him and chopping him up into pieces.

He shivered at the thought of what they would do to him when they found him. He kissed his wife on the cheek and silently said his goodbyes to her. He had to get out of town. "I'm sorry, Gladys. I haven't been the best husband to you. I sure hope you make it through this. Maybe I can come back for you."

With that, he walked away. His heart ached for the wife he had known for twenty-five years, but he had no remorse for the girls he had imprisoned and raped for years.

Within minutes, a security officer employed by John Sands arrived at the farm's surveillance house. He had called for backup on the way there, and a team of six guards were just a few minutes behind him.

He opened the door and walked straight to the surveillance room with his gun drawn. He radioed the other men.

"Go straight to the house. If the girls are gone, start looking in the woods in all directions. Someone has destroyed everything in here," said the officer.

"ETA five minutes."

"Speed it up. Every second counts."

The officer sent a text to Judge Sands. "Arrived. Communications have been sabotaged. Will update more soon."

Six men arrived in a windowless van. They searched the house and found nothing. They drove the van all the way to the edge of the woods. Two men jumped out and ran into the north end of the woods. The van drove along the tree line. Two more men entered another area of the woods, and another entered at the south end. They moved deliberately, looking for any signs of the girls. They stopped to smell and listen. There were no sounds of heavy breathing, no crumpling of branches or leaves, no sounds of scurrying squirrels. Just silence.

After nearly an hour of searching, a booming voice rang out into the forest. "Don't move." With an automatic weapon pointed in their direction, the man stood thirty feet away from the girls. Huddled in a small bunch, with their backs against a tall wooden privacy fence, their scared whimpers could be heard as the gunman approached. The man took out his radio and called the other officers. "I have them. West end. Cornered against the fence."

"Please, let us go! Please!" I begged.

"No talking."

One of the girls began to scream, which triggered another scream. Before they could stop us, we were all screaming at the top of our lungs.

"Shut up. All of you. You're going to make it worse for yourselves."

We couldn't hear him above our screams. Maybe someone nearby was hearing us and would report it. I was so proud of the girls for fighting back the only way they knew how.

We were escorted out of the woods and shoved into the back of the van. We didn't know where we were going, but it wasn't back to the house we had come to accept as our home over the past weeks.

A text message was sent to the judge.

"Call when you can?" asked the officer.

The judge was still sitting in his chamber, and he called the officer.

"What did you find?" asked the judge.

"I talked to the guard. He left because his wife was in an accident. It's possible she was a target, and this was an elaborate scheme. These girls may have had help from someone. I don't see how they could have pulled this off alone."

"How could there possibly be someone who would help them?"

"I'm not sure sir. It just doesn't add up."

"Where is the guy now?"

"He was at the hospital when I talked to him. No idea where he is at this very minute. He's probably headed to Mexico. He knows how serious this is. We're looking for him, sir."

"Don't let him get away."

"I'll keep you updated. This woman is a problem, though. She sliced his face. She's got a fire in her that we haven't seen before. A real troublemaker. I'm afraid that if someone doesn't put the fear of God into her, she's going to be a serious problem."

"Sliced his face? How the hell would he be in a situation where a woman overpowered him and sliced his face?"

"I had to rewind the footage to find out. He wasn't being exactly honest about it."

"And?"

"He went to the house one night to take a girl for his own pleasure, and one of the little ones hit him in the head with a frying pan. Caught it all on camera, of course. He fell down limp and the woman sliced him."

"You have got to be kidding me!"

"No, sir. It's the truth. He took off holding his face."

"Serves him right for trying to mess with the girls. Those aren't his girls, they're mine! Find him."

"I'll do my best, sir."

"I'm coming to Waco. I need to deal with this girl, Braydee, myself."

"Okay, sir. Just let me know the details. I'll let Mr. Pateo know, and we'll arrange for a car to pick you up. Let me know once you finalize your travel plans."

Chapter Seventeen

We were unloaded at a long metal building. About two hundred yards away, I could see Braxton. I could see picnic tables and a small gazebo that looked like a break area. Next to it, was the barn with goats and sheep. We could hear them making noises far off in the distance. We could see several eating hay from the trough.

I was so relieved to see that we were somewhere familiar. Somewhere near people. It gave me hope.

"Line up."

We formed a line.

"This is where you're going to stay until we get communications running at the farm. You won't be nearly as comfortable here, but that's your fault."

"Nothing is our fault." Baily sounded off.

"Yes, it is. You had a nice place to stay until someone pulled some shenanigans."

"No. It's not a nice place to stay. It's not." She was adamant about making her point.

"You know exactly what happened back there. Someone thought they could help you by tearing down all the surveillance. But guess what? You're worse off because of it. So do the right thing."

"YOU do the right thing," Katrina yelled with all the tiny might of her 40-pound self. The guard laughed.

"Well, aren't you all a feisty little bunch?" He looked at his partner. "We have had a lot of classes come through, but I think this class is the spunkiest of all." The men laughed.

One of the guards opened the door. The metal building was longer than it was wide with a big roll-up garage door. The door opened, and we were escorted inside at gunpoint. It reeked of gasoline and oil mixed with fertilizer and hay. There were tractors and lawnmowers inside on one side of the building. On the other side was nothing but hay bales. The door closed and it was completely dark for a few moments.

"Everyone find someone's hand to hold." We fumbled for each other's hands. "Now close your eyes and count to ten. When you open them, we'll be able to see a little better."

We all closed our eyes and when we opened them, it wasn't as dark anymore. Our eyes adjusted, and there was light coming in from around the garage door. There was light coming from a window in the very back of the garage. It was enough for us to see.

"Don't let go. Let's walk slowly towards the window back there." Everyone moved very slowly. "Okay. I know you're scared. So am I. But we're very close to people. Did you see the barn next door with the sheep? Next to it is where I've been working." No one responded.

We walked closer to the window, and I could see bales of hay stacked and strewn on the floor.

"I'm going to make us a great big bird's nest, and we're all going to pretend to be baby birds in the nest. We can snuggle up together and figure out what to do next."

"How are we going to make a bird's nest?" Jill always asked the questions first.

"We're going to get some of this hay and form it into the shape of a nest."

We gathered the hay bales and formed the most perfect nest. The sides came up high around us. We left one little space where we could all gather inside, then we pulled the hay up to fill in the gap. We hugged each other. I can't tell you how the others felt, but for me, I truly felt like a momma bird. My wings were wrapped around the girls. This was my nest, and anyone messing with it would pay dearly.

I started to sing. "Hush little baby don't say a word. Momma's going to buy you a mockingbird." My song was interrupted by the sound of tiny meows. In the dark, we could see four tiny figures moving closer to us.

"It's baby kittens!" shouted Marlea. "Here, kitty kitty."

The kittens inched carefully in our direction. One by one they jumped up on the ledge of our nest and joined us. The girls giggled and took turns petting the kittens. The kittens crawled from child to child as if they had known us their entire young lives.

"Can we name the kittens?" asked Jill.

"Of course, we can!" I was so thankful for the sudden distraction. Nothing could have been more perfect or comforting in that moment. We named them Shadow, Peep, and Coco.

As night fell, the building became eerily dark. There were noises coming from the corners where rats had made their homes. With only a little bit of moonlight coming in, I walked the girls back to the front of the building near the door so that they could use the bathroom.

There were some paint cans and five-gallon buckets near the lawn equipment that I had seen before the lights went out.

"If anyone needs to use the bathroom, now is the time." I fumbled with the bucket and placed it where we could get to it easily. When we were done, we all held on to one another and headed back to the nest.

Snuggling in, one by one, we rested in our nest. I don't know if anyone slept, but at least we were safe for another night.

We awoke to the sound of the door rising and light flooding in. A man stood at the entrance. We could only see the silhouette of his body and the smoke he was blowing from the cigarette he was inhaling. It was a haunting sight.

"Hey." He shouted, and it vibrated against the metal. With the wooden baton in his hand, he beat the side of the building. The sound was deafening. The kittens scurried to their hiding places. I responded.

"We're here."

"Just you. Let's go."

"Where am I going?"

"To work."

"Like this?" My scrubs were dirty from running and hiding in the woods. "Do you think I can honestly do my job knowing these girls are here hungry and thirsty? I can't focus. Please get them some food and water. I need to speak with Mr. Pateo immediately."

"No! You aren't giving the orders here. I am. I have orders to take you to the side entrance of the campus. You'll be able to shower and put on clean scrubs. There will be snacks in the break room if you need to eat."

"What about the children?"

"Let's go." He pointed the gun at the nest of girls.

"Take care of each other. I'll see you soon." I hugged them all before I left.

"Let's go!" he yelled.

I was escorted into a side entrance of the building and down a dimly lit hallway. There were metal doors on each side. Just before we entered the main area of the facility, there was a small shower area. Inside the bathroom was another white lab coat and a pair of scrubs.

"I'll be waiting right here. Hurry up," said the stranger.

After showering and getting dressed, I was escorted through the large metal doors and suddenly found myself back in a hubbub of activity. Everything looked like a normal working facility. There were people everywhere in white lab coats, some with stethoscopes and lanyards around their necks.

I couldn't figure out the dynamics of who was working under pressure like me and Tate, and who was here of their own free will. How many people here knew what was going on? It just didn't make sense.

There were people laughing and talking as we passed by. They certainly didn't look as if they were being held against their will. There were women with highlighted and styled hair. Their makeup was perfectly done. Men who were clean-shaven and healthy. These people definitely weren't living in the situation that the girls and I were living in.

Then there was me. No makeup. My hair is in a tight, thick bun with no jewelry or nail polish. Working only to stay alive and keep the children safe.

I walked into my research room, and there was Tate.

"Tate." I ran into her arms. We hugged each other as we had done the previous days. "Are you okay?"

"As good as can be expected. No one has harmed me in any way if that's what you're asking," said Tate.

After our long hug, we separated and began working. Side by side we worked, discussing our experiments and sequencing results, just as if we were still at Baylor.

"Did you ever tell the guy in San Diego that you had decided to decline the position they offered you?" asked Tate.

"No. I honestly wasn't quite sure of my decision yet. I was still weighing all my options and the salary package. I'm sure they've tried to call more than a few times to see where I stood on that," I said.

"You know, there are so many people looking for us right now."

"I know! I called 911 the night I was taken."

"What?" Tate was genuinely surprised.

"Yes. I saw a young girl getting kidnapped. I started following the car. I called the police and described everything I saw."

"Seriously? You followed the kidnappers? I don't think I could have done that!"

"Well, I couldn't just let them drive away. The worst part about it is that I was intentionally wrecked by a police officer. He pulled me out of the car and was the one who zip-tied my hands and feet."

"Oh God."

"He acted like he didn't have a clue he was a part of the whole thing. He's either that naive or just played a good part. I went from seeing him and feeling safe to realizing there was no hope all in one breath."

"That's crazy! So, if an officer helped to kidnap you, do you think there's a chance the 911 operator was in on it and never called for help?"

"It's possible, I guess. Who knows, really? The operator was very sincere and kept telling me they were coming. It certainly would have been an elaborate scheme."

"Um...this is pretty dang elaborate."

"You know what I mean. There would have to be a huge cover-up in place for a random 911 operator to be in on it. What about you? How did they take you?"

"I was waiting on an Uber, and someone pulled up and said my name. I said 'yes' and I got into the car. There was a man already in the back seat, so I just got into the front seat. The next thing I knew, I was in a van. I guess they must have drugged me because that's all I remember. They kept me in some sort of bunker for a few days. I'm not really sure how long. Then they brought me here.

"Do you know where we are?"

Tate shook her head yes.

"Do you?"

The intercom sounded and a voice rang out.

"That is enough conversation for today. You will remember the rules, or there will be consequences."

We just stood staring at each other.

"They're listening. How quickly we forget."

"Of course, they're always listening."

Five hours passed, and I could feel my stomach beginning to rumble.

"There's a break room here somewhere?" I said. "I'm so hungry. I don't see how they expect us to work while they're starving us in a cell."

"Where are they keeping you?"

Again the voice interrupted on the intercom, so we stopped talking.

We ventured into the hallway, and an undercover guard sat nearby, watching us. We approached him.

"Where is the break room? I asked.

He pointed.

"Go down this hall and take a left. It's the fifth room on your right."

"One of you stay. You aren't allowed to leave together."

"I'll stay," said Tate.

I walked down the hallway counting the doors. I turned the knob and opened the door to what I thought was the break room. Startled by what was sitting in front of me, I jumped.

"If you're looking for the break room, it's next door. This happens all the time."

His voice was like something I had heard on the radio. Something that soothed. No, it wasn't his voice. It was his face. Smooth, but with a sense of maturity. Nicely shaven, with dark curly locks, unkempt and loosely falling around his neck. I stared for an uncomfortably long moment. So long, in fact, that he repeated himself.

"The break room is next door." He smiled. Slowly he stood up from his desk.

I could see his lips were moving, but I couldn't hear the words. There was utter silence in the room. The only other sound I could hear was the booming of my heart, beating a rhythm in my ears. I involuntarily smiled. It wasn't just a smile. It was a half-smile that took a few seconds for the other half of my mouth to catch up. He must have thought I was deaf because he asked me if I was okay and if I could hear him.

"Oh, I'm sorry. Thank you. Yes. I was just. Um." I was frozen. I'm unable to speak because you're quite possibly the hottest guy I've ever met' I said to myself.

"Um..." I stopped.

He casually licked his lips and pushed his hair away from his face. Again, I lost my words and stood with nothing but 'um' filling the room.

"No problem." He chuckled. "I can't say I've ever had this effect on a woman."

"I'm sorry. I swear, I know how to make complete sentences."

"I think that's one of the requirements to work here, although I'm not sure how some of these people got hired now that I think about it."

"You're new around here, aren't you? I know I haven't seen you before. I would've remembered if I had seen you before." He hadn't flirted in so many years, but this felt like what he remembered it to be. There was a strange hotness in his body.

"Yes, very new. You?"

"Oh, I've been here for nine years."

"What do you do here?" I asked.

I was smitten in an instant. I can't explain it. It was truly a moment I have never felt before. For that brief moment, I completely forgot that I was a slave, trapped in a metal building and forced to kidnap young children.

"I'm a biomedical engineer," he said. "I came here from Stanford University. I was recruited by Kingston Health, but in the end, these guys offered more money. I help design software to run medical equipment and computer simulations to test new drug therapies."

"That sounds interesting."

"It's useful, but not interesting."

"And you? What do you do here?"

"I'm a biomedical engineer, I..."

The security guard entered the room. "Are you lost, Miss?"

"No, not anymore. This gentleman was just telling me where the break room was. By the way, you were one room off. It's six doors down, not five."

Confused, Chandler looked from me to the officer. Why would an officer walk into his office and interrupt a conversation between him and another employee?

"My name is Chandler Grey, like the color. If you ever want to sit down for a cup of coffee, just come ask. I'd love to join you and learn more about you."

I swooned as much as I could with an armed guard at my back. "I'd love that. My name is Braydee Quinn." I gasped. I had been warned never to speak my name under any circumstance. I couldn't bear to think about the consequences of what I had just done! I said my name for the first time since I had been kidnapped. What would they do to the children, me, or Tate?

"Nice to meet you, Braydee." I cringed at the sound of my own name, but the officer was texting on his phone and had missed the conversation completely.

"I'll see you soon, hopefully?" He stuck out his hand. It was as if I was drowning in the ocean and his hand was the life vest. I could feel safety in his touch. I wanted to just say 'Please help me' and collapse into his arms. Instead, I said, "Hopefully."

The officer pointed me to the break room, and I walked away.

There were donuts, some sausage biscuits from Hardees, and several pots of coffee. It smelled heavenly. There were vending machines and a Keurig with various blends of coffee and tea pots. I felt so guilty for eating a biscuit and drinking coffee knowing the girls were locked away hungry.

I studied the room. I was right. Not everyone here was being forced to work. Many of these people were there of their own accord. They had no idea of the atrocities that were being committed under this very roof. Or maybe they knew and just didn't care. I chose to believe the first scenario.

The guard left, and I stuffed as much inside my pockets as I could possibly carry. I would take these snacks to the girls, just in case we still didn't have any food.

I was terrified over the possible consequences of mentioning my name. I knew someone was watching me all the time. I was certain of that.

"Well, how was the break room?" Tate asked.

"It's pretty good. There's a ton of snacks and things. You'll have to check it out."

"Yeah, I'm going now."

"Okay. Down that main hall. Take a left and it's the sixth room on your right."

I wanted to tell Tate about the gorgeous man behind the fifth door, but I didn't want whoever was listening to hear me discussing him. That would be a conversation I would have with the girls when I got back to them.

Chandler sat at his computer running some tests. He was trying hard to put Braydee out of his mind, but every single detail of her was on a loop in his brain. Maybe five feet, eight inches. Thin, from what he could tell in the lab coat. High cheekbones and perfectly shaped lips. A golden vacation tan. Graceful, piano-playing fingers. Shiny, long blond hair. Green eyes. No makeup. He had been extremely observant of every detail.

His thoughts were coming in short bursts of excitement. What was her job here? What did she say her name was? He wondered what she looked like with make-up on. Did she even wear makeup? Was she single? He didn't care how old she was, but she looked to be in her late twenties or maybe early thirties. Her name was Braydee. Wasn't it? Braydee Quinn.

He tried to focus on the computer in front of him, but all he could think of was the dumbfounded look on the woman's face as she stood there in his office. Why had she drawn such a blank when she entered the room? Could she have been as Cupid-struck as he was? He could almost feel the arrow that had pierced his very being. The last time he'd felt this way, it had ended a twelve-year marriage, with utter heartbreak bringing it to an abrupt end.

He had married his college sweetheart. His true love. Together, they had built quite a nice life for themselves. Five years into their marriage, they had a baby girl, and life could not have been better. The three of them moved to California, and he took on a job at Stanford University. His heart was full of love and peace. There was nothing better in this world than walking through the door and seeing the love of his life playing with his baby girl. One afternoon, as his wife was coming home from picking up their daughter at school, a texting driver hit them head-on. Their daughter was killed instantly. One year later, consumed with grief, his wife committed suicide. He had thought about his wife and daughter every day for nine years.

There was nothing he could have done differently to save his wife or daughter. Still, he wondered if he could have said something to his wife that might have saved her life. Could he have held her a little more? Could he have taken off work longer to spend more time with her? He had missed so many of the signs of impending suicide. He blamed himself for not coddling her more after the accident. He was dealing with his own pain, which meant working more and staying out of the house.

Now, at thirty-six years old, he was beginning to believe he was ready to feel love again, or at least something like it. He had taken the job at Braxton Therapeutics nine years ago. His hopes of saving lives with new medicine and helping children through cloned organs is what kept him going every day.

He sat fumbling with the computer keys. He had not felt any emotions, other than pain and sadness since his wife died. Something was stirring deep within him. He wanted to know more about Braydee.

He pulled up the computer database of employees. He wanted to see what section she worked in so that he could casually drop by and say hello. Maybe he would spy on her office and casually bump into her in the hall or show up at the cafeteria and pay for her lunch. He smiled at the silly thoughts going through his head. He carefully studied every department, but there was no one on the list named Braydee Quinn. The only employee with the last name Quinn was a male.

The afternoon was passing slowly. I was so worried about the girls, and all I wanted to do was get back to them to make sure they were safe. Tate was saying something, but I didn't hear her.

"What were you saying?"

"I was saying that we need to process these for two more hours." She was pointing to a set of glass vials in a tray. What has you so distracted? You haven't responded to several things I've said in the last hour."

"I'm just so worried about the girls, I can barely function."

"I know you are."

A siren rang out, but it wasn't a siren just for them. They quickly realized it was a fire alarm. Everyone began moving hurriedly from the building.

"Is there an actual fire?" I asked someone who was walking out rapidly next to me.

"I'm not sure. Seems like every so often we get these alarms, but since I have been here, they always turn up false."

It was chaotic as we exited the building. I looked for Chandler but didn't see him. Standing outside under the canopy with what looked like possibly a hundred other employees, I locked eyes with Tate. Our eyes said it all.

"They can't hear us out here. This could be our chance to say what we need to say and make plans to escape."

We began to talk quickly.

"Yes. They have me in a metal room at the end of a hall. I can't figure out exactly where it is in reference to our lab because they walk me down all these halls and locked doors. I know it's in this building."

"Okay, Tate. We're in Texas. You said you knew that already. I think it's Lubbock, though."

"Yes."

"They were keeping me and the girls at a house about twenty minutes away, but two days ago, I busted up all the surveillance equipment, and they moved us all to a metal building in the back corner of the property here."

"What?"

"Yes. All the girls are there right now. No food or water. No bathrooms. These people are insane."

"Oh God, Braydee. What are we going to do?"

"I don't know, but we can't stop trying."

There was a motion for everyone to come back inside. Our time outside lasted less than five minutes. Maybe next time there would be a real fire, and we would have more time to talk. Maybe I would be the one to start a fire and burn the place to the ground.

Chapter Eighteen

Whit pulled out of the ballpark and headed down Highway 59 North towards the interstate. It didn't take long for him to notice the gray SUV on his tail. This was going to be an adventure. He wondered if it was a good guy or a bad guy following him.

After about forty minutes, he pulled onto I-20 West traveling in the opposite direction of Pensacola. Duke would have to wait. He needed to shake whoever was following him. He exited on the first exit and pumped gas. The gray SUV parked on the side of the gas station and sat there, waiting, and watching. Whit got a good look at the person driving, but that didn't help much.

He finished pumping gas and started the car. Immediately, the engine of the SUV started up, too. Whit exited his vehicle and walked toward the man following him. He motioned for him to roll down the window.

"I'm not sure who you are, but you've been following me since I left the ballpark earlier. You should work on being a little more discreet." Whit walked back to his car.

"What are you talking about?" asked the man, and he rolled up his window as Whit walked away. He waited for Whit to pull out. Whit sped away. He turned off at the next exit, waited until he was sure no one saw him, then headed to Pensacola. No one was following him this time.

One hour later he was slipping off his flip-flops and walking towards the meeting spot at Dog Beach. He scanned the area and suddenly recognized Duke's profile. He was sitting on a towel, far off in the distance.

As he approached, he whistled, and Duke stood. The two men embraced briefly and then sat down on the towel.

"Thanks for coming, Whit. I know you're risking a great deal to be here."

"Yep. Everything."

"I know, and I'm grateful to you. Have you heard anything new? Learned anything about the Judge?"

"I left him a message." Whit chuckled, and Duke's eyes were wide with excitement.

"What did ya say?"

"I said Bob was at the bottom of the ocean."

"No way! What did he say then?"

"Oh, I told his secretary."

"That's even better! She can get the rumor mill going. Have folks chattering around the courthouse about what that could mean."

"Yep, I agree." Whit pulled the phone from his backpack. "Here's your new phone. I have one, too. I'm going to ask you not to call me unless it's an absolute emergency. If you need to meet, just send me the numbers - the day of the week and the time. So, if you need to meet on Monday at seven p.m., you will text 1-7. Tuesday would be 2-7 and so on. Does that make sense?"

"Yes."

"We can meet out here on the beach. Park as far away as you can and walk."

"I don't have a car. I'm walking everywhere."

"Okay, well, keep it that way. If you go paying cash for a car, it's definitely going to trigger suspicion and a call to the police. Lay as low as you can and keep quiet. They are flashing your picture on every news station."

"Believe me, I am."

"No, you aren't. You've already called your best friend, who has now delivered a burner phone. That can get us into all sorts of trouble."

"I know. I get it."

"There was this guy following me when I left the ballpark earlier," said Whit.

"No way. How did you shake him?"

"I just walked up to him and said, "Stop following me, you son-of-a-biscuit eater."

"No, you didn't."

"No, I didn't. But I did confront him, then I just took a few turns until I knew I had lost him."

"I'm sorry I've dragged you into this, Whit. I swear you are the only person who would believe me."

"I think you're selling yourself a little short. Melissa would believe you."

"I don't think so. Not this time. This crosses the line."

"Crosses the line on what? She loves you. She knows you better than anyone. She came over the other night and wanted to talk about everything."

"I can't imagine what this is doing to her."

"She's stronger than you think. I told her I didn't think you were capable of doing what they were saying you were doing. I sort of walked her through my theory, according to what you had told me, and asked her if she knew anyone you would trust wholeheartedly and not ask questions if they asked you to do something."

"What did she say?"

"She blurted out 'my dad' before she even thought about it."

"Wow. She's one hundred percent correct on that. I really trusted Pops."

"It's those dang rings you took that has everyone convinced you're guilty."

"I swear, I've never done anything like that before. I've heard stories from others about taking valuables from prisoners or from crime scenes. The dude snatched them off the girl's hand, and I was holding them before I really processed what was happening."

"Hey, don't beat yourself up about it. Look where it's leading. You would have never known the judge had it in him to kill you, and you would have never known he was part of some elaborate human trafficking operation if it wasn't for those rings and your fingerprints on the door. Those rings may have messed you up, but if it's going to bring down the big dog, then it's a good thing."

"You're so right. I'll gladly go to jail if it means exposing John."

"So, what's the next move? Is there a plan?"

"I need you to get a message to Capt. Marshall. You've watched crime shows, right? You know about DNA and all that?"

"Well, yeah. But what are you suggesting?"

"I've written a letter and I've got the address here. I just don't have an envelope and stamp. I could get one from the hotel owner, but I wanted to give it to someone I trust. Be sure to write Attn: Captain Gary Marshall on the envelope."

"Understood."

"This letter tells him everything I know about the judge, which isn't much. Either he believes me and begins trying to uncover the truth, or he thinks it's all a lie and continues to focus on me as the main suspect."

"That's a gamble we'll just have to take," said Whit.

Duke dropped the plastic bag containing the handwritten letter in Whit's backpack.

"Remember not to touch it with your bare hands, and don't lick the envelope or stamp. I don't want you connected to me at all. When you get home, just put on some gloves, and take the letter out. Type a copy for me. I want a record of what I sent."

"You got it. I'll take care of it. I'll take a picture of it as well."

"Good idea."

The two sat looking at the waves in silence for several minutes. Whit tried cheering his buddy up.

"Not a bad place to be hiding out, bro."

"How did I get to this place in my life?"

Whit's phone rang, and he looked at the name.

"It's Melissa."

"Answer it. I want to hear her voice," said Duke.

"Hey M." The speaker was on.

"Hey. Are you busy?"

"Not so much. What's up?"

"I was up all-night last night thinking about what you said."

"What part?"

"About whether or not I believed Duke was capable of kidnapping someone."

"Yeah."

"Whit, I don't think he is. I swear he had some issues that nearly destroyed me, but he was a good man."

"He IS a good man, not was."

"I feel so helpless. If he was put up to something by someone, I couldn't live with myself knowing everyone had him convicted, including me, before we even knew the truth."

"I was right there with you, Melissa. We all were. It's going to take more than a hunch and a feeling to clear him."

"Right, and I don't know how many people he has in his corner."

"No one but me and you are right now."

Melissa listened to the waves in the background. She could hear the seagulls off in the distance. There was only one reason Whit would be at the beach and not jump at the chance to brag about it. He was with Duke, and she could feel his presence very near.

"Would you tell me if Duke reached out to you?"

"No."

"I didn't think so."

"Will you tell him I love him, and I know he's not the monster everyone is saying he is? Tell him I'll be waiting for him when this is all over. That is if you happen to hear from him."

"I will. That is if I happen to hear from him."

Duke mouthed the words "I love you, Melissa. I'm so sorry" as he hung his head, listening to his wife on the phone.

When Whit hung up, the two men looked at each other in silence.

"I'm going to be okay. She believes in me."

"We both believe in you."

The two parted with a bro shake and a quick hug. Things were about to get dicey.

Whit pulled into the driveway well after dark. He had stopped to get groceries on the way home. As he unloaded, he spotted a man halfway down the road sitting in his car. "I see you," he said to himself.

Once inside, he put away the groceries, sat down at his computer, and took the handwritten letter from his bag. He began to type the words that Duke had written.

Capt. Marshall,

I know this looks bad. I'm guilty of taking the rings, but let me explain. My father-in-law, Judge John Sands, called me several months ago. It was from a blocked number, but I answered it anyway. He explained to me that he had been secretly working on a case with the Baldwin County Police. I didn't question it because I had no reason not to trust him.

He told me that the police officer in charge of the operation had "fallen ill" and would be unable to proceed with his task. He assured me that although it was a very simple job, it was also top secret. He instructed me not to tell anyone about it, not even Melissa, and not anyone on the force.

He explained how the department had been corrupted by a mole who was tipping off the criminals before they could be apprehended. He chose me because I was someone he trusted.

I told him I was in. He gave me a location in Foley, and I was to go down the road exactly eight miles, and park on the right side of the street. I was waiting for orders to throw out a tire shredder.

He told me to wait for the call and that I would have to move quickly. There would be a black Chrysler passing by, and the person following the Chrysler was the target. I didn't know what that vehicle would be, or who was in it, but I would get a phone call the night of the operation, verifying the target vehicle.

That night, I got a call from an unknown number, and I was instructed to throw out the shredder and once the car was brought to a halt, drive away. That's where I messed up. After the accident, I ran to the car and pulled the woman out. It was a natural instinct. A van pulled up, and I saw two men walking a girl to the back of the van then I helped load the woman into the van.

My father-in-law gave me five thousand dollars for the job. He said he was overpaying me because I was his daughter's husband. I put the money in a post office box because he suggested it. He told me he'd had a box for years. He was going to help me open an account in Switzerland to avoid taxes if I wanted to continue helping with secret assignments. I was all in.

Don't ask me why I didn't question that much money. I trusted my father-in-law completely, and that's all I can say.

When I saw the news about the girls, I knew something was wrong. I tried asking him questions when we were at the cookout, but he turned belligerent and told me not to worry about it.

Taking the rings was so very wrong, but that's what brings me to the next point.

When he found out about my fingerprints on the car, he sent Bob Seagrave to kill me. Thankfully, I was able to defend myself. According to the guy he sent, Judge Sands is heavily involved in a human trafficking ring along the coast. Bob also told me that Kasey Kendall, the missing girl from 2019, is alive and living with a family in Tyro, Kansas. He said you could go to West Olive Street, and tell them Bob sent you, and they would have the girl. He also directed me to a place behind a dresser where the little girl's shoes and Woody Thomas's badge was hidden.

All I'm asking is that you do some digging and trust me. I promise I'll turn myself in once I can prove the judge is a criminal. I just need some help.

Duke Davis

Whit printed the letter for Duke and placed it in a drawer in his desk. With rubber gloves on, he placed the handwritten letter in the addressed envelope to the police station as he was instructed.

He took the envelope to the mailbox and raised the flag. It never occurred to him that someone would still be watching his home at this late hour.

When the last lights were turned out, and the watcher was sure that Whit was in bed, he pulled up to the house, retrieved the envelope from the mailbox, and sped away.

The watcher pulled into a McDonald's parking lot and stared at the envelope addressed to Captain Gary Marshall. He would wait until morning to let his boss know what he had found out.

The watcher called the judge.

"Hey, I think this guy, Whit, has been in contact with your boy, Duke. I'm holding a letter addressed to the captain."

"How did you get it?"

"Whit put it in his mailbox. I just took it out. Do you want me to bring it to you?"

"No. I don't need anything happening around me right now other than work and family. Open it."

The envelope was opened. "Yep. It's a handwritten letter from Duke."

"Send me a video of you burning the letter. Keep an eye on Whit. He'll lead us to Duke," said John.

"You got it."

"Whatever you need to do, do it. I don't need either of them getting into my daughter's mind and corrupting her thoughts. Duke doesn't have another ally that I know of, so if he loses Whit, he'll start to get messier than he's already getting."

"I understand."

The watcher set his alarm to get some rest in the parking lot, then he would head back over to Whit's house later to continue watching.

As Whit sat drinking his coffee and watching the morning news, it occurred to him that it was Sunday, and the mail wouldn't be running. He started to worry that the watcher may have seen him put a letter in the mailbox late at night. He didn't want to take a chance on whoever had been watching his house getting curious about his outgoing mail. He went to the mailbox to retrieve the letter, but it was gone.

He shuddered at the thought of someone being so bold as to take a letter from his mailbox. It was then that he decided to meet with Capt. Marshall in person. He would have to take a chance that the captain would believe Duke. He hated putting himself in the middle of it, but it had to be done.

He called the station to set up a meeting.

Within minutes, the captain called back and wanted Whit to meet with him and Det. Cory Knotts immediately.

Whit placed the typed letter in an envelope and headed to the station. Thankfully, no one was following him.

"Hello, Whit. Thanks for coming in. We have some questions for you, so this worked out great. Do you want to start?" asked the captain.

"Sure. I've been in contact with Duke."

"Really? Where did you see him?"

"I met him yesterday. That's all I'm saying right now."

"If you're aiding and abetting a fugitive, you'll be in serious trouble, you know that, right?"

"I know that, but just listen. He called me to explain that he's not guilty of taking those girls. I listened to him, and I believe him. We decided to meet in person, and he sent this letter to you."

He handed the letter to Capt. Marshall, and he read it. He passed it to the detective. They both sat in disbelief staring at one another for a few seconds.

"Those are some serious allegations. Do you believe him?"

"I do."

"So, why didn't you just mail the letter and stay out of it."

"That was the plan. I put it in the mailbox around eleven p.m. last night. Then I realized the mail wasn't going to run on Sunday, so this morning I went to retrieve it, and that's when I realized it was gone."

"Someone took it from your mailbox?"

"Yes. I didn't know if it was the good guys or the bad guys, but I've had someone watching me for the last twenty-four hours, at least. They followed me from my kid's ballgame yesterday. Late yesterday evening, someone was watching the house. I thought they had left because I didn't see them when I went to the mailbox. I figured whoever it is was just trying to watch for Duke, to make sure I wasn't harboring a fugitive."

"Well, I can tell you, it wasn't the good guys. We don't have anyone keeping an eye on you. Although we did consider it. Did you notice if they followed you here?"

"Definitely not. I took every back road and whipped into crazy places just to be sure I didn't have a tail."

"If they took the letter, you're their target right now. You know things they don't want you to know. You know where Duke is, and assuming all this is true, Duke is public enemy number one. They'll be coming for you. They need answers, and you may have them."

"But I don't know where Duke is. I just met him one time to get the letter. He could be anywhere by now."

"Where did you meet him?"

"In Pensacola."

"Any way you look at it, you're in too deep right now."

"What do you suggest?"

"You're going to need to disappear for a while. Give us a chance to do some work on what Duke is alleging. We have a few questions for you before you go if you don't mind."

"Sure. I'll do my best."

"The night the girls were taken, Melissa said Duke came to stay with you."

"That's right. He had gone to The Keg and had way too much to drink. It was late, and I was already in bed."

"How did he get in?"

"The door was unlocked. He was sleeping on the couch when I got up."

"What did he tell you about that night?"

"He said he had been working on something, but he couldn't tell me what. I jokingly said a secret mission, and he said yes."

"He didn't tell you anything else about what it was?"

"No. There were no details at all. That was it."

"Okay. We can see who was bartending at The Keg that night. Maybe he got loose lips while he was drinking."

"How much eminent danger do you think I'm in?"

"On a scale of one to ten, you're at a ten. Again, this is assuming a hit was put out on Duke for possibly exposing the judge."

"Duke told me about a syringe with a sedative he used on the hitman. He said he was ambushed by a guy who had the syringe, but Duke was able to use it on him during their struggle. He said he buried it in the sand over in Perdido Key, where you guys found the truck."

"I'll bet there's DNA from both of them on it, assuming this is all true. We may be able to find the guy in a national database. We'll send someone over there now. Do you have somewhere you can go and hide out for a while until we get all this sorted out?"

"Yeah. I have a brother up north I can go stay with."

"No. That's the first place they'll look. Keep your family out of this. Are you married? Kids? Think your job will let you take off?"

"Divorced. Yes, one six-year-old. I work for Servpro. They'll be fine without me."

"I'd give them both a call when we're done here. Tell your ex-wife you're going away for a while, but not to worry. That's it. Nothing more. Tell her you'll explain more when you're able."

"Okay. What about Melissa? Do you think she's in any danger?"

"No. She's the judge's daughter. Not a chance."

"True."

"Thanks for coming by Whit. If I were you, I wouldn't even go home. I can send someone by to make sure everything is turned off and locked up for you. We can make it look like we're there to search the place just in case anyone is watching. Grab you some shorts, T-shirts, and flip-flops from Walmart, and just disappear for a while."

"Okay. If anything develops, will you give me a call? I'll be waiting to hear when the coast is clear. No pun intended," said Whit.

"I hear ya. Yes, I'll call. Do you think Duke is suicidal at all?"

"No. He's not. He's very determined to clear his name."

"And you feel certain he'll turn himself in after a reasonable amount of time if we can't find any proof?"

"Duke believes that you'll find proof pretty fast because the proof is out there."

"Okay, but if not, he's going to have to come home. He's a fugitive as it is, but I'm going to focus the investigation on the judge and not Duke at the moment."

"Thank you."

Whit was escorted out of the station and to his car.

He picked up his burner phone and sent two numbers to Duke. 7-1.

Duke looked at his phone. 7 is today. That's Sunday at one o'clock. He was anxious to hear what his buddy had found out. He headed to their meeting spot and waited.

Whit arrived early and saw his friend already sitting on the sand waiting.

"Hey, man. That was quick. What's up?"

"I put the letter in my mailbox last night, but this morning I realized it was Sunday, so I decided I was just going to take it to the post office mail drop, because some guy is watching my place. When I went to get it was gone."

"Seriously? Oh God. You're in trouble."

"Yep. I decided to take in the one I printed."

"I'm speechless."

"I hand-delivered it to the detective and Capt. Marshall."

"You did not. Are you being serious right now?"

"I'm dead serious. I wanted to sit down and look him in the eye and tell him I don't believe you're guilty."

"Wow. You really did that for me?"

"Yep. I did that for you."

"How did he react?"

"He didn't show much emotion, but I could tell he and the detective were pretty shocked. They were just staring at each other after they read the letter. He said he was going to do everything he could on his end to find out if any of what you said is true."

"The judge is smart and sneaky. He's busy covering any little shred of evidence that could be out there."

"Right. There's more. He told me to disappear. Whoever has been following me is on the bad team, and they'll stop at nothing now that they know I've met with you."

"Whoever took the letter is employed by my father-in-law, and that's dangerous."

"I know."

"What about your son? Does your ex know what's happening?"

"Capt. Marshall said he would take care of discretely letting her know."

They both stared at the breaking waves in silence for a few minutes.

"I think we may need to change locations. My place is too small for the two of us. It definitely wouldn't work," said Duke.

"Let's head to Panama City Beach. We can blend in pretty good with all the riffraff down there."

"Let's go."

Det. Knotts gathered a team and headed to Perdido Key. After searching the sand, they found the syringe, just as Duke had said. It was placed in a plastic bag and sent to forensics.

Back at the station, Capt. Marshall made a phone call to Tyro, Kansas.

"Hello, sir this is Capt. Marshall. I'm calling from Orange Beach, Alabama, about a little girl who was kidnapped in 2019. We have reason to believe she's living in your town."

"Why? How?

"We got a tip from an individual. His name is Bob Seagrave. He told us to go to West Olive Street and ask for the girl. Told us to say that Bob sent us."

"Okay, that's easy enough. This is the smallest town in Kansas, so we all know each other. There's a girl living with a family there. I've seen her on many occasions. They told us she was orphaned and that her family was killed in a house fire."

"How old is she?"

"She's an elementary school kid. She goes to school at Trenton Elementary. There are probably about 160 kids in the school."

"She would be eight years old right now," said Capt. Marshall.

"I can go get her and hold her here at the precinct, but I'm going to need proof."

"I'll get you proof. Just wait until I can get everything arranged. Is she safe?"

"Oh yes. She's with a good family. She's not in any danger, that's for sure."

"Okay. Thank you, sir. I'll be in touch as soon as I get everything arranged with the little girl's momma."

"I'll be waiting for your call. This is pretty shocking. Nothing like this ever happens around here."

"Before I go, do you know Bob Seagrave?"

"Everybody knew Robert. He was a bad seed. Put his parents through hell. Everyone was glad to see him get locked up."

"He went to prison?" asked the captain.

"Sure did. Best place for him."

"I appreciate your help. I'll be in touch soon."

Chapter Nineteen

Braydee

The door of my lab room opened, and I recognized the lady who had given me my scrubs at the first meeting with Gavin Pateo.

"Hello, Braydee. I need you to follow me. You have a meeting with someone."

"Right now?"

"Yes."

"What's this about?"

"It's about you learning to do what you're told. Now let's go."

Tate looked terrified. I wondered if she had been lying about them not hurting her. The look on Tate's face sent a chill down my spine.

I followed the lady down several halls and ended up in another area of the facility I had no idea existed. The place was full of little mazes of corridors. She stopped and knocked on a door.

"Yes?" The man's voice bellowed through the closed door.

She cracked the door and stuck her head in. "I have the lady."

"Bring her in."

I walked in with my head held high and shoulders back. Today was no time to lack confidence. I wasn't broken yet.

Across the desk from me was a heavy red-faced man with a scowl.

"How are you, Braydee?" The voice was deep. The way he said my name was unnerving.

How dare he ask how I was doing? I stared at him with contempt, not speaking a word.

"Have a seat. I'm going to ask you some questions," he said. "If you answer me truthfully, there will be very little consequences for what was done to my property. However, if you lie to me, those little children you're trying so hard to protect out in that metal building will be carved up and placed on a platter. They will be sent to the four corners of the world, and it will be your fault. I will only ask you once. Do you understand?"

I nodded.

He had a strong Southern accent, and his breath was foul with liquor and coffee. He smacked his jaws as if he had pieces of old food stuck in the crevices of his teeth.

"First question. Did you destroy the communication equipment on the farm?"

I hesitated then answered. "Yes. It was me."

"Did anyone else help you?"

"No. I acted alone."

"How did you get access to it?"

"A driver picked me up. He was unfamiliar with the place. He said his brother was supposed to be picking me up, but his wife was in an accident. I put two and two together and realized his brother was supposed to be watching the monitors in the house."

"So, what did you do?"

"I went in and cut the wires."

"And what else?"

"Busted the monitors."

"And what made you think it was okay for you to destroy my property?"

Before I knew it, I was on my feet, screaming across the desk. "And what makes you think you can take people to be your personal property and destroy their lives?"

The judge stood up and walked around the desk. With his fat red palm, he slapped me hard across the face. I fell backward to the floor, and I pulled myself up with the chair.

"Don't raise your voice to me, young lady. Now apologize."

I couldn't speak.

"I said apologize!"

He slapped me on the other cheek, but I didn't fall this time.

"You will apologize, girl."

I could see his long nose hairs moving in and out, as his foulness permeated my nose.

"I'm sorry."

"What? Louder."

"I'm sorry, sir."

"What are you sorry for?"

"For being disrespectful, sir."

"And what else?"

"For destroying your property."

"Very good. Now where were we? Oh yes, I was asking you if you acted alone, and what gave you the right to destroy my property."

"No one knew I was going to do it. It just happened. I saw the chance and took it."

"You've got spunk, I'll give you that, but I'll beat the spunk out of you if anything like this happens again. You're lucky I don't do it now." He stepped close to my face again.

I could no longer look him in the face. He was wretched to the eye. One eye cocked to the left and his yellow teeth were protruding. His reddish hair was mashed on one side. He walked back to his seat.

"I just needed to be sure you acted alone. I can assure you, I'm in no mood for your nonsense." He pulled a taser out of his desk drawer. He tased me and I crumpled to the ground. He stood over me and laughed before he yanked me back to my feet. I steadied myself with a chair.

His phone rang and he silenced it.

"I came a long way to put my eyes on this operation and look the person in the eye who has cost me so much time and money. There's a lot at stake here. More than you'll ever know. If I hear of another mishap involving you, you'll cease to exist, and those kids will pay for your actions. Am I clear? I'll find someone else to fill your place, just like I found you to fill the last girl's place."

"Yes, sir."

His phone rang for the third time during our meeting. It was on silent, but still vibrating on his desk. He finally answered it.

"I told you not to call me when I'm working unless there's an emergency. This better be an emergency."

"It is," said the woman on the other end. "I just talked to Millie. She said you canceled all court hearings today because of an emergency. She was surprised I didn't know. So, it seems at least one of us has an emergency. What is it?"

How many times had he told his secretary not to share anything with anyone?

"Yes. I canceled everything on my schedule to handle important business. It's something that concerns all of us. In case you forgot, our son-in-law is missing and in a heap of trouble right now. So, I need you to pull the hound dogs off me and let me do my job. I'll be home late tonight like I told you."

"Where are you, John? I'm your wife, so don't say it doesn't concern me. It does concern me. Saying you'll be home late tonight isn't working anymore."

"I'll have to call you back. Stop your worrying."

"No! Tell me where you are right now."

"Why can't you just stop being so damn nosy and leave me alone. I'll tell you about it later."

He hung up and breathed a sigh of his heavy, nasty breath into the air.

I banked every word I had heard from him and what I could make out from the person on the other end of the line. His name was John. He's obviously married. He has a secretary. He canceled court. He's possibly a lawyer or a judge. His son-in-law was missing. If only I had someone to tell any of this to. I rehearsed it in my mind.

He stood up tall and leaned into my personal space. His attempt to look intimidating only served to make him look more ridiculous, as one of his eyes was cock-eyed looking to the right of me.

"I will not have any more disruptions. Do what you were brought here to do. Find ways to help others through cloning, or we'll be forced to continue selling organs in other ways."

"What other ways?"

"I'm trying to do a good thing here. For many years we have had to harvest organs from donors. It is my goal to create organs so that we no longer need so many donors."

"You're a monster," I said so softly he could barely hear it, but he heard it.

"A monster?" He smiled big enough for me to see the specks of tobacco in his brown crooked teeth.

"Go." He pointed to the door, and I walked out. Waiting for me outside was my escort. She walked me to the front of the building. A car picked me up and drove me around to the back side of the metal building where we were now all staying. I knew Tate would be worried sick that I didn't return.

When the metal door was rolled up, I ran to the nest. Inside the nest were seven children and three kittens all huddled together.

"Are you guys, okay? Did they bring you some food and water today?"

Nikki spoke for the group. "We're fine. They brought us some water and sandwiches earlier today."

"I'm so very sorry." I reached into my pocket and pulled out the break room snacks.

"I found these today. Peanuts, a few biscuits, and some crackers. It's better than nothing."

The girls eagerly and respectfully shared everything.

"The water is over there." Baily pointed to a case of water.

"Okay, drink if you're thirsty, but remember, we have to drink sparingly." Everyone nodded. "Wait. I just noticed we have much lighter coming in today."

"Yes, two men came in earlier and took the wood off the back windows. It's so much better now!" Clara was happy to inform me.

"Well, it's a good thing they did that, because I'm ready to have some fun! Who wants to go on a scavenger hunt?"

All the little hands were raised, and their faces lit up! A chorus of me, me, me, echoed throughout the building. I laughed at the sound and sight of my girls. Our bond was growing so strong and with it our will to survive.

"Wait here, and I'll walk around and make a list of things that you'll need to find."

As I walked around the dimly lit barn, I realized it wasn't the safest place to have children walking around. I was afraid of what we might stumble across.

"On second thought, I think it'll be better if we all go together on a nature hunt. Let's just see what we can discover in this big, beautiful barn!"

It would've been a great adventure under different circumstances, but I was determined to make the most of every single moment I had with the girls.

We began our journey. Everyone was holding hands with someone. "Don't let go of your partner. If you see something interesting, let me know."

We saw an old spinning wheel, a broken-down lawn mower, all kinds of old farming equipment, sling blades, rakes and hoes, a doghouse, old lumber, fertilizers, a wheel barrel, some big metal oil barrels, and pieces of a metal roof. My mind was spinning. How could I use these things?

"Guess what we're going to do? We're going to make the most amazing playground ever!"

"How?"

"You'll see! First, let's decide where we want to set it up. I say over here near the window." The girls all agreed that it was the best place. "First we'll drag some lumber over and roll one of the barrels over here."

"What for?" asked Jill.

"That's going to be our seesaw." The girls smiled. "Next, we'll bring over the wheelbarrow. That is going to be a special princess carriage ride."

Everyone laughed as Katrina jumped into the wheelbarrow. I picked up the handles and began pushing as she giggled excitedly.

"And we are off to the palace!" I rode her over to the see-saw and she got out.

"Me next!" shouted Clara.

"Let's wait until we get everything in place, and then I'll be happy to ride all of you. Even you, Princess Nikki." Nikki smiled at the silliness of it all.

"Let's all work together to get the doghouse over there. It's very heavy." We pushed and pulled until we had walked the doghouse little by little, inch-by-inch, over to the playground.

"I used to have a playhouse," said Marlea. "I played in it with my sister before you took me from her." She started to cry.

"Marlea, I told you I didn't have a choice. I promise. I'm so sorry."

I tried to console her, but she pulled away.

"I'm going to help you get back to them. I'm trying to keep you safe. I'm trying so hard." The mood had suddenly shifted. I could feel the heaviness of what Marlea had said and how it affected everyone.

I looked around at the junk we had pulled together, and the magic of the playground suddenly disappeared. The barn felt eerily quiet.

Baily, the eleven-year-old beautiful blond, began to speak. "I'm really scared." Her voice was shaking. The others joined in, letting me know they were all scared. We held hands and walked back to the nest.

"We can set up the playground another day."

We all piled into the nest.

"I want you to know I'm scared, too, but together we're brave. Let's fix our nest up a little bit better, and I'll tell you the story of Rumpelstiltskin. It's a story about a tricky little imp who spins straw into gold and tricks a woman into giving up her firstborn child."

I thought it would be a good story to know since we had seen a spinning wheel stashed in the corner of the barn. We could move that to the playground tomorrow.

Piling into the nest together was both exhilarating and terrifying. Never before could I have imagined this journey and how I would be forced to use my imagination to save my sanity. I loved being able to pull scriptures, stories, songs, and experiences from my own life to help us all keep our sanity. Still, it was terrifying knowing that every day could be the last day I spent with them.

Our days were numbered. I thought of Samantha and how there had only been a few questions about her the day after she had been taken. After that, everyone just accepted that she was gone. It was horrifying.

I was sure that everyone was afraid to know the truth. The truth was, her organs had been sold on the black market, and that was the most terrifying thing imaginable. It was something I hoped none of the kids ever found out.

If there were any more questions about Samantha, I vowed to lie. I would tell them she was adopted by a wonderful family. They needed to hear something with a happy ending.

As we snuggled in the nest, I rehearsed everything I heard during my meeting with "John". I was sure that John was his real name because that's what the lady on the other end of the line called him. I recounted to myself every detail of what he looked and smelled like.

John Sands packed up his belongings and called his driver.

"Take me to the airport."

He arrived at Waco Regional Airport and boarded his plane headed to Alabama's Foley Municipal Airport. It was a private plane, as usual. The pilots were not known to him, just random individuals employed by the airport.

When he stepped off the plane in Alabama, he immediately felt the shift in momentum. Things felt like they weren't running smoothly, and when that happens, someone usually gets caught. The call from his wife had left an uneasiness in his chest.

Chapter Twenty

It was nearly three a.m. when John Sands stepped through the door of his home. His wife was sitting in the recliner in the den with the TV on.

"Where have you been?" Her voice was flat and monotone.

"Not now."

"Where have you been?" A little louder this time.

"I'm tired and like I told you on the phone, I've been doing my best to save this family. I said, NOT NOW."

"Saving us how?"

"You wouldn't understand if I wrote it in crayon. Now go to bed."

"Don't treat me like I'm stupid, John. It's not that hard for your wife to call the local airport and ask questions. They didn't have any trouble letting me know when your flight was leaving and when it was arriving. Benefits of living in a small town. Now why do I need to call the airport to get this kind of information about my husband?"

He stopped in the hallway and slowly turned around, staring at her with his beady half-cocked eyes.

"Why were you in Waco?" Her words were slow and deliberate.

He glared without blinking. He was shocked that she knew he was in Waco. He stood staring as she rambled on.

"So, you aren't going to tell me? Same old excuses? It's private information. Do you know, I've kept a log of every time you've gone to Waco in the past six years? Do you know that, John? What are you up to?"

"You're an idiot."

She picked up her coffee mug and hurled it across the room at him, sending coffee everywhere. It missed its target, and she screamed as the mug shattered into pieces against the floor.

"I hate you! I hate you!" she screamed.

He whizzed around, moving quickly, and grabbed her with both hands around the shoulder and forcibly jerked her up out of the chair. He shoved her against the wall. Her back hit a picture frame, and it fell off the wall onto both of their heads. Rhonda cried out in panic and pain, but John didn't stop.

"Have you been spying on me? Do you think that's smart?" He squeezed her shoulders harder and banged her back into the wall three times. She screamed louder and tried frantically to pull away.

"You're hurting me! Oh God! Stop it, John!" He slapped her hard across the cheek. She was stunned. It had been well over a year since she'd seen this side of him. She had hoped it was finally over, but deep down, she knew the sleeping monster was always inside him. He slapped her hard across the face again.

"John, stop! Stop!" She doubled over in an attempt to shield herself from him. "I'm sorry! I shouldn't have been spying on you."

"Spying?"

"It wasn't spying. I just wanted to know where my husband was and what he was doing. It won't happen again. I trust you. Please!" She was crying now, hoping that his rage had ended.

"Do you know what I should do to you right now?"

"Please, John. I said I'm sorry. It won't happen again." His fat hand squeezed the back of her neck and hair.

"I told you; I was trying to save this family. There are things going on that you would never understand. You sit around sewing and watching soap operas, and you have no clue what it takes to keep this family running."

He continued to squeeze her hair and neck tighter. "Do you see what's around you? Do you think any of this comes easy? NO! There's a price to pay. Now leave me the hell alone, and let me get some rest so that I can continue to do what I do for this family!" He shoved her to the ground and kicked her in her ribcage. Rhonda screamed in pain and lay curled up on the floor, unable to move.

John had taken out his frustrations on his wife, once again. He didn't care. She'd get over it. She always did, because he knew she would be lost without him.

Melissa was sleeping upstairs but was awakened by the yelling and the sound of glass breaking. She listened from a distance. She knew not to get involved when her dad was acting like this. Her mom had told her it would only make things worse for her, so she always just listened and cried from a distance.

She waited until the yelling had stopped and then eased down the stairs just in time to see her mom lying on the floor and her dad standing over her,

"Dad! No!" She rushed over and flew at him with both fists. He grabbed her, held her by the arms and twisted her around into a bear hug. She screamed and kicked.

"Calm down."

"No! Let me go! Mom!"

"I'm okay, baby. I promise." Rhonda sat up holding her side hoping her ribs weren't broken again.

"Let me go!"

"I'll let you go when you calm down."

Melissa took a deep breath. She knew the worst had passed, and now it was time to just be with her mom as she recovered.

John felt his daughter's body go limp, and he released his grip.

"I didn't know you were here, Melissa. Your mom is fine. Aren't you, Rhonda?"

"Yes. I'm fine. It's okay. I'm fine, I swear."

Melissa knelt by her mom and helped her up off the floor. She led her to a chair and helped slowly lower her to the seat, as her face grimaced in pain.

"Oh, come on, now. It wasn't that bad. I'm sorry, Rhonda. I really am. It's been an exhausting few weeks. I apologize for my outburst." He looked at Melissa. "You know how your mom can push my buttons. I'm in no mood for this."

He left the room. The ladies held each other and cried.

Melissa had seen this side of her dad way too many times to count. The beatings were always taken out on her mom, though, never on her.

Morning came and John left for work early. Melissa sat at the coffee table with her mom.

"My heart breaks for you, Mom. Why do you stay with him?"

"He can't help it. He's a good man. He's been a wonderful husband and a good father to you. What else would I do with my life at this age?"

"You would live! Travel and enjoy yourself. Find a new husband. You're a beautiful woman."

"I can't."

"Yes, you can. What started it all last night?"

"Your dad told me he would be in late. My gut told me to call his office and just ask some questions. Milly told me he had canceled his schedule because he had to make an emergency trip out of town."

"And you didn't know anything about it?"

"No. I told Milly I had no idea he was going out of town. She said he didn't actually tell her he was going, but that she heard him booking a flight."

"That's odd."

"I called the airport and told them who I was and that I just needed to verify John's flight information for him, and they gave it to me."

"Where was he going?"

"Waco, Texas. What's even more odd is that your dad has been going to Waco for many years. I don't know why he goes, but it bothers me that he won't admit it's not work-related."

"You've known for years and never asked? Do you think he has a girlfriend out there?"

"If he does, there've been no signs of him spending money or taking care of her financially. I don't think that's it. My gut tells me it's something else. I've asked about the trips, but he's always said they're work related."

"Waco? That's the second time I've heard of that town in the last week."

"When was the first time?"

"That woman who was kidnapped was living in Waco. She worked there and was vacationing with friends along the coast when she was kidnapped."

Melissa and her mom paused simultaneously and glanced at each other. Neither of them spoke aloud what they were wondering. Could Dad's trip to Waco be somehow related to the disappearance of the woman?

"Mom, I'm going to tell you something that I can't believe I'm saying out loud. Something weird is going on and I think Dad is involved. I can't explain it, but I can feel it."

"What are you suggesting?"

"What if Dad is involved in the kidnapping of that girl Braydee and the other girl."

"Why would you say such a thing? That's not possible."

"Because Mom, Duke was involved, and he's the last person in this world I would have suspected."

"That's true."

"Anything is possible at this point. I found out through a reliable source, that Duke was waiting for the vehicles to arrive that had both women in them the night they were taken. He opened the car door and likely dragged the woman out of the car for someone else to take her."

"I just can't picture Duke harming another human being," said Rhonda.

"Right. Unless he was tricked into it, or believed he was doing it for the department for some reason."

"So, maybe someone put him up to it?"

"Yes, someone he trusts."

"Like your dad." She rubbed her hand along her side, over what she believed were broken ribs. Melissa continued.

"Maybe. The girl's rings were in Duke's possession, and the police told me that the last call he made was to Dad."

"That's odd."

"He's now missing or dead. Dad went to Waco, and it just so happens that the girl is from Waco."

"Yes, but your dad was going to Waco long before there was a missing girl involved."

"I heard you say that you've been keeping a log of Dad's trips to Waco. Is that true?"

"Yes. It's true. I've also kept up with many of his other trips. There was a time when I even had a private investigator follow him from the airport because I was just so curious."

"Where did he go?"

"He went from the airport to a medical facility. He stayed there for six hours, went to another office nearby, and then boarded his plane and came home."

"What was the name of the facility he visited?"

"It's called Braxton Therapeutics. I remember because it reminded me of the singer, Toni Braxton."

"Okay, this is a great start."

"To what?"

"I'm going to get to the bottom of why he's going to Waco. When was the last time you remember him taking a trip out there?"

"It was three years ago. He was acting all fidgety and cranky. He went out there at least three times within six months."

"I'm sorry, Mom. I know this is a lot to digest right now."

"I don't want to believe it, but I have to admit, something feels weird about all this."

"I need to go. There's something I need to do," said Melissa.

"What? What are you going to do? I see that look in your eyes."

"It's okay, Mom. I just need to talk to Whit about some things. Can you get me the information you gathered on Dad?"

"What are you going to do with it?"

Melissa looked at the woman in front of her. Her mom, her best friend, and a fragile wife afraid to start over. She sat holding her ribs and talking softly, so as to not create any more pain than necessary.

"I'm going to take it to the police station. If there's nothing there, then Dad is fine. But if he has done something bad, he needs to be brought to justice."

"I can't let you do that. Do you know what your dad would do to me, and probably you, too, this time? If he found out we were snitches, he would take his anger and revenge out on us! I can't even imagine what he might be capable of."

"He's not going to find out. Just tell me."

"No. I won't be a part of this. You've already lost Duke. Do you really want to lose your dad?"

"I don't WANT to do this. I WANT the truth to come out, no matter what it is. Without our help, the truth may stay hidden."

"I just can't."

"Then why have you been saving this stuff all these years? Why have you been watching him?"

Rhonda Sands sat with her head down. She knew why. There was something suspicious going on in Texas and she knew it.

"Look on the top shelf of my closet. Everything is in the metal box I got from Germany. Please be careful."

Melissa went to her mom's closet. Sitting on the top shelf in plain sight was a beautiful metal box with pictures of Germany's Rhine-Main River covering it. There was a castle and a café. It had been the trip of a lifetime for her mom.

The box had once held a German cake and so many great memories. How ironic that now it was full of questions, suspicion, documents, and pictures that could possibly incriminate her dad.

She pulled the box down from the top of the closet and just stared at it for a while. She wrestled with whether to call the detective or just put it back up on the shelf. Turning it into the authorities won out and she closed the closet door.

As she turned to leave, she was startled at the sight of her dad standing in the doorway.

"Whatcha got there, hon?"

"Just some old keepsakes and pictures. Mom and I are going to look through 'em."

"Sounds like a good thing to keep her occupied and out of trouble for a while."

"Yeah. We're going to have a girl's day. Go out for wine and reminisce about the good old days." She stated the last part sarcastically, but her dad was typically self-involved and didn't catch her meaning.

"Everyone wants to look back on the old days as the good old days. One day you'll look back on today and say it was the good old days."

"I doubt that." She brushed by him, carrying the box. She needed to speak to Det. Knotts or Capt. Marshall before she got cold feet.

Chapter Twenty-One

Capt. Marshall stuck his head inside the door.

"I just got off the phone with the Tyro, Kansas, police department. They think Kasey is there. The chief told me there is an elementary-age girl who has been living with a family there for a few years."

"That's crazy! Man, this is great news. Maybe a happy ending for a change."

"Let's not get ahead of ourselves. We still need to see if it's her. We need to talk to her mom and let her know what's going on. She'll want to be with us when we go up and retrieve her. The chief said that she was safe and living with a nice family, but we don't know how they'll react when we try to take her from them."

"Right. I'm sure they don't know the circumstances of why she's there."

"They were told she was orphaned and that her family had burnt up in a fire."

"I'm sure the girl has let them know what happened."

"Probably. But that doesn't mean they believed her."

Det. Knotts pulled up all the old files from years back and began reading.

"Missing girl: Five-year-old Kasey Kendall. She was taken from a Walmart parking lot. She had been left in the car while her mother ran inside. Prints were found on the door of an officer but were suggested to be old prints from a previous meeting at a bar."

He dialed the phone number on file for Mrs. Kendall, and she answered.

"Mrs. Kendall, this is Det. Knotts with the Baldwin County Police Department. I need to tell you something about your daughter."

"Someone called earlier, and I've already told them everything."

"No, this is something else."

"What about her? Have you found something that could help us find her?"

She had never given up hope. Each year she had posted new signs with an age progression of Kasey. She would be eight years old now.

"Possibly. We haven't been able to verify-"He trailed off as Mrs. Kendall interrupted.

"What have you found?"

"Someone gave us a tip that your daughter is alive in Kansas."

"What? Who? Who has her? What kind of tip?"

"The details aren't entirely clear. We were told she is living with a family. The police chief has verified that there's been a young girl living with a local family and that she moved there roughly three years ago."

"Oh God! Thank you, God! My prayers have been answered." The tears began to flow. Her words were broken as she choked back gasps of air.

"I want to go now. Take me to her."

"Yes, ma'am. That's why I called. We're making arrangements now to go and get her if we find that it's really her."

"How soon can we go?"

"Just as soon as we can make the flight plans. Are you available to leave tonight?"

"I want to go now." She sobbed into her hands and tears streamed down her cheeks.

"Ma'am, I don't want you to get your hopes up and then find out it's not your daughter. We're waiting for the chief to email us a picture of the girl. Once we have that, I'll send it to you for verification, and then we'll book the flight."

"I understand. I'm so overwhelmed right now." She was trembling with excitement and fear that it could all be nothing but false hope.

"I'm going to hold on to the false hope for now. I need this moment, even if it turns out to be someone else's little girl."

"I understand."

"I hate to ask this, ma'am, but did you know Woody Thomas went missing?"

"No. How would I know that? It was all I could do to get out of bed and feed myself. I wasn't keeping up with what a scumbag like Woody was up to."

"I'm sure, ma'am."

"Disappeared, huh? Just gone?"

"That's right. He was just here one day and gone the next, according to the records here at the precinct."

"Sounds a whole lot like my little girl. Here one day and gone the next. I'm believing with my whole heart that my little girl is waiting for me in Kansas."

"Thank you. I'm truly sorry for all that you've been through. I'll send you the picture as soon as I get it. What's your email address?"

The detective took down her email address. "I wish someone was there with you during this time. Do you have someone you could call?"

"Not really. I've pushed everyone away. Everything just felt so pointless once she was gone. I couldn't even have a conversation with my husband, much less my friends."

"That's understandable."

"Friends slowly quit calling or texting me."

"And your mom and dad?"

"They live in Tennessee. I'll call them as soon as we hang up."

"Don't tell them anything about Kasey yet. We need to identify her. It shouldn't be too much longer, then you can call them."

"Thank you. I'll be waiting for your call.

Det. Knotts stared at his coffee mug. His heart ached for Kasey and her mom. The trauma they had experienced was something no child or parent should ever have to endure.

He fumbled through the papers in front of him. There was no new evidence on the missing officer.

He turned back to his current case. There were no emails or pictures, no incriminating text messages, or anything unusual. He called the bar that Duke had visited the night the girls were kidnapped, according to Whit. He knew the manager, and needed to see who was working the bar and if they had heard Duke say anything that would give them a place to start.

"Hi, Rob. It's Cory Knotts."

"Hey, man."

"I'm working on the case against Duke Davis. I was hoping you could pull the logs and tell me who was working the bar on a certain date?"

"Sure, I can do that. What's the date?"

"September 8 is the date the girls went missing."
After a few minutes he was given a name.
"It was Jenn Williams. She came in at six p.m. and didn't leave until four a.m. She would have talked to him. You know how she flirts, anyway, but she goes overboard with Duke."

"Oh, I know. I've seen it in action. I've got her number in my phone, so I'll give her a call off the record. Thanks, man."

"Yeah, no problem. Come see us sometime."

The detective called the bartender, Jenn.

"Hey, there. What can I do for ya?"

"I was hoping you could answer some questions about one of your patrons."

"Oh, well, unless they were belligerent or handsome, I'm afraid all the days and nights just kind of run together at work."

"The person we're inquiring about is Duke Davis."

"Oh, God, yes! I can remember him!"

"Well, okay."

"That didn't come out right. I can always tell you when he comes in, because he always sits at the bar, he's always chatty, I always try to flirt, and he always drinks too much."

"Well, hopefully, in this case, he said something useful. Do you mind if I record this conversation? It's off the record, but I may need you to come in and make a statement."

"I don't mind at all."

"Okay. Duke's friend, Whit, said that the night the girls were kidnapped, Duke came to his house. He was very drunk, and he said he had been to the Keg. That would have been September 8. Do you remember seeing him?"

"Yes, for sure. He came in before midnight and stayed for a few hours."

"How did he seem? I mean what was his demeanor?"

"He was sad. Very off from his usual self."

"How could you tell he was sad?"

"He was just more to himself. Wasn't smiling. Wasn't really picking up on my funnies. He was just staring at his drink mumbling to himself off and on."

"Did you hear anything he was mumbling about?"

"No, not really."

"He did tell me that he was afraid he had done something he shouldn't have done. I was just trying to be a good listener. You know, that's what we bartenders are known for. But we don't hear half the things we're nodding and responding to."

"Was there anything said about where he had been?"

"No, nothing like that. He did say something about his father-in-law. The only reason I remember is because he specifically said not to mention it to anyone. I wouldn't be telling you now except I feel like this is a different situation with him missing."

"It could help him in the end. What exactly did he say?"

"He asked me if I knew Judge John Sands. I said I only knew that it was his wife's father. I remember him asking me if I had ever done something I thought was right, but it turned out to be very wrong."

"What about John Sands? Why did he ask you if you knew him?"

"He said his father-in-law had him doing something, but that his gut instinct was saying it felt off."

"Anything else?"

"I gave him another couple of beers, and then he left. That was it. I had never seen Duke like that. He's always so upbeat and full of energy."

"Thank you."

"I just can't believe Duke would do something like this."

"Let's hope there is a good reason behind his actions. You have been very helpful. I'm going to need you to come into the station and fill out a formal statement. The time may come when Duke needs witnesses. This was just the kind of information I was looking for."

"Is Duke alive?"

"Yes, we think he's still alive."

"Oh, that's great."

"I need you to do me a favor. Don't tell a soul about Duke coming by the bar. You could be in some serious danger if the wrong people find out Duke was talking about his father-in-law. There's some shady and dangerous stuff going on around here right now."

"I won't say a word. I haven't told anyone anything, I had forgotten all about it until now."

"Okay. Come by anytime in the next few days. The sooner the better, though."

The email notification popped up and Knotts opened it up. There was a picture of what looked like an older Kasey, but he wanted Ms. Kendall to identify her to be sure. He forwarded the email.

She immediately called him. He could barely understand her on the other end of the line.

"That's my baby!! That's her! That's Kasey!" She was hysterical with excitement and had begun to hyperventilate.

"Oh, God! Thank you, thank you!"

"Breathe deeply, ma'am. I don't want you to pass out."

She attempted to steady her breathing.

"When do we leave?"

"I'm making plans now. I'll email you the information and I'll send someone to pick you up.

"I'll be ready," she sobbed and hung up the phone.

She called her ex-husband first.

"Dale, are you sitting down?"

"I'm at Publix. What is it?"

"I need you to go to your truck."

"What's this about?" He was pushing his buggy out of the way and walking to his truck as she spoke. She wasn't one to be irrational or tell him to do something for no reason.

"Tell me when you're there."

He could tell she was crying.

"Okay, I'm here."

"The police just called. They found Kasey. She's alive in Kansas and we're going to pick her up."

Tears began to fall uncontrollably. Together they cried for nearly five minutes. Just holding each other through the phone. Time stood still and nothing else mattered.

"I'm coming to the house," he choked out the words.

"I'll be waiting."

When Kasey's dad pulled up to his old familiar house, all the pain of losing Kasey rushed back. The fights with his wife and the way she had pushed everyone away flooded over him, but in the same instant, it was pushed aside, and joy overtook him.

He was a praying man and outside of his home he bowed his head.

"God, please restore my marriage. Let us be a family. I want to be the best version of myself I can be for my family. Make me more like you and keep us in your will."

His ex-wife opened the door and stood on the porch. She had never looked more beautiful to him in his entire life.

They ran into each other's arms and cried. Dale began to pray for the two of them and the Holy Spirit covered them, washing them with a peace they had never felt before.

"I love you, Dale. I'm so sorry for the way I've acted."

"I love you, too. You don't have to apologize. No one knows how to act in these situations. You're going to be okay, though. You look beautiful."

"Even with this puffy face and these red eyes?"

"Especially with that puffy face and those red eyes."

He held her hand looking at his beautiful wife. Oh, how he had missed her touch and everything about her.

"I've missed you so much, Dale."

"I'm glad to hear you say that. I've missed you every day," he said.

"What would you say about getting your clothes and coming back here with us."

They started to cry again. Us. That was a word they never thought they would say again.

Standing in front of the Tyro County, Kansas, police station was surreal. The Kendall's held hands as they walked inside to see their daughter for the first time in three years. The chief introduced himself and shook their hands.

"I've had a very long conversation with the family Kasey has been living with. It's an older couple. Family of a guy that used to live here many years ago. I believe their story," said the chief.

"And what's their story?" asked Dale angrily.

"A local guy named Robert brought her up. They were told she lost her parents in a house fire. He said she had been in his care, and she was in a state of shock and that she believed her parents were still alive."

"Dear God! Did they not see the news coverage that first year? It was on every major network for several months because of the officer that was accused."

"No, sir. It's a small, simple town. They were completely unaware. They're pretty shook up over the whole ordeal. You're welcome to press charges, but I could tell you, if you knew them, you'd understand. They're farmers, not kidnappers."

"Can we just see our daughter?"

"Of course. She's in here, guys." The gentle elderly police chief pointed down the hall. "This way."

They walked down the hall and into a small room where Kasey sat eating an ice cream cone. When she saw her parents, she dropped the cone and ran to them, throwing herself into their arms. The three of them hugged and cried.

"Daddy!" yelled Kasey. She ran into his arms.

"You look so beautiful, baby girl." Dale held her face in his hands. "Look at you so grown up."

"Mommy. I didn't think I would ever see you again."

They held each other for minutes. Cheeks were wet with a steady stream of tears.

"I want to go home." This time when she said it, it was actually going to happen. She had spent three years saying she wanted to go home.

"That's where we're going." Her mom picked her up and Kasey wrapped her arms and legs tightly around her.

"I'm not too big for arms and legs!" said Kasey.

Her mom laughed.

"You'll never be too big for arms and legs."

It was something she had always said to Kasey when she wanted to be hugged really big. She would say use your arms and your legs, and she would pick her up. She had done that since she was three years old. Now after all these years, Kasey was hugging with her arms and legs again.

In the room next door, an elderly couple sat crying. Taking on the young child had been hard at first, but they had grown to love her as a granddaughter.

"I need to tell Nana and Papa bye," said Kasey.

"Who?" asked her mom.

"Nana and Papa."

The Kendall's knew she meant the two people who had been keeping Kasey from them for the last three years.

"Okay. Let's go. I want to see them," said Dale.

The chief escorted the couple into the room. Holding on to each other they looked much older than their age. They were frail and leathered. We woman held out her hands to Kasey and she ran to her.

"I'm going to miss you, Nana. I love you," she said. "Are you going to visit me sometime?"

"I love you, too. I don't know if I'll be able to visit." She looked at Kasey's parents. "I sure hope so."

Kasey hugged the man she had called Papa for three years and everyone could tell there was genuine love between them.

"It's time to go," said Dale.

The little old man and woman sat holding each other as Kasey walked away. Tears filled their handkerchiefs, and they waved their final goodbyes.

Chapter Twenty-Two

Melissa was filled with confusion, pain, delusion, and regret as she pulled up to the police station. There was confusion as to what was going on, and pain because it involved her family.

It was the most difficult thing she had ever done in her life. What if she was wrong? What if she was betraying her dad in the worst possible way?

Just because he had been a horrible husband had nothing to do with what a good dad he had been over her lifetime. He had never laid a hand on her or treated her the way he had treated her mom.

She thought about the abuse she had witnessed by her father against her mother. It was more than she could bear alone. She had held the secret for as long as she could. Her heart ached and her knees were wobbly as she stepped out of the car and walked into the station.

"Come in, Melissa. You sounded troubled on the phone earlier." Det. Knotts led her to a chair across from his desk.

"Yes. I want to talk about my father." She was shaking.

"Do you mind if I record you, or is this off the record?"

"You can record me, and no, it's not off the record."

He pulled out his recorder and sat it on the desk. "Go ahead."

"I think my father is somehow involved with the girls who went missing."

"Okay. Why?"

"Last night he flew in from Waco, Texas. As it turns out, he's been going there for years. He doesn't tell my mom, but she knows. The trips are very secretive, according to her. She's been keeping a record of these trips, and on one occasion, she had him followed."

"Does he know this?"

"I don't think he knows she had him followed, but he does know she's been keeping tabs on him. He found that out last night. They got into a fight, and my dad hit her in the face a few times. He shoved her into the wall. He kicked her. She thinks she has a broken rib, but she doesn't want to go to the hospital. He has a bad temper. We know how to keep from making him mad. He always hurts her in places where no one can see, but last night it was in the face."

"So, your dad physically abuses your mom?"

"Yes."

"How often?"

"Maybe three times a year? I don't know. It used to be pretty rare, then it would happen a lot, then we would think he had stopped altogether. There's just no way to predict it."

"Why hasn't your mom come forward and pressed charges?"

"Because he's the judge. Because if she does, she'll lose everything, and he'll lose his job. She's afraid."

"I see."

"And mainly because she loves him and wants to be with him. He's a good dad, and we have a good family life most of the time."

"I understand. We see it a lot. Did your mom tell you any details about when she had him followed?"

"Yes. He took a plane from Foley to Waco. She said that when he got off the plane, he went straight to a medical facility, and then to someone's office."

"What was the name of the facility?"

"Braxton Therapeutics."

"Is there any chance your dad could have a medical condition he's being treated for that he's keeping a secret?"

"I don't think so. My mom would be the first to know if that was the case. He's a bit of a whiner, so I feel like that would have given him reasons to whine and make her feel bad about making her do things for him."

"But it's a possibility."

"I guess it's a possibility."

"Is there anything else about your dad that you would like to share?"

"Duke being involved doesn't seem right. It's so out of character for him. I know him down to the core. He's a really great guy. You can ask anyone. I don't believe for a minute he knew he was helping to kidnap someone. He and my dad have been very chummy in the last few months."

"In what way?

"Well, Dad didn't think Duke had the brains to be the right husband for me. He said it all the time. It wasn't until I walked down the aisle that Dad accepted that Duke was going to be my husband. He practically threatened to write me out of the will if we had children. He said he didn't want brain-dead grandkids."

"Why did he think Duke wasn't smart?"

"Just things he would say when we were growing up and dating in high school."

"I'm sorry you're having to repeat all this."

"It isn't even relevant to the case, but I've never told anyone. Not even Mom. Anyway, the night the lady disappeared; Duke didn't come home. The friend he stayed with that night said he was drunk and babbling about a secret mission. It was just silly talk that meant nothing until now."

"Whit Thomas?"

"How do you know him?"

"Small town. People talk. I just know him from a distance. Seems to be a good guy." He didn't want to say anything that would give away the fact that Whit had come into the station and brought a letter from Duke.

"One of the best. I don't want anyone to know that I've said anything against my father, though. I know it's crazy to be saying all of this based only on a hunch."

"Many cases are solved based on a hunch."

"When I heard that Duke had taken Dad's boat, the hair on my neck stood straight up. There's a connection somehow."

"Do you think your dad could have had something to do with the way Duke disappeared with the boat? Your dad said he stole the boat with help from someone."

"Honestly, I'm so confused by all of this. I don't see Duke stealing a boat and I don't see my dad or him kidnapping a girl. I can't even believe I'm here right now." Her hands started to tremble.

"Is it possible for you to stay with your parents for a while so that you can keep your ears and eyes on your dad's activity for a while?"

"I'm already staying there."

"Perfect. Can you get with your mom and find out any other details of what your dad did on his trip to Waco?"

"Yes, I can do that. I want all of this to be over." She held her face in her hands as she propped her elbows on the desk in front of her.

"I know you do. Does your mom know that you're here?"

"No." She lied. She wanted to keep her mom out of it.

"Do you think she'd be okay with you being here? Would she cooperate with us if we need her to?"

"No, she's not okay with it. She's so destroyed inside that I would even suspect something like this. She's so loyal to him. It doesn't matter what he does to her, she just keeps silent because she's scared she wouldn't be able to survive without him."

"I understand that. Typical victim thinking process. Can you think of anything else before we wrap this up?"

"Yes. The most important thing. The box."

"What box?"

"I have a box in the car that mom has been putting all kinds of stuff in for years regarding Dad's trips. Let me go get it."

"Great." He held his poker face.

Melissa retrieved the metal box from her trunk and placed it in Det. Knotts hands.

"Thank you, Melissa. I need to tell you something."

Melissa froze. She wasn't sure she could handle any more bad news.

"We found the missing five-year-old, Kasey Kendall."

"Where? How? Oh, my gosh!"

"It was Duke that tipped us off about where she was."

"Oh, God, no. Did he have something to do with it?"

"We don't believe he did. The little girl's shoes were found in a secret compartment on your dad's boat. I think your hunches could be correct."

Melissa steadied herself against the car and held back the emotions that formed a huge lump in her throat.

"I'm lost right now."

"I want you to think about something. A little girl was just found, all because Duke was involved. Sometimes things look so bad, and the path is so thorny, but it's actually meant to produce a beautiful rose at the end of the journey. Does that make any sense?"

"Yes, it does. I thought Duke was at the wrong place at the wrong time, but really, he was at the right place at just the right time."

"Yes, that's what I'm saying."

"If Duke had never touched that car or stolen those rings, that little girl would never be found." She had started to whimper out her words. "I would gladly give up my marriage, and Duke would go to jail if it meant finding that little girl."

"I believe it. Let me give you a hug. You deserve one right now."

She hugged the officer affectionately.

"Thank you. I'll see what I can find out. I'm so nervous though. I feel like I'm losing my mind. I love my dad. I swear I do. I felt like I was seriously unraveling. You are telling me Duke helped you find the girl has given me so much hope."

"That's why I told you. Anyone would unravel under these circumstances. Stay focused on keeping you and your mom safe at whatever cost."

"I'm not afraid of my dad. In all the years of abuse, he has never once hurt me. I'm truly his little girl, and I'm not worried about me at all. I'm just afraid for my mom."

Later that evening, Rhonda and her daughter sat on their large wraparound porch, enjoying a glass of Chardonnay. It was the perfect time for Melissa to bring up her concerns once more.

"Mom, I looked up Braxton Therapeutics online. It's some sort of research facility. Something about cloning and organ transplant research."

"What? Why would Dad be visiting a place like that?"

"Are you telling me you never googled the place?"

"No, I didn't."

"Why? Weren't you a little curious? I mean you paid someone to follow him. Did the investigator not tell you this years ago?"

"I'm sure he did. I swear I just dump things when I no longer need them. Once I found out how quick the trips were, and that there was never a woman involved, I just kind of stopped thinking about it until now."

"Well, why does it matter now?"

"Because he's been acting so fidgety. He doesn't want to talk, and he's preoccupied with something in his mind. It's different than when he has a hard case going on."

"I agree. Something's off, Mom. You know it. You can feel it. There are just too many coincidences right now. Taking a trip to Waco, when someone who's been kidnapped is from Waco - well, that's a big red flag."

"That is enough! Yes, I do feel like something is off, but your father is a good man. He has his issues, but do you know how badly you could damage this family if someone heard you saying such things about your dad?"

John Sands stepped onto the porch and repeated the words Rhonda had said.

"Heard you saying such things about your dad, Melissa?"

"John, you're home early!"

"Shut up, Rhonda. I'm talking to my daughter. What could you possibly be saying that could badly damage this family?"

"That you are a beast, and if you lay a hand on my mother again, I will go public. I promise you! I'll tell everyone that the Honorable Judge John Sands is a wife-beater and has been his entire married life!"

She stood up and went straight to her room. John watched her walk away. She listened for his footsteps coming up the stairs, but never heard any, and finally relaxed on the bed, with her door locked.

John had never been threatened by his daughter before. He looked a bit confused as Rhonda made her way into the kitchen and emptied the rest of her wine down the sink. She fought back a tear as she thought about the times, she had wanted to walk away but couldn't.

She wished she had the courage like Melissa to speak up for herself, but she didn't. All the years she had wasted believing he would change, but he never did.

Melissa called Capt. Marshall.

"I want to leave town and take my mom with me."

"What's happened?"

"I'm really nervous about all this. I feel like my dad is a little unhinged right now."

"Unhinged? How?"

"He's just acting out of character. He's on edge and it's making things uncomfortable for me and mom."

"I understand, but being there at the house is crucial."

"You obviously don't know my dad. He's not discussing anything at our house, nor is he conducting secret meetings or sacrifices. Whatever he has going on, he's been very careful to keep us out of it. I'm telling you we just need to get away right now."

"I understand. Where are you going?"

"Costa Rica."

"Oh, wow. You're taking a serious vacation!"

"A forced vacation, but mom and I will make the most of it. Dad walked in on me and Mom talking about him, and it was a close call. He was very upset. I threatened to expose him if he laid another hand on Mom. I'm in my room right now. I'm so scared, I'm shaking."

"Did he hurt your mom?"

"No, he just yelled and told her to shut up in front of me. He gave her a death stare that scared me enough to want to leave until he cools down a bit."

"I see. Yes, it might be a good idea to get away for sure. When are you leaving?"

"I'm not sure yet, but I'll let you know. Just as soon as I can make it happen."

"Okay. Let's keep in touch."

Chapter Twenty-Three

I emerged from the shower room wearing a pair of clean scrubs and a fresh, white lab coat. I felt a sense of confidence and relief, but nothing had changed.

Maybe it was because I felt like the girls were safe today, and they had enough water to survive. Or maybe it was because of Chandler.

I was escorted to my room, but Tate wasn't there. I decided to visit the break room. Maybe I would run into Chandler.

"I'm going to the break room. Be back in five minutes."

The guard near my room nodded.

My meeting with cock-eyed John was still on my mind. This was not the time to do anything stupid. I walked as slowly as I could, hoping that at any moment Chandler would open his door and say 'good morning.' It didn't happen.

The break room was once again filled with smiling faces, and the sounds of various conversations merged into one. The scent of coffee and Danish filled the air. For a brief moment, I was a normal person on a normal job.

I secretly stuffed my pockets again, which was a quick reminder that I wasn't normal, and many little mouths were depending on me. I slowly made my way back to my room. Tate was still not there, and I was beginning to worry. I would have to begin without her.

I pressed the call button next to the door and spoke into the box, not knowing if anyone would even answer.

"Where's Tate?"

"She's in a holding chamber."

"Why?"

"Because she was a very bad girl last night."

'What did she do?"

"That doesn't concern you."

"Oh, but it does concern me. I can't stay focused, and I need her for the project we've begun together. It's important."

"She'll be back by Friday."

"What's today?"

"It's Tuesday."

With Tate gone, I was a mess. I couldn't even imagine what a holding chamber was, but I knew it was meant to be something awful. What had she done? Would she have attempted an escape? If so, she had not given me any clues about it.

It was nearly quitting time, and I made one more attempt to see Chandler on the way to the break room. As fate would have it, from the end of the hall, I saw his profile as he entered the break room. My heart skipped a beat, and I moved quickly in his direction.

He was standing in the back of the room stirring a cup of coffee.

I eased up next to him, and I reached for a packet of tea. "Hi, Chandler." My smile was reflexive and genuine, and my voice was nearly a whisper.

He smiled back. "Oh, hi, Braydee."

"Please don't call me that. I'm sorry. I can't explain it right now. I'm in danger, though. That's all I can say." My whisper was barely audible.

He looked confused. I know I must have sounded completely psycho.

"Danger? From whom?" He whispered back.

I placed the teabag in the hot water and turned to go.

"Some very bad people," I whispered, as I turned to go. I touched his hand. "Please help me."

I left as quickly as I could, hoping and praying that no one had caught the slight touch of the hand on the break room monitor.

The large metal door rolled open and two men entered. The girls scattered in every direction, hiding behind anything they could find. The voices bellowed inside the metal barn.

"Come on out, girls! We aren't going to chase you, but we aren't leaving until you come out."

No one moved. They were frozen with fear.

"Stop wasting time. You're only making it worse for yourselves." The men began walking to the hiding places of two of the girls and pulled them out by their hair. They dragged them to the center of the barn as the girls screamed.

"I'm taking this one with me. When your keeper comes back, tell her that if she's caught fraternizing with any of the employees again, every one of you will be chopped into pieces. Tell her she should be thankful only one of you was taken."

Baily was screaming as the man grabbed her around the neck with his forearm and began pulling her towards the car. She wriggled her face down and bit his arm until she tasted his blood in her mouth. He screamed and let her go. She ran as fast as she could out of the barn, but her little eleven-year-old legs were no match for the men.

When they caught her, they slapped her until she easily submitted to being put in the car. Baily was driven over to the facility and was taken through the same back door Braydee had been entering.

Down the hall, there were so many metal doors that resembled freezer doors. Each one had a set of letters on them. There were padlocks on a large bolt. The man took out a large ring of keys and quickly found the master key. He opened the chamber and shoved Baily through the door. Inside there was a mattress on the ground, a metal toilet like you would find in a jail cell, and a small slot where food was slid in from somewhere on the other side. Bruised and battered, Baily took her spot in what would be her new home until someone decided otherwise.

Next door, Tate could hear everything. She sat on her mattress and hugged her knees to her chest. She wondered if the person next to her was Braydee.

At quitting time, I was picked up as usual from the front entrance. I looked around often to see if I could spot Chandler anywhere. He looked so confused when I told him I was in danger. I knew he had no reason to believe me. I only hoped he could sense the seriousness of the words "bad people" and that he wouldn't talk about it with anyone.

My driver unlocked the side door of the building for me. It occurred to me just how many people were involved in keeping us locked up because I had never seen that driver before. I walked into the building, and the girls began screaming. They were crying and babbling all at once, and I couldn't understand anything that was being said.

"What? What has happened? Where's Baily?" I noticed right away that she was gone.

"That's what we're saying. They took Baily. They took Baily because you're fraternizing. What's fraternizing?" Nikki was speaking for the group.

"Oh, God, no! They know."

"They know what?"

"Let's go to the nest. I'll tell you everything."

We all piled up together. The girls were all still sobbing.

"When did they take her?"

"Not too long before you got here."

"Okay. I met a man yesterday. I stumbled into his office. It turns out that the place where they have me working is full of normal people who are working there because they want to. I don't know who's a prisoner and who's free, but I'm trying to figure it out."

"So, why did they take Baily?" Katrina's gray eyes were red from crying so much.

"Little Katrina, my sweet baby girl, they took her because they told me not to talk to anyone, and I did."

Again, my actions had caused pain to come to the girls. "I'm so sorry."

"Why were you talking to him if they said not to?"

"Because I think he's someone I can trust to help us."

"He doesn't know you or us. Why would he help?"

"It's just a feeling we shared. Something I can't explain. I saw him in the break room today, and I whispered to him that I was in danger and needed help. That's all."

No one spoke.

"I was just trying to help us. I promise."

"You keep saying that, but do you think it's helping at all?"

"I don't know. I want to believe that this time Chandler is going to be the key to getting us out of here."

"Is Baily going to be, okay?"

I didn't want to lie to them anymore. I wanted to say I don't know anymore. I just don't know. Instead, I said

"Of course. We're all going to be okay."

Twenty minutes across town, back at the "farmhouse" where Braydee and the girls had been kept, a fifteen-year-old boy flew his drone over the wooded acreage and into the clearing as he had done several times before. He had seen the girls outside playing on multiple occasions, but today they were gone. In their place were the words 'Help Us' formed out plainly for him to read. He took a video of it and ran to his mom.

"Mom, I need to show you something."

"What is it?" She looked up from her computer at her son.

"It's probably nothing, but I would love for you to take a look at this."

He first showed her the video he had taken weeks before of the girls sitting in the circle outside the house playing.

"Stop. Zoom in right there." He did. "I've seen posters of that little black girl at the Walgreens. She's been missing for weeks. Where is this?"

"It's just over the trees west of here. But look at this." He pulled up the footage of the words 'Help us' and paused it.

"What the heck?"

"Yea, they made the words out of their clothes! I've seen all the girls there a few times. They just come out and play every now and then. They always stay close to the house. When I saw this, I kind of freaked out. I took some footage around the house from a distance."

"I'm calling the police." She dialed 911.

"911 What's your emergency?"

"I think one of our neighbors has been holding some girls hostage."

"Where are you, ma'am?"

The address was given, and officers headed to the house where the 911 call originated.

The operator continued.

"Why do you think your neighbor has kidnapped girls?"

"I'm looking at a video of the little girl, Marlea, who went missing from the park a few weeks ago. It looks just like her."

"Okay. Sit tight. Officers are just around the corner."

The officers arrived within ten minutes of the call.

"Hello, ma'am. You reported potential hostages?"

"Yes, sir. My son has drone footage of the little black girl, Marlea, along with some other girls sitting in a circle in the backyard of a house due west of us."

"When was the footage taken?"

"He's right here. You can ask him."

The boy stepped forward.

"I've seen them a few times. They've been there for a few weeks. The first video was two weeks ago, then again last week. I really wasn't paying attention much, just flying my drone. I looked back at the footage today and saw 'Help Us'. The video is about five days old."

"You know it's illegal to fly drones over other people's property like that, son? That's an invasion of their privacy."

"No, sir. I didn't."

"Yes. Can't do it in neighborhoods like this. Take it out to the country. In this case, it's a good thing you were flying it.

"Do you know who lives at the house your son videoed?"

"No, I have no idea."

"Can you show me the footage?"

"Yes. Here you go."

As he watched the children sitting in the circle with the words 'Help Us' near the house, he grabbed his radio.

"I'm going to need backup. I need several units at 1342 Franklin Circle. We can all go together to the residence in question. I have footage of at least three missing girls that I recognize. It's possible all of them are on a missing persons list."

"Ten-four. Units in progress."

Fifteen minutes later the house was swarming with cops. They lined up and filed out to encompass the house. With weapons drawn, they surrounded both houses on the property. Two officers busted down the door to the first house and officers flooded into every room. They quickly surveyed and announced 'all clear' in each room.

"Hey, guys. I just found something. It's a big metal door."

There was a large sliding bolt with a padlock, but it wasn't locked, and they opened the door. The stench was overwhelming. As flashlights lit up the room, they could see chains bolted to the ground. There were ten chains on each side of the room. The small room was a prison. There was human waste all around.

The officers fought back the urge to throw up as they quickly surveyed the room. "Let's get someone over here to take pictures and get some fingerprints. Let's head to the house in the back and hope we find the girls alive inside."

The officers found only signs of where the children had been but no children. They took pictures of everything inside the house.

"What do you think these rock piles are for? There are eight piles of them."

"Not sure. Could have been a part of some game or counting system. Could have been the number of days they were here."

"Let's get these clothes bagged."

After pictures were taken of the words 'Help Us' that had been placed near the back of the house, all the clothes were placed in separate bags. There would be DNA evidence that would help identify who the clothes belonged to.

I distributed the small snacks I had saved from the break room, and everyone was able to eat something. The girls had begun to lose weight quickly over the last five days, and without enough water, they were becoming weaker and weaker. I picked pieces of straw out of their hair. It broke my heart to think that we had all come to this. Living like caged animals at a zoo, sleeping in a bed of straw.

"Remember when we made the words 'Help Us' at the other place?" Nikki asked.

"Of course, I remember."

"Well, do you think whoever was flying the drone ever found it?"

"I've been wondering the same thing. There's a chance it's been seen. Let's hope if they did see it, they took it seriously and reported it."

The mind is like that. When something was happening across the globe with someone, I could often feel it in my spirit. So many times, I have been about to make a phone call, and suddenly that person will call me. If satellites can connect computers, maybe we can connect with minds. It was worth a try. I'd try anything at this point.

"I need everyone to do something kind of crazy right now. I need you to think about the one person who loves you more than anything. Picture them finding you. Take a mental picture of this metal barn and send it to them with your mind. Focus so hard on describing with your mind where you are. I'm going to tell you a few things that I want you to think about."

I described the health facility a few hundred yards away from us and asked the girls to think about it. I described the barn with the sheep and the goats. We all did our best to send a mental signal to our loved ones.

I wondered if the girls had anyone who was worried about them. I knew Marlea did, but I didn't know about the others.

"Okay, now let's focus on Baily. Where is she? What does it look like where she's being held? How far away is it? Can you feel her thinking about us, too? Focus. Let's let her know we love her."

Clara squinted her eyes and took my hand. "She's close by. I can feel her. She's lying on a mattress in a small room. It has a metal door with the letters SR on it."

I felt her tiny hand squeezing mine. Her eyes were still closed. I stared at her in disbelief, but I believed her. I had seen metal doors down the hallway where I entered the facility, and they had random letters on them.

"Clara. There are metal doors at the building where I work. I'm going to look tomorrow and see if there is one with the letters SR on it. Have you ever done anything like this before?"

"Done what before?"

"Have you ever pictured something in your mind that turned out to be true?"

"No, I haven't. I've never really tried to think about much though."

"Let's hope and pray that you're right."

The girls were weak from hunger and thirst, and I was beginning to lose all hope of finding an escape.

Morning came with a jolt. The doors were opened, and outside was a van. "

"Everyone up. We're leaving."

It was still dark outside. We didn't have a choice but to follow the flashlight to the van.

"What's happening right now? Where are you taking us?"

There was no answer.

"Why are you moving us?"

"You didn't think you were just going to live in the metal barn for the rest of your time here, did you? That was temporary until we could get your rooms ready."

"What rooms?"

"That's enough questions. Too bad you gave up a great situation at the farm."

We pulled up to the back side of the facility and unloaded. Nikki, Jill, Marlea, and Clara were put in one small room. Katrina, Lexi, and I were next to them.

"Am I going to work today?"

"Nope, not today. Today you're going to sit in this room and think about how good you had it back at the farm.

Sitting on the mattress, I cried silent tears. The girls didn't see them.

I had heard about modern-day slavery, but never really understood how someone could be a slave in the twenty-first century. What keeps a person from running away? Fear. I remembered watching the story of Elizabeth Smart, and how she had been kidnapped from her bedroom by a local contractor her parents had hired.

She was raped repeatedly, forced to marry her captor, and wear strange clothes in public. Yes, that's right, in public. She was out and about many times. She interacted with people, but she was too scared to speak up. She was convinced her family would be tortured and killed.

That was me. Seeing what they were doing to the children had me paralyzed. I couldn't tell a good guy from a bad guy anymore. People who seemed very normal were far from it. I prayed to God to please make a way. Let Chandler become inquisitive and begin searching for answers on his own.

I wanted to just start screaming and tell the girls to scream with me. Maybe someone good and kind would hear us and come running. But the result of such action was that we would be gassed to death in this chamber, or worse. I lowered my head a little more so that the girls wouldn't see my face, even though their eyes were closed as they lay next to me.

Chapter Twenty-Four

Chandler Grey arrived at 7:55 and went straight to the break room. He lingered as long as possible, looking for Braydee, but she never came. He strolled around down the halls and poked around in areas he had never been before, but still, there was no sign of her.

The words she had spoken to him yesterday had sent a shiver down his spine. The intensity and pain in her eyes was something he recognized immediately. He had seen that same look in the eyes of his late wife in the months before she had committed suicide.

"Help me."

That's what he saw. He went to his computer and began another search. Again, he pulled up the employee data list. There was no Braydee Quinn. He did a Google search and up popped her name, along with everything happening in the news.

There was a Braydee Quinn missing person article, with her picture. There was an article about a missing Waco, Texas woman kidnapped in Alabama. Baylor University Scientist Missing. The list went on and on.

His heart raced, and his first instinct was to call the police. Since he didn't know where she was, he decided to wait. Whoever had taken her had brought her here by force. They wouldn't just let her walk away. He had to think it through and come up with a real plan. Her life was in his hands. He would need to carry on as if he didn't know anything until he could put the pieces of the puzzle together and make some sense of what was happening. He would have to move slowly to keep from alerting anyone. Maybe Braydee wanted to disappear. But then why wouldn't she be using a fake name to conceal her identity? No, he had seen her cry for help.

He had made the mistake of not doing enough for his wife and had lost her. He wouldn't make the same mistake this time. He had to find Braydee. It was going to be very difficult in a place this size, with so many people working behind closed doors.

He decided to prop his door open and keep watch to see if she walked by, but she never did. Two days passed, and still, Braydee had not passed by.

He became obsessed with listening to the footsteps coming down the hall in hopes of seeing Braydee pass. He had come to figure out the difference between the sounds of a man approaching and the sounds of a woman. Days passed and still no Braydee.

The girls and I sat waiting. Waiting on food. Waiting to breathe clean air. Waiting for toilet paper. Waiting on all the things that just a month ago, I took for granted. We could hear noises of activity, but I couldn't make out any voices. Dinner never came, and I knew more days like this would send us to the grave.

I'm not sure how long we were locked in the rooms together. There were no windows in the chambers. Every few hours, the lights would come on. Blinding us for a moment and then going off again, leaving us sitting in pitch-black darkness. It was their form of torture. Maybe it was days, maybe only twenty-four hours. All I know is that it was pure hell. We were finally given food and allowed to rest.

Someone came to the door and motioned for me to follow them. I showered, and put on my scrubs, as I had done so many times before. I was led back to my workstation.

Tate was still missing. I was pretty sure she was dead by now, although I knew it would benefit them more for her to be alive. What had she done to be locked away, or worse, killed?

Around midday, I took a break and walked around the lobby area.

I nodded to the guard at the front end of the building. He smiled and it seemed genuine. Good guy, I made a mental note. I smiled at the undercover guard near the fountain. He stared at me, motionless. Bad guy, I said to myself.

I would begin today by putting together a mental picture of who was the slave labor and who was here because they wanted to be.

I walked slowly around the very large lobby area. There was an enormous water fountain in the center with a beautiful waterfall creating the most soothing sounds. I breathed in the droplets of mist rising from the fountain. I touched the water. Only the bad guard paid me any attention. He watched me carefully.

There were pennies and dimes down at the bottom of the fountain. I remember wanting to run away when I was a child. I had a plan to run away to the mall. I would hide out in the bathrooms when they locked the doors, then I would sneak out and take the money from the fountain. I would then use the fountain money to buy food at the food court. It was the perfect place for a runaway, or so it seemed to my thirteen-year-old mind.

I smiled at the nonsense of running away from great parents and a wonderful life. I guess every teenager has those thoughts. The problem with teenage runaways is that they are the biggest targets for human traffickers. I shook off the image of Nikki on the streets, along with all the other children who don't have a place to call home.

As I slowly strolled around the large lobby, I saw a white van pull up to the entrance of the building. A woman in her mid-fifties unloaded six passengers, all under the age of thirteen, it seemed. They walked fairly slowly together as a group down the hall. I looked around. Not one person showed any interest in where these children were being taken.

"I need coffee." I mouthed to the guard from a distance and pointed down the hall. He nodded.

Entering the break room, I saw Chandler sitting with his laptop in the corner of the room. He was alone. He looked up and smiled.

I smiled and nodded. I hoped he could read into my face that I wanted to do more than just smile and nod.

"I've been looking for you," he said.

"Really?"

"Yes. You're a hard one to find," he said with a wink.

"I guess I am, in more ways than you know."

I wanted to sit down and chat, but I passed him by and went straight to the coffee pot.

"Do you want to meet up for lunch later?" he asked.

Oh, if he only knew how much I would love to meet up later.

"I wish I could."

"Are you taken?"

Was he deliberately using words as a signal? My heart raced. Could he know? I mean, I had given him my real name. It was possible he did a Google search and there was something on the internet about my disappearance. I fumbled with my coffee mug thinking of the best response.

"Yes, you could say I'm taken, but not in the way you think," I said very quietly, trying to pleasantly smile for the cameras that were probably watching us and at the same time, signal for help.

He stood up and silently joined me at the coffee Keurig. He pulled out a cup and sat it in front of me.

He looked at his watch.

"Well, would you look at the time? I thought I had time for coffee, but it looks like I need to ska doodle."

He brushed up against me as he turned to get his computer. It was slow and intentional contact.

He grabbed his computer and left the room. My heart sank. I had wanted so badly to see him, and now he was gone.

When I reached for the cup, he had left, I saw there was a folded piece of paper inside it. I turned away from the camera and slipped the piece of paper into my coat pocket.

After loading my pockets with crackers and cookies, I went back to my station. I couldn't take a chance reading it at work, so I would have to wait until I got back to the barn.

I was beaming with excitement when I heard my door open. I turned hoping to see that Chandler had found my workstation. My heart sunk when it wasn't him.

"Hi! I hear you're one of the new kids on the block."

"Hello. Yes, that's me."

"My name's Brandon. I just like to introduce myself to people I don't know?"

"Thanks, Brandon." I fiddled with Chandler's letter in my pocket.

There was a long pause. "This is where you tell me your name." He chuckled.

"Oh, sorry. I'm Grace. You can call me G."

"Nice to meet you, G. You'll see me around. Let me know if you would like to meet up for lunch at the cafeteria sometime."

"Sure will. Thank you." I didn't even know there was a cafeteria.

"Welcome to Braxton."

"Thank you!" Oh, if you only knew.

The evening finally came, and the car picked me up out front, as usual. I was brought around to the back of the building and escorted to the chamber where the girls were waiting for me. Once I was settled inside, I pulled the note from my pocket.

"What's that?" Lexi asked.

"Shah," I whispered. "It's a note someone gave me today."

"It's going to get us in trouble again," she whispered back.

"No, it's going save us."

I read it to myself.

"Braydee,

I found you on the internet today. I know about how you were taken in Alabama. So many people are looking for you. It's a very big story. I want you to know that you're going to be okay. I'm scared to go to the police just yet, but I'll help you. The article I read reported that a police officer in Baldwin County, Alabama, is missing, and they found your rings in his post office box. If this is true, there could be police here that are also involved. Please find a way to communicate with me. I need to know where they are keeping you.

Your new friend, Chandler."

I felt intense relief flood through me. I started to cry, but I held my breath until the urge passed. Someone knows. Someone is going to help us.

"We're going to be okay." I hugged the girls, still whispering.

"What's going to happen to us when someone finds us? Are they going to send us back to our homes?"

"Do you want to go back to your homes?"

"No. I hate it there. It's bad."

"Then you won't have to go. If you want to stay with me, we'll make that happen."

"How?"

"I don't know how. You just let me worry about that."

I closed my eyes and felt the little arms around me and heard the tiny breaths of air that were seeping from Lexi and Katrina's little nostrils as they slept, so trusting. I finally felt hope.

Tomorrow, I would tell Chandler where we were being held. The problem was, I really wasn't quite sure where we were. Somewhere in the building was all I knew, and there was an entrance in the far back right corner that we always used.

I stuck his letter in my bra close to my heart. It would give me strength until we were rescued.

The following day, I waited until 10:40, since that was the time I had seen Chandler in the break room the day before. There he was, sitting at his computer and drinking a cup of tea. He smiled and nodded as I entered the room.

I smiled back, but this time, the connection between us was a powerful force beyond anything you can imagine. I had hope. His eyes gave me strength.

"How's it going?" he asked nonchalantly.

"It's getting better. I'm finding my way around."

I made my coffee and dropped a note in an empty cup next to the pot. I couldn't wait for Chandler to read it, but when I turned around, an officer stood in the doorway.

"Whatcha got there?" he said.

I stood paralyzed as the officer asked again.

"Whatcha got there?"

"I believe that's a chocolate Danish," Chandler interjected as he stood to check for a note from Braydee. He quickly slipped the note out of the cup and casually made a cup of tea for himself.

"Oh, this? Yes, it's, um, really good." I smiled at the officer as I passed.

Chandler gathered his things and went to his office. He closed his door and pulled out the letter from Braydee.

"Dear Chandler,

My heart is so full right now. To know you took the time to find out who I am and help me is beyond belief. I'm being held, along with seven children, in something they are calling a chamber. We enter through an entrance at the back right side of the building. They take me down a long hall to a private entrance with a number-coded lock. Along our hall are many rooms with letters on them. I have no idea who or what is in them. There could be other children.

Be careful. They're watching my every move. They could be watching you as well. Please call my mom, Lea. 212-334-6789 and let her know I'm alive and well. We have friends in the police department in my hometown. They will help you. Don't trust anyone other than my mom with this information."

Your forever friend,
Braydee"

He gathered his things and walked to his car. He cranked his car and began pulling out of the parking lot. He pulled out his phone to call Lea Quinn and heard a voice behind him.

"Drop the phone and drive."

He felt the cold steel on the back of his neck, and he dropped the phone.

"Drive."

"Drive where?"

"Go left and keep going until I tell you to turn."

After an hour of turning left and right, he was directed down a long-isolated road. He could see that someone was following them.

"Stop."

"Please, sir. I'm begging you. Why are you doing this?"

"Get out."

Chandler opened the door and stepped out of the car.

"It doesn't have to be this way."

"Shut up and walk." He took several steps and stopped.

"You can kill me here as well as anywhere. I'm not walking for you."

"Suit yourself."

The gun rang out two times and Chandler fell to the ground. Blood gushed from his stomach. The gunman dragged him to the woods and left him there. He then waited on his buddy to pick him up as he watched as Chandler bled to death on the side of the road. He pulled the body near the tree line and walked back to the car. Within minutes a trusted friend of the gunman picked him up and they drove away. Chandler lay motionless until they disappeared from sight. Once they were gone, he crawled on his belly back to his car. He pulled himself up and opened the car door. There was his phone. He called 911 as he slumped down on the ground outside the driver's side door.

"I've been shot. Come quick."

"What's your address?"

"I don't know. I'm in the middle of nowhere. Can I share my location with someone?"

"Yes. Stay on the phone until we get your location."

There was coughing and gurgling as Chandler did everything he could to focus on staying conscious.

"We have your location, sir. An ambulance is in route. They're ten minutes away. Stay on the line."

"I can't stay on the line." Chandler hung up and took the piece of paper Braydee had given him from his pocket. He called Mrs. Lea.

"Mrs. Lea?"

"Yes?"

"I'm a friend of Braydee's. She's alive."

She gasped into the phone.

"What? Alive where? How do you know? Who is this?"

"She's being held prisoner at Braxton Therapeutics in Waco, Texas. The entrance to where she's being held is in the back of the building."

"What? Hold on, please. I need to write this down." She grabbed a pen.

"Please tell me again."

"She's at Braxton Therapeutics in Waco, Texas. She and seven girls are being held in a room with metal doors with letters on them. The entrance is in the back right side of the building. That's all I know."

Braydee's mom was crying, and Chandler was coughing.

"Sir! Are you okay?"

"I've been shot. The ambulance is on the way. I'll be okay, though. Braydee gave me a letter and told me to call you. She doesn't trust anyone here."

"How do you know her?"

"We met about a few weeks ago at work. I had no clue she had been kidnapped."

"How is she?"

"She's okay. She looks healthy."

"Thank God! Have you called the police?"

"No. We don't know who we can trust here." He gurgled again and wheezed heavily. "Since there was a police officer involved in the kidnapping, we're afraid the police here could be involved. Braydee said for you to contact the police there, because you have friends and people you trust on the force."

His words were getting weaker, and it was taking everything in him to keep up the conversation. He could hear sirens off in the distance, and he knew he was going to be okay.

"Yes."

"I'm going now, Mrs. Lea. Call the police now."

"Thank you. What's your name?"

"Chandler Grey."

"Thank you, Chandler, from the bottom of my heart."

Lea Quinn hung up the phone and immediately called the police chief and long-time friend.

"Hey, Sam, it's Lea. Someone just called me and told me Braydee is alive!" She was speaking fast.

"Seriously?! Lea, you trust this person? Who was it? Where is she?"

"Yes, he said he'd been working with her at a place called Braxton Therapeutics. It's in Waco, Texas. Do you know people on the police force in Waco that you trust?"

"I know some people in Texas I can call."

"I'm afraid, Sam. The guy who called said they don't know who to trust and Braydee has given instructions to call us instead of the local police."

"I can understand that with the police being involved down in Alabama."

"Hurry, Sam. If they get wind of this, they could move her, and I may never see her again." She began to cry.

"I'm on it. Just breathe. My guys can't do this, of course. It's out of our jurisdiction. I know some people at the federal level. I think this is a job for them."

"Thank you, Sam. I haven't even told my husband yet. You were my first call." Braydee's dad, Tim, walked in the room as she was hanging up.

Sam called some friends at the FBI and set up a raid on the facility.

"What haven't you told me?" asked Tim.

Lea ran into her husband's arms and collapsed.

"Braydee is alive," she whispered. It was all she could say. Tim held his wife as they cried. He didn't ask how she knew. He didn't know if it was true, but seeing his wife broken and limp again was beyond gut wrenching. He would stand there for as long as she needed him to.

After several minutes Lea wiped her eyes and sat down. She began to share the story of Chandler calling and Tim squeezed her hand.

"Our baby is alive," he said as his tears fell uncontrollably.

I stood over my microscope pretending to work. I moved methodically from file to file in an effort to appear busy. I was too anxious to concentrate on anything other than Chandler reading my letter. Very soon my mom and dad would know I was alive. My heart was so full of hope.

Chapter Twenty-Five

John Sand's phone rang. He was waiting for the call.

"Hello?"

"Everything has been taken care of, sir," said the gunman.

"Give me details."

"The woman was communicating with a man during break time."

"I'm past all that. What did you do with the man?"

"He's been eliminated. Out of the picture for good."

"Thanks. Just keep watching her. She's a sneaky one. Do me a favor though. Drop by the facility and pop your head in the door. Tell her the boss is watching, and Chandler Grey is dead. Make sure she knows it's her fault. That ought to shut her up."

"Will do, sir."

"You made sure this couldn't come back on you, right?"

"Of course, sir, I took him out in the middle of Timbuktu."

"And?"

"I shot him several times."

"Where's his car?"

"Left it there."

"What the hell? Where's the body? Don't say 'left it there' or I'm going to lose my mind here."

"Um. Yes, sir. I drug him into the tree line where no one would see him. It's very wooded. If anyone saw the car, they would just think someone ran out of gas."

"I'm so tired of everyone being idiots these days. Did you NOT think to maybe take the car off somewhere and burn it or run it off a cliff where no one could find it? You didn't think that maybe leaving a car on the side of the road would likely draw attention and make someone suspicious about where the driver was? I'm sure there was blood. Someone will find the body." John was furious.

"I swear it's in the middle of nowhere. There's no traffic in the area at all. No chance of anyone finding it anytime soon. When they do, well, it's just another murder."

"Anytime soon is not the issue. WE DON'T WANT IT FOUND PERIOD! We don't need another murder tracing back to a Braxton employee this soon. We dodged a bullet earlier this year. This would be a little too coincidental. I need you to go back out there and do something with the car and the body. Now!"

"Okay. Do you want me to go by and let the girl know he's dead first? I'm not far from Braxton."

"Yes. Make sure she's clear that we're closely watching her."

"Okay. I'm sorry boss. I should've thought that through a little better, but I'll take care of it."

"And if you think you left DNA evidence somewhere, even though it wasn't in the instructions you were given, be sure you wipe it down. I suggest torching it afterward. Sticks the body in the car and burn that SOB to the ground. I shouldn't have to say make sure it's not anywhere close to civilization. The last thing you need is the fire department showing up."

"Got it."

"I hope so." John hung up knowing the level of incompetence among the people working for him was on the rise.

Braydee jumped at the sound of the door opening. She half expected Chandler to walk in and give her a coded message about something her mom had said or about her being rescued. Instead, in walked a large man wearing leather gloves. He handed her a letter.

"This is for you."

"Thank you," she said.

As quickly as he entered, he was gone.

She opened the note with excitement, and she read:

"Chandler Grey is dead. You did this to him. We're closely watching everything you do. This is your last warning. The children will be next."

She crumpled the letter into a ball and fell to the floor. She screamed as loud as she could. Tate rushed over and knelt beside her. "Braydee!"

Someone stuck their head in the door. "Is everything okay?"

"It's fine. I'm okay."

"Did you fall? Are you hurt?"

"Yes, I fell. I'm fine. I'm terrified of rats, and one ran across my foot. I'm okay," she lied.

"A rat? Okay, just checking. That was a nasty scream."

"I'm sorry. I'm good now." Braydee stood up and braced herself with a chair. Tate looked on in horror. She had no idea what had just happened, and she dared not ask knowing people were listening. They exchanged a long pitiful stare and went back to working on their projects.

After giving Braydee the note, the gunman who shot Chandler stopped at the gas station and filled up a can of gas. He would use it to torch the car. He then went to Arby's and grabbed a roast beef sandwich for him and his friend, and the two of them drove back to the location where they had left the car and the body. He could see the car in the distance.

"There's the car up ahead."

"I see it."

"You can drive my car. I'm going to put his body in the trunk. Just follow me. I'm taking it to this place I know in the middle of the desert, about sixty miles from my old home place. I'll burn it. Just follow me."

"Alright."

They pulled up and parked next to Chandler's car and walked around to the spot where he had seen Chandler fall. There was no body. Only a pool of blood. He looked at the trail of blood that led back to the car and all over the car door.

He ran to the car and opened the door searching frantically for the phone he had seen Chandler drop on the front seat. Adrenaline shot through his body, and he was paralyzed with fear. He had forgotten to grab the phone before he left. Chandler must have called an ambulance. There was a good chance he would survive the gunshot if the ambulance had gotten there quickly enough.

"Oh, God, no!"

The passenger got out of the car and approached his friend.

"What is it? What's wrong?"

"Nonoo!" he yelled.

"What the hell is wrong?"

"The guy I shot is gone. I left him over there." He pointed near the tree line.

"Get in the car. Let's go now. I'm not getting charged as an accomplice to this stupidity. Come on!"

He was already getting in the car while the killer was standing there slapping himself in the head.

"No. No."

"Get in the car."

"Hold on. I've got to call the judge. I've got to tell him."

"Not this minute you don't. Get in the car NOW!"

"Wait!"

He took the gas can out of the back and ran to Chandler's car, drenching it with gasoline. He lit the fabric seat with his cigarette lighter, and they pulled away as the car burst into flames.

"I don't know what to do. If I tell him the body is gone, he's going to have me killed."

"And if you don't tell him?"

"He's going to have me killed."

"Right."

He picked up the phone and called the judge.

"What is it? I'm headed into court." He was sick of being bothered by incompetent nonsense.

"I stopped by Braxton and told the girl what you said and then when I got to the guy's car ... well, the body is gone, sir?"

"WHAT?"

"I said the body is gone."

"I heard you; you freak in idiot!"

Chandler was quite possibly alive and now everything he had worked for was about to come crashing down.

He hung up the phone and called Gavin Pateo at Braxton.

Gavin picked up on the line that was only to be answered in case of an extreme emergency.

"Wipe the place clean. Now."

"I'm on it."

Braxton Therapeutics was a legitimate organization doing many great things for the world in medicine, science, and health. There would be no signs or evidence left that would lead investigators back to John Sands. He had gone to extreme measures to make sure that Gavin Pateo did exactly what he was trained to do.

With the touch of a button, the computer system used to traffic the girls would be loaded into an emergency van waiting out back. The girls would be relocated, and a cleaning team would initiate a wipe-down of any trace of the girls. Animals would be moved into the large barn where the girls had been sleeping. Dust and dirt would be strewn to present a feeling of abandonment in the rooms.

An assortment of various old boxes and bins would be placed in the rooms where the girls had been staying. It would have all the appearance of storage rooms. Braydee, Tate, and the girls would be taken to a holding facility in New Mexico until they were assigned a new location. They wouldn't be returning to Braxton.

The entire operation had been put at risk, and it all led back to Braydee. Many clients would be waiting on organs and girls, and production would slow to a crawl because of this one woman. She was turning into a total liability. He made a phone call.

"Get rid of Braydee Quinn. I'm done with her."

"You got it."

"Don't kill her. Take her to the nanny hole."

"Ok, sir."

It was a place worse than death. A place where she would be shot up with drugs and be forced into a sex role until death.

He tried to clear his head as he headed back into court. He was confident with his team's ability to clean things up in Texas, but he still had no idea what the authorities had found on his boat, and that had him very worried.

Chapter Twenty-Six

The news broke about Kasey Kendall's recovery. Every news station was reporting it. There sat the mother and father with their eight-year-old daughter.

Interviews from news organizations across the nation were featuring the reunion. The little girl explained in detail how a police officer had approached her car on the day she was taken.

"He knocked on the window of our car and asked me if I would open the door. So, I did," explained the little girl. "He told me that I needed to ride with him to the hospital because my mom had gotten sick. I got into his car and later I was taken to a boat."

Kasey's mom and dad sat next to her holding her hands as they relived the horror of that day.

She explained how she had stayed on the boat with a nice man who then took her to a new family.

John saw the interviews and was furious! He had been betrayed and lied to. Bob failed to do his job. The kid was never supposed to have survived that boat ride.

He sat in his office thinking about his boat and what they might find on it. It had been cleaned many times over, but he knew every fool that had ever been convicted had missed one small detail. He had tried enough cases to learn how not to be caught.

There were two other officers involved with John over the years before Duke. He liked having someone on the inside of the police department. It helped to know what was going on around town. He had been fed vital information about girls that had been picked up for prostitution or drugs. The last officer he recruited decided he didn't want to be a part of John's plans any longer. His conscience got the best of him, and he wanted out. He remembered the conversation with the officer very well.

"I just don't want to be a part of this. I'm getting my life together, and this doesn't feel right," said the officer.

The officer didn't really know the extent of the operation, or exactly what he was involved in, but he knew enough to know that it was shady.

"This is going to catapult you to the next level in life. You'll have more money and power than you'll know what to do with," said John.

"I'm sorry, I can't. I have a daughter now. I'm trying to focus on being a good dad, cop, and husband."

"You know I can't let you out, right?"

"I'm walking away, and that's final. I've done enough for you. That's it. No more."

"Once you're in, you can't get out."

"Well, you should have mentioned that before you brought me in. I want you to know, if anything happens to me, I have a flash drive stashed with some pretty incriminating things on it."

"Are you threatening me right now?"

"Take it however you want to take it. I'm saying that as long as I'm safe, you're safe. My lips are sealed unless you do something stupid."

"You think you've got me by the balls right now, don't you. Watch your back at all times, son."

"I'll do what I have to do, but I want you to go about your life and let me go about mine in peace."

"You better think long and hard about releasing any information about me. You're linked to me now. You were involved in everything on that flash drive. Do you know how devastated your family will be to find out what you've been doing? You've been part of a sex trafficking. It doesn't matter who you point the finger at. Your reputation as an officer, dad, and family man is over."

The officer shuddered at the words. It started with the judge wanting information about prostitutes and homeless girls that were brought in, as well as information on parties that were being raided. The next thing he knew, John was bailing the girls out of jail and having them picked up at the station.

It wasn't until one wild night on John's boat with underage girls that the officer recognized some of the girls and realized what was going on. That's when he wanted out.

"I'm out, John. Go ahead and roll the dice. See if I won't bring you down. I'm telling you now, don't contact me again."

Click.

The officer moved his family out west somewhere and was never heard of again. He shook his head as he thought about the other officer he had tried to groom over the years and what a disaster it had been, but nothing had been as bad as his son-in-law, Duke Davis.

The official forensic report came back on the boat. Capt. Marshall looked at the report. He opened the manila envelope and then the box that came with it. Inside the box, in a plastic bag, was a police badge. He pulled it out and looked at the number then he placed it back in the box and pulled out two more bags. In one was a child's shoe, and in the other was a stack of cash.

He read the report.

Fingerprints in various places including fingerprints of children. Three matches in the database of girls who were arrested in the last year. The police officer's badge matched the badge number of the missing officer Woody B. Thomas. Missing since May of 2018. It was found in a compartment along with the child's shoe. The description of the shoe is as follows: Size two tennis shoes with Disney characters on them. DNA skin cells match Kasey Kendall, missing since 2019.

Numerous cloth fibers were found in the carpet below the deck. Hair and fingerprints match known felon, Robert Seagrave. Fingerprints and hair matching Duke Davis. Various clothing fibers are found throughout. See the attached pictures.

This was enough to bring the judge in for questioning.

Capt. Marshall called John.

"I was wondering if you could make some time to swing by the station this afternoon when you get off work."

"What's this about?"

"It's about some things we found on the boat. We'd like to ask you some questions."

"Absolutely. I'll be there somewhere around six this evening. Still nothing on Duke?"

"Nope. Nothing yet."

"Okay, talk to you soon."

When John arrived, he was smiling and shaking hands with familiar faces. He was escorted into a side room.

"Hey, John. Thanks for coming." They shook hands and had a seat.

"This seems a bit formal. This must be pretty important if you couldn't tell me over the phone?"

Capt. Marshall placed the box on the table. "We found these things on your boat. Do you have any idea what could be in this box?"

"No idea."

First, he pulled out the badge and laid it on the table.

"Duke's badge," said the judge.

"No. It's not Duke's badge. It belonged to an officer who went missing several years back. His name was Woody Thomas."

"Huh?"

"Have you ever heard of an officer by that name?"

"Never." He lied.

"So, you have no idea how or why his badge is on your boat?"

"No." It was too late to say yes, he knew him, and he had loaned him the boat. That would have made more sense. Now he had to stick to the lie he had started.

Next, the shoes were pulled out of the box and placed on the table.

"Do you have any idea how these shoes got on your boat?"

"I'm sorry, but where are you going with this?"

"I just need to know, have you ever seen this shoe?"

"Absolutely not. I have no idea who may sneak on my boat at night and play games. I don't know if the attendees at the marina might take it out on occasion. I don't know Marshall. Who does it belong to?"

297

"It belongs to the little girl who went missing several years ago. There was a DNA match. I guess you saw they found her."

He sat stone cold. "What little girl? You'll have to tell me more than just a girl went missing."

"Her name was Kasey Kendall. There was an accusation of an officer who may have been involved in the abduction. His fingerprints were found on the car, similar to the way your son-in-law's fingerprints were found."

"And what does all this have to do with me?"

"Because all this was all found on your boat."

John stared into the eyes of Captain Marshall and never blinked.

"Like I said, I don't have a clue. Maybe the officer who left the badge took the little girl out on my boat, molested her, and thought he would dump her at sea. Maybe he changed his mind. Who knows? Not me. You could have asked me these things on the phone."

He stood up to leave.

"I could have, but I wanted to look you in the eyes."

"You're treading on thin ice here, sir. Disrespect is not something I take lightly. False accusations could ruin your career."

"I apologize. It's not my intention to make you feel attacked or insinuate that you could be guilty of something. I'm simply asking questions. Trying to solve a crime here."

"Well, if you're done, I have a wife with supper waiting at home for me."

"Have you ever met Woody Thomas?"

"I don't know. It's possible we could have met somewhere at some time. Baldwin County is not that big."

"But you don't remember him?"

"No, I don't."

"And you're sure about that? You have never seen him in a social setting?"

"Absolutely not."

There were surveillance pictures of John and Woody boarding a plane together and talking at the airport, and another picture of them having dinner in a little dive joint in Texas. Melissa had provided them via the metal box.

"So, you would go on record saying you don't know him personally in any capacity."

"That's what I'm saying."

"So, he would have no reason to be on your boat or boarding a plane with you. No reason the two of you would be at dinner together. Right?"

"Look, Duke and Melissa are friends with a lot of people and hang out with plenty of officers. They take the boat out on occasion, and I really don't keep tabs on what's going on with it. If you're asking if I took him out, the answer is no. I didn't know the man period. End of conversation." He was visibly bothered.

"I understand that. But you realize both of these things are opening up a lot of questions."

"Yes, I understand that.

"One more thing." The captain was just about to let the judge know that they had found the clothes of some missing girls in Waco but thought he had better wait.

"What is it?" The judge paused at the door.

"Oh, it can wait."

"You started to say it. What is it?"

"I was just going to say we have a lead on the missing woman, Braydee Quinn."

"A lead how?"

"I'm afraid I'm not at liberty to discuss the details, just that we're hoping it's not a false lead. Someone called and said they had spotted her."

"Where?"

"Near Chicago." He didn't want to give away the location of the lead. That might spook him if he was guilty of something.

"Oh, okay. Well, good luck. Are we done here?"

"We're done. Thank you for coming in."

Walking to his car he remembered the day the girl, Kasey Kendall, had been taken by Ofc. Woody. Woody was such a good asset except on the days he chose to act on his own. Kasey had never been a part of the equation.

He would never forget that call.

"I got a girl. She looks like she's about five years old."

"Are you a complete idiot? You got a girl?"

"Sir? No, sir. I mean, yes, I got a girl, but no, I'm not a complete idiot. She was just right there sitting alone in the Walmart parking lot. I thought you would be happy."

"I'm not happy when you do independent thinking. I run this show. You don't make a move unless I tell you to. There is a whole process that requires a lot of coordination."

"I'm sorry, sir."

"What do you think we're supposed to do with a kid right now? This isn't a pick-up month. Where did you think we would hide her?"

"I don't know. I thought you had somewhere you could take her."

"No, I don't have somewhere to just put kids! Take her to the "town square" and I'll have Bob meet you there with the boat. You can put her on the boat, and let Bob take care of her until I can figure out what to do next."

"I'm sorry, sir."

"Just get her there out of sight. Bob can take her out to sea for a while until I can figure this out."

"Yes, sir."

"I'm going to repeat, you don't act unless I tell you to act. Is that clear?"

He was furious. He would've chopped off Woody's head himself if he could have gotten to him.

Bob met them at the "town square" which was the abandoned dock in Perdido Key. Every so often, girls had been transported by boat, but it was rare. The boat was mostly used for wild sex parties before the girls were taken to their final destination.

After a week on the boat with Kasey Kendall, Bob had been given the signal to just get rid of the girl. It was a lot easier than the logistics of moving her when everyone in the nation was looking for her. She didn't fit the profile of kids that could easily disappear.

John couldn't figure out why Bob left the shoes and the badge on the boat. It seemed more deliberate than careless. It looked as if he was setting him up to be caught.

He knew the law, though. There was no way to connect him when so many people had borrowed his boat, and possibly without his knowledge. Still, it was a close call. He needed to hear from Bob and Duke needed to be found ASAP. He was a walking, talking menace to life at this point. John drove home to an empty house.

Melissa and her mom sat on the beach in Costa Rica drinking a fruity drink with an umbrella. They didn't talk much, and there was nothing to celebrate. They just stared at the water, wishing things were different in their lives.

"Mom, what if Dad isn't the person we think he is?"

"I don't want to go there, Melissa."

"There's a reason you were having him followed, and I don't believe it was because you thought he was having an affair."

"I was curious. That's it. Things felt a little off with John, and I did some digging."

"I'm not trying to upset you right now, I just want to go back with a clear and open mind, and I want you to do the same," said Melissa.

"It doesn't seem like you're trying to be open-minded. It seems like you're set on your dad being guilty of something. Don't forget, Duke is the one missing right now - with a warrant."

"Ouch. I get it. I deserved that."

"Sorry."

"I just want to talk to you about everything I'm feeling right now, but I don't even know what to say."

"The only thing that really matters to me right now is that I'm on the beach with my favorite person in the entire world. You're my light and my joy. I don't want John reaching out from Alabama and ruining my time here with my daughter."

"I agree!"

"I don't know what we'll face when we get home. There may be some really bad things coming our way, but right now, let's make a toast."

Melissa raised her hand and clinked her glass against her mom's glass.

"Here's to the best daughter a mom could ask for. Cheers!"

"Here's to the best mom a daughter could ever have! Cheers!" The two ladies smiled and stared at the ocean. In the distance, they could hear singing.

"Let's go find the music!" said Rhonda.

They linked arms as they headed in the direction of the music. They were both so thankful for the moment, but wishing they could indulge themselves during their time together without worrying about Duke and John.

Chapter Twenty-Seven

Undercover officers along with federal agents and local officers quickly surrounded Braxton Therapeutics. There had been no time for Gavin Pateo to remove evidence of the girls. Too much time had passed since Chandler had alerted the authorities.

I could hear sirens off in the distance.

I stared at Tate, wondering if she was thinking the same thing I was thinking.

"Could they be coming for us?" Tate asked it first.

"I was just thinking the same thing," I whispered.

"But how would they know about us?"

Braydee took Tate by the hand, and together they walked out of their room to stand near the fountain. The guard watched from a distance.

"Tate, there was this guy in the office next to the break room. I met him a few weeks ago." I was trying to talk fast. I knew I only had seconds before the guard would motion for us to go back to our workstation.

"I saw him one time when I walked by. Very handsome guy. What about him?" asked Tate.

"He and I exchanged a few notes. I told him who I was, and I gave him my mom's phone number."

"Oh, my God, Braydee! You may have saved us!"

"No. The note that the guy gave me this morning said he was dead, and it was my fault. His name was Chandler. That's why I screamed." Tate hugged me, and I didn't care who was watching.

"It's not your fault. You know that. These people are monsters."

"It is, though. I was warned not to make contact or attempt to cause any more trouble. I was told this would happen, and I did it anyway. They're coming for the girls next. What have I done?"

"You were trying to save us all."

"Instead, I got him killed. A man is dead because I was so selfish that I couldn't keep from involving him in my problems."

"Please don't think about it that way. You saw a way to possibly save the girls, and you took that risk." The guard rushed in our direction.

"Oh, my God the girls! What if something has happened to them too?"

The guard quickly reached us. "Walk down the hall, and don't look back. Keep walking until I say stop."

The sirens were surrounding the building now. Something big was happening. There were officers with guns approaching the front entrance. I don't know why, but I believed they were coming for us. I didn't move. I planted my feet in defiance.

"I said walk."

I stared at the officer with a clenched fist. "No!" I said.

He shoved me, but I didn't flinch.

"Your next move better be towards the hall, or it'll be your last move." The officer was in my face. Tate grabbed my arm.

"Let's go," she said.

"No." I repeated.

Officers began to enter the building from every entrance. Within minutes every exit was blocked. One officer had a bullhorn and began speaking. The words echoed through the building.

"*Braydee Quinn, you're safe. Come to the fountain area of the building if you're free to move on your own. Tate Livingston, you're safe. Come to the fountain area of the building if you're free to move on your own.*"

He continued to repeat himself, and we stood frozen. Neither of us could move at first. Then we realized that they had truly come for us. The officer repeated it again "Braydee Quinn ..."

"HERE!" I screamed. "OVER HERE!"

Tate and I ran to the officer, and he placed his weapon in the holster and hugged us. "Come with me, ladies."

"That officer by the fountain. He's one of the bad guys." I pointed. Within seconds he was surrounded, handcuffed, and in custody.

"Are there other victims inside the building?"

"Yes! Hurry! This way."

"Let's go!" Officers began following us as we jogged down the hall and made several turns.

"I've never entered the holding area from this direction. I've always been taken around the back of the building, but this was the way I was brought in to work each day. I remember passing all these sliding glass doors."

"So there's a back entrance where the girls are being held?"

"Yes."

He called out on his radio, "Be sure you have eyes on every area of this building. There are multiple victims inside who haven't been retrieved yet and an escape could be underway."

"Roger. The building is surrounded."

We entered an area labeled "Biohazardous Storage Area Authorized Personnel Only". There was the red door I remembered.

"This is it. They're back there in small rooms."

The officer tried to open the door. It was locked.

"Gavin Pateo is the man in charge around here. His office is at the other end of this hall."

"Quickly. Get Gavin Pateo in custody. We need access to the hazardous material area. Go. Let me know when you have him."

Several officers ran towards Gavin's office. The door wasn't locked, and they stormed in. Gavin sat at his desk.

"We have him sir."

"Bring him. We need him to open the red door."

Gavin Pateo sat with both hands flat on his desk. Weapons were pointed at him.

"Stand up slowly and put your hands on your head."

He did.

"Now turn around, and face the wall."

It was too late to let John Sands know what was going on. There were enough eyes and ears on the property, so John would be notified soon enough. Gavin wondered why security had not alerted him that the property had been breached? There were camera's a mile away.

The security guard had seen the approaching officers. There were so many coming. He was hired to keep an eye on the property and report any suspicious activity. He didn't consider officers of the law suspicious. On the contrary, he assumed they were there to help with something. Therefore, there was no need to report to his boss, Mr. Pateo.

"Where are the keys to the red door?"

"There are no keys. Just a switch."

"Where's the switch?"

"Over there." He pointed with his head.

There was a panel on the wall with a small door and inside was a switch labeled 'Bio Storage'. The agent flipped the switch, and the door clicked unlock.

When I heard the door click open, I rushed past the officers down the hall. I was yelling for the girls.

"Clara! Katrina! Marlea! We're safe!"

I yanked open the latch on the first door, and three little girls with dirty, thin faces ran out and grabbed me around the waist.

We all hugged and cried.

"We did it! We're going to be okay," I sobbed.

I quickly moved to the other two doors and freed the other children. We cried some more and then I began laughing hysterically. I was so happy. Nothing else in this world mattered at this moment. The children were safe, and we survived. I knelt down, and we held each other.

"These officers are the good guys. They're here to help us all."

Nikki held my hand. "I don't want to go home. I'm scared. I want to go with you. Don't make me go back home."

I could see that she was terrified of leaving me.

"You're coming with me." I stood up. "Sir, all of these girls, with the exception of Marlea, have been sexually abused or neglected by family and friends. We've spent a lot of time together, and they are scared to be returned to their families or foster care. I want them all to stay with me. I'm not letting them out of my sight."

"We completely understand. We have some very competent people ready to help them."

"No, sir. You don't understand. They're coming with me. That's just how it has to be."

"Okay, that's perfectly fine for now. They'll need to be checked out and cleared by our medical staff."

"I mean you no disrespect, but these girls have been in my care all this time, and I intend to make sure they are taken care of and seen by the best doctors and therapists' money can buy. For now, they aren't leaving my sight. We will all be seen by the doctor together."

"Understood," said the officer.

No one said to hold hands, but we all did. One long human chain of love and relief walked toward the exit to freedom. Tate held hands with the last of the girls, which happened to be Baily.

"I love you, Braydee." Hearing my name being said by Katrina was heaven on earth. My heart melted.

"I love you, Katrina."

"I love you, too, Braydee."

"I love you, too, Clara."

"I love you!"

The words I love you were spilling from our mouths as a child to a mother and a mother to child. It was as if I had birthed each one myself. Every cell in my body felt connected to theirs. We sat on the floor hugging as officers watched. Tate kneeled and joined in our group hug.

We went from a secret circle in a field, to a nest in a barn, and now a cold hard floor in a medical facility. No matter where we were, our love, resilience, faith, and imagination held us together.

As the girls loaded into the van, the officer explained to me that we would need to go to the police station and give a statement. They would need descriptions of anyone we could remember. I couldn't wait to describe the man with the red face, cocked eye, and foul breath.

"Tate and I need to call our families and let them know we're safe. Do you have a phone I can use?"

"Of course. Here you go."

I dialed Mom's number.

"Mom?"

Nothing but crying on the other end of the line. Sobbing. Then yells for my father.

"I love y'all. I'm okay."

"We love you so much. Where are you? We've been waiting for your call!"

"Waiting? Did someone already tell you they found me?"

"Your friend, Chandler, called us about two hours ago. He said you had given him a note and that we needed to contact the local authorities. We've been a nervous wreck ever since."

"What? Chandler called you?"

"He had been shot. We now know that was left for dead. But thank God, he survived. He was the one who saved you."

"Mom! My heart is so full right now. They told me he was dead! I'm in shock. This is crazy. He's alive?"

"Yes! We're all in shock right now. Are you ok?"

"I'm just fine. I love you guys so much."

"We love you." Mom and Dad said the words in unison, and I began to cry again. The time to be strong was over, and all my pent-up emotion was unstoppable.

"I can't wait for you to meet your grandkids." I laughed.

"Grandkids?"

"The children I've been taking care of. I'll tell you more later. I just wanted to hear your voice. I love y'all so much. I have to go now."

"I love you, Braydee!" my parents yelled again.

I turned to one of the officers that was with us and asked about Chandler. "So, the guy that reached out to my mom, Chandler Grey, is he alive?"

"Yes, he's recovering at Providence Hospital from multiple gunshot wounds but he's going to be fine."

"I need to call him! I need to talk to thank him."

Tate squeezed my hand. "This is all too much to take in."

"Sorry Tate. Here. Call your mom."

I handed her the phone.

"Mom."

"Tate! Tate. Oh God, is this really you?"

"It's me. I'm okay. I'll fill you in as soon as I see you. I'll be home when they're done questioning me about everything. Maybe late tomorrow. I love you so much."

"I've cried everyday thinking I would never hear your voice again."

"I've cried every day too, Mom. I'll see you soon."

"I love you baby girl. Can't wait to see you! Whose phone is this?"

"It's a police officer. I'll call you soon. Love you."

Tate's mom began calling everyone letting them know her daughter was alive.

None of the girls asked to call home, but Marlea's family was waiting for her at the station when we arrived.

Marlea ran into her parents' loving arms. She smiled at me as she left the station. I knew she had left me out of the description of her kidnappers because I was never questioned about it. I guess it was her way of saying thank you for taking care of her during those weeks we were being held.

As we settled in at the station, I was allowed to go inside with each girl as they described in detail how they were taken and from where. I held their tiny hands as they relived the joy of the secret circle and the horror of hiding in the woods until men with guns loaded them into the van and took them to the dark barn.

Listening was surreal. This was my life. I had really lived this nightmare and survived. My mind immediately went to Samantha. The tiny organs lying so neatly in the special cooler. I shook the image from my mind. My focus had to be on the ones who survived.

It was finally my turn to describe the men who took me and the man who had slapped me at the health facility.

The officer started the recorder.

"Tell me anything you can that will help us find the men who took you, and also any of the men running this operation. We already have Gavin Pateo in custody, but so far, he isn't talking. He's lawyered up," said the officer.

I described the man with a funny laugh and tattoo on his forearm of a mermaid drinking beer and everything I could remember about the bar that night.

"What can you tell about the people you had interactions with at Braxton?"

I went into detail about the nurse and what I was expected to do while working for them, which was horrific.

"After I destroyed the cameras at the house where we were being held, I was in a lot of trouble. I was led to a room to meet with a man who seemed to be calling the shots at Braxton. He was about six feet tall. A big guy. Fat belly and a red face, like he was a drinker. He had a slightly cocked left eye and bushy white eyebrows. Breath reeked of coffee and liquor. Yellow, crooked teeth."

An artist drew the picture on a computer as I spoke.

"He was pure evil, and he told me that if I didn't do what I was brought here to do, that the girls would be chopped into pieces." I breathed heavily and focused on my need to destroy this man.

"I'm so sorry. Can you continue?" asked the officer.

"Yes. He took a phone call while we were together. I could hear a woman on the other end of the line call him John. She was talking loudly. I heard her say something about being in court and his secretary telling her he was out of town."

"Oh, that's great."

"He mentioned settling some trouble they had been dealing with. Maybe family trouble or something?"

"Could you tell anything by his accent?"

"He was definitely a southern man."

"Is there anything else?"

"I don't think so."

"Okay. You did great, Braydee. There are a few people who will want to talk to you later, but tonight we need to get you all to the hospital to be checked out. Once you've been cleared to go, we have a suite rented for you and the girls at Waco Hilton. It has adjoining rooms and plenty of space."

"Thank you so much. The girls are going to love it."

"We also have bathing suits and fresh clothes being brought in for you guys."

"Oh, wow. The girls are all so weak and fragile right now. I don't imagine they would be able to swim, but I can't thank you enough."

"It's the least we could do. You'd be surprised at how resilient kids are. We just need to make sure they haven't suffered any long-term damage."

"I've been sneaking them food from the break room. They fed us sometimes, but not on any sort of regular basis."

"I can't imagine what you've all been through. You go on and enjoy being with the girls. The van that will take you guys to the hospital will stay there until everyone is released."

"And if they have to keep someone, we'll all stay together until she's released."

"That's perfectly fine. I get it. In the meantime, I'm going to send this sketch to the detective in charge of your missing person case in Orange Beach. Maybe they know someone who fits that description."

The officer called Orange Beach PD.

"Can I speak to Det. Cory Knotts?"

"One moment, sir. Can I tell him who's calling?"

"Yes, this is Ofc. Bateman calling from Waco, Texas. It's concerning Miss Braydee Quinn."

"One moment."

"Hello, this is Det. Knotts."

"Hey, there. I know you guys have been waiting to hear from us."

"Yep. Been on pins and needles. We saw a little bit of the national coverage earlier. That was an impressive operation the way your team handled the place."

"Been one hell of a day. I sent the report over to your office about two minutes ago. We did our best to get as many details as we could, but Braydee was so tired, we limited it to what was the most important for us right now."

"I'll check the wire and see if we have it yet."

"I also sent over a sketch. She described a man that she had some dealings with. He could possibly be the head of the entire operation. We don't know, of course, but she had some great details about him that she remembered. Very specific things that would identify him."

"Oh, really?"

"Yes. He even took a phone call while they were together, and she heard a woman on the other end call him John. She said their conversation sounded a lot like a husband and wife. The wife was upset because she didn't know he was out of town, and thought he was in court."

"Hmmm."

"Just take a look and pass it around."

"Will do. I'll let you know something. I appreciate it."

"We'll talk soon."

Det. Knotts grabbed the report and the sketch and met up with Capt. Marshall.

"Take a look at this."

"John Sands," he said without even seeing the description.

"Yep. Pretty candid description of him. Cock eye. Crooked teeth. Redish hair. I think it's him. Braydee said she heard a woman on the other end of the phone call him John."

"Insane. Do you even realize how insane this is?"

"Who else knows about this?"

"Just me. It just came in."

"Don't say a word to anyone. If this is John, and I believe it is, we have no idea who he's working with. There could be someone right here in the department feeding him information."

"Exactly. I'm going to pull up a video clip of him. I know I can find something online. I'll see if Braydee can positively identify him from it. If so, I don't want to take a chance on him getting wind of this and skipping the country."

"Right. I agree. If she says he's our guy, let's go get him."

Det. Knotts called Waco. "Do you still have Braydee there with you?"

"She just got in the van with the others. Why?"

"I'm emailing a video clip of a Baldwin County judge. His name is John Sands. The sketch you sent over is eerily similar to him. I think it's our guy."

"Is that so? Let me go grab her before she leaves. I'll let you know shortly."

"Miss Braydee, we have a video we want you to look at. There is a judge in the video who could possibly be the John you met with. Do you mind stepping out and taking a look?"

"Of course." Braydee got out of the van and waited as the officer pulled up the YouTube commercial of John Sands running for office.

Braydee gasped. "That's him. Without a doubt that's him. That's his voice. I'll never forget it as long as I live. Those are the fat fingers that slapped me across my face."

"You're one hundred percent sure?"

"More than one hundred percent." She was shaking with anger. "Who is this man?"

"His name is John Sands. He lives in Foley, Alabama. He's a local judge."

"That would explain why the woman said she thought he was in court."

"Yes. It would. I'm going to let the officers know that you've positively identified him as the man you met with at Braxton."

"This is really happening right now!"

"It sure is. They're going to need you to be in Orange Beach within the next few days. They have a lot of questions. I'm sure they'll arrest him immediately. We're certain someone has already tipped him off that the place was raided, and I'm sure he had people in place to take the fall for him if anything came out."

"I'm in shock right now. Thank you, God."

"I don't think he ever anticipated your will to escape and save these children."

"I guess not."

"Go get some rest. You have a busy week ahead of you."

The phone call was made to Alabama, and a warrant was issued for the arrest of Judge John Sands.

There were no lights flashing or sirens blasting down the streets into the quiet neighborhood where John Sands lived. Just city cops and a SWAT team. John was backing out of his driveway when officers arrived.

He rolled down his window and greeted them.

"Officers."

"Keep your hands on the wheel and don't make any sudden movements."

"What's this about?"

An officer opened the door. "Get out and put your hands on the car."

"Again. What's this about?" John sat staring at the officers as if he were untouchable.

"Get out now!"

John slowly unfolded and stood up facing the car. The officers handcuffed him quickly.

"What the hell is going on here? Someone better start answering me or your jobs are on the line," he growled.

"You have the right to remain silent. Anything you say can and will be used against you in a court of law..." the officer continued reading him his Miranda Rights.

"I don't need a damn lawyer. I need someone to tell me why I'm being dragged off my property with no explanation."

"Sir, you have been charged in the kidnapping of Braydee Quinn for starters."

"Oh, God! Are you serious right now? Do you have any idea how idiotic that sounds?"

"Save it for the station."

Within minutes of the judge being arrested, a neighbor called a reporter friend, the reporter called the police station, and the news began traveling like wildfire.

"John Sands, who has been a judge here in Baldwin County for more than twenty years, was arrested tonight at his suburban home in Foley, Alabama. He was taken into custody and has been charged with the kidnapping of Braydee Quinn, who went missing two months ago. We'll keep you posted," said the NBC news anchor.

Duke and Whit sat in the corner of a little dive bar in Panama City Beach eating supper. It was Duke who noticed the closed caption breaking news in Alabama.

"Whit! Look!"

Whit twisted around in his seat to see the TV flashing images of Duke's father-in-law.

"They got him!"

"Whoa. They sure did. I just hope they have enough evidence to keep him."

"Bet they'll hold him without bail. He's definitely a flight risk."

"No doubt," said Whit.

The next image that flashed across the screen was of Duke. He was wearing his police uniform in the first image and standing with Melissa in the second picture. The closed caption said they were still looking for Ofc. Duke Davis in connection with the kidnapping. Duke was considered armed and dangerous. There was a number flashing to report any sightings of him.

"Dang, man. I hate seeing that. Especially the picture of you with Melissa. She doesn't deserve any of this. I feel so helpless to protect her right now. Knowing I brought all this shame on her is killing me."

Duke looked around the bar.

"You don't think those guys recognized me, do you?"

"Not a chance. You don't look anything like that picture."

Duke's hair was unwashed, and his face hadn't been shaved in over a month. His ball cap was pulled low over his eyes, and he certainly didn't resemble his police academy graduation picture.

"We'll still have to lay low until everything is settled."

"Of course. He's got his tentacles everywhere. He's too smart to get caught," said Whit.

"He's caught already, so he wasn't that smart. He may end up outsmarting the system in some kind of way. At least they've found something that has them confident enough to put him behind bars."

"I wish you could call someone on the force and find out something. Is there anyone you trust right now?"

"I trust my partner. He's a great guy and a great friend. I just don't want to put him in any kind of situation."

"True. I can't imagine what Melissa is going through right now." Whit shook his head as if he was picturing the whole scenario right there with her.

"I don't know how she's going to handle this on top of what I've done to her. I just want to hold her."

"You will soon enough."

"Hopefully."

"You will. Just be patient."

"I'm going to turn myself in, Whit. Whoever was looking for me is most likely scared to death because his boss is in jail. John could start chirping to get less time and start pointing fingers at people to make a deal."

"Good point."

"I'm going to serve time regardless of my part in all this, but I've got to get my life back. I need Melissa. It's time."

"I'm hiding because of you. The quicker you turn yourself in, the quicker I can see my boy and get back to work and life."

"Man, I don't know how I would've done it without you. We've had some great conversations. I truly feel closer to God because of you."

"Sitting in front of the ocean, talking about how fragile we all are can make you realize what's important in life. I don't see how anyone survives this life without God and their faith."

"I'm with you on that, for sure."

The men nodded and exchanged a stare that said more than words could ever say.

"Let's get out of here. The quicker we do, the quicker I get to see Melissa."

It was just after midnight when Whit dropped Duke off at the police station. Duke walked in with his hands up. The lady at the front window spoke first.

"Hey, Duke, haven't seen you 'round in a while. Oh, shoot, Duke!" She instantly remembered why she hadn't seen him in a while. She pressed a panic button, and two officers were there within seconds.

"I'm turning myself in, guys." Duke's hands were still raised. One of the officers grabbed his cuffs and placed them on his wrist.

"This way, buddy. I hate to be the one doing this to you. You know what we have to do, though."

"I know. Mugshot and fingerprints."

"That's right."

Duke was led down the familiar hall he had walked a thousand times. He took off his clothes and put on the orange inmate clothes.

"This way."

Passing the isolation rooms, Duke caught a glimpse of his father-in-law. He paused long enough to make eye contact. Duke blew him a kiss and gave him a wink. John flipped him the bird and mouthed some obscenities.

"Hard to believe my father-in-law and I might be cellmates. What are the odds?"

"You'll be in here tonight." He was placed in a cell with five other men. "Don't worry, we're right here. If anything starts up in here tonight, you'll be okay."

Duke knew what he was referring to. A cop in jail was a recipe for disaster.

"Is there anyone you need to call?"

"No. I've already called my lawyer. He'll be here in the morning."

"Have you talked to Melissa?"

"I tried calling her a couple of times today, but I didn't get an answer. I was calling from an unknown number, though. Went straight to voicemail."

"Rumor is she's in Costa Rica with her mom. At least that's what I heard someone saying at The Keg the other night."

"Oh, okay."

"I'm sure she wants to talk. She loves you, man."

"We'll see."

"Night. Glad you finally turned yourself in."

"I was waiting on the bastard in the other cell to get caught first."

"Hope we got the right guy."

"You did."

"Night."

Duke nodded and took a seat on the cold, hard bench.

Chapter Twenty-Eight

After we were all checked out by the doctors and released, we settled in at the hotel. We showered, swam, relaxed in the hot tub, ate pizza, and all piled into one bed for movie time. The officer was right. The children were so resilient!

As everyone began to fall asleep, I began making plans for the future.

The first call would be to Providence Hospital.

"Hi. Can you please ring the room of Chandler Grey?"

"One moment, please."

"Hello?" Chandler's voice was weak, but it was his voice.

"Hey, Chandler. It's Braydee."

"Braydee. You're safe?"

"I'm safe thanks to you. I owe you so much."

"You owe me nothing. I wanted to help you. I could see the pain in your eyes. I knew something was terribly wrong."

"The nightmare is over because you took a chance. I just can't believe you would do that for a total stranger."

"Do you feel like we're total strangers? Because I don't. I was connected to you from the moment you walked into my office, looking for the break room." He chuckled and then grimaced at the pain of laughing.

"Honestly, I've never felt more connected to a person in my life. I couldn't even speak properly the day I met you."

"I noticed. It was cute."

I blushed through the phone, and I was sure he was imagining my skin turning a new shade of pink.

"It was embarrassing."

We both spoke the words at the same time.

"I want to see you." We laughed, and it felt so good. So normal.

"I'm leaving for Alabama tomorrow or Friday, but I'll be back."

"Can I go with you?" It was the most forward thing he could ever remember saying to a woman.

"I would love that, but would you be able to travel so far? Are they releasing you tomorrow?"

"I was kidding. The doctor said I was so lucky the way the bullets went in, but no, I'll be here for a while. At least a week. I just wanted to see what you would say."

"Well, I said yes, and I meant it."

"Any chance I could see you before you leave tomorrow? Just a few minutes?"

"I don't think so. I have six girls with me. I have so much to get together within the next few days for us to head out."

"Us?"

"Oh, yes. They're road-tripping with me. No chance I'm letting them out of my sight."

"Oh, wow! I understand. Do what you have to do, and I'll see you when you get back," said Chandler.

"That sounds good. Can't wait!"

"And I can't wait to meet the girls."

Braydee smiled.

Chandler smiled.

"Talk to you soon."

"Wait. How will I get in touch with you when I get out of here?"

"I'll get a phone tomorrow."

We exchanged cell numbers.

"Okay, bye, Braydee."

"'Bye."

We hung up with such a sense of peace and comfort in our hearts.

Morning came, and there was much to do. I explained everything to the girls.

"Guess where we're going first?" They were giddy with excitement. "First, we're going to my house. I want you guys to see where I live."

"How far away is it?"

"Literally five minutes away."

"Why didn't we stay there last night?"

"Well, the officer already had the hotel booked for us as a special treat."

"Then what are we doing?"

I knew from experience that the questions could go on forever.

"The first stop is my house where we'll pick up my car."

"You have a house and a car?" Lexi seemed truly surprised.

"Yes, I do, and guess what, it has a third row and we'll all fit." When I bought the Buick Enclave, I bought it with the intention of needing enough space to travel across the country. I never imagined I would be traveling across the country with six children. The thought was exhilarating.

Arrangements were made for officers to drop us off at my home. I found out later that my parents had been paying the bills and keeping everything up to date in case I returned. It had only been less than two months, but it felt like a lifetime.

My three-bedroom, two-thousand-square-foot home, suddenly felt like a mansion. After several hours of visiting my home, we loaded up and headed to Orange Beach, Alabama.

"Our first stop is Verizon for a phone for me and one for Nikki as a backup communication. The second stop is Providence Hospital," I said.

"Why are we going to the hospital?"

"Because I want you all to meet the man who saved our lives."

"How did he save us?"

"I gave him a note explaining how much trouble we were all in. The bad men found out and shot him. They thought he was dead, but he called my mom and told her to send help for us."

"You have a mom?" Katrina's little inquisitive eyes pulled me in another direction.

"Yes, baby. I have a wonderful mom, and you will meet her very soon. She and my dad are going to join us at the beach!"

The girls took the news of meeting my parents with great excitement.

The seven of us rode the elevator up to the sixth floor and everyone knocked on Chandler's door together.

"Come in."

We pushed open the door and Chandler greeted us with his warm, beautiful smile. He raised the head of his bed so we could talk.

"Hello, ladies! This is a surprise. I'm so happy to meet you!"

The girls circled around his bed, and I grabbed his hand.

"I just needed to see you in person to thank you. We all wanted to thank you," I said.

The girls began telling him thank you, each in her own way. Everyone was so chatty and full of life. I had never seen them so excited. They talked about our beach trip, dogs, cats, and everything in between. There was such a spirit of gratitude for what Chandler had done for them.

"I can't wait to celebrate with all of you. As soon as I get out of here, we're going to do something so fun!"

Baily reached out and grabbed his other hand.

"You're a real live hero. Like Superman, really."

"No, I'm not. I'm just an ordinary guy trying to do the right thing when I can."

"You're anything but ordinary," I said. I pulled his hand to my lips and kissed it. Baily pulled the other hand to her lips and kissed it.

Lexi said, "I think Miss Braydee likes you," and all the girls giggled.

We visited until the nurse told us we would have to leave, then we reluctantly said our goodbyes.

Pulling out of the hospital parking lot, I could feel a part of me being left behind. Without a doubt, I knew I wanted to know everything I could about Chandler Grey. I knew I wanted him in my life forever.

It was late Saturday night when we arrived in Orange Beach, Alabama. I had greatly underestimated the amount of time it took to travel with children. We checked into our beach house and spent some time on the beach with flashlights, looking for crabs. Tonight, I would rest my mind because tomorrow would be brutal.

Melissa and her mom boarded a plane headed back to Alabama. Their trip had been cut short by the news of her dad being arrested. They prayed to God it wasn't true, but their gut was telling them that something evil had invaded their family.
"Mom, I'm scared." She whispered as she held her mom's hand on the plane.
"I know you are. So am I. Life, as we know it, is about to change. Do you know how much I love your father?"
"Yes, of course. With all your heart, just like I love him with all my heart. I just don't want to see you hurt. That's all."
"We share way more love and good times than pain. I don't let his moments of rage define our relationship."
"Do you even understand how backward this is? If it was me, he was hitting, would you have stayed with him and made excuses?"
"Of course not! I'm not making excuses."
"Yes, you are. You tolerate his bad behavior because it's all you know."
Her mom began to sob. "That's not it, Melissa. I'm scared. I'm scared of him."
"You told me you were scared of trying to live life alone at your age." She put her arm around her mom and tried to comfort her.

"I'm scared of that, too, but I'm more scared that he wouldn't let me leave. He's told me as much."

"I had no idea," said Melissa.

"There's a lot you don't know, but I do love him. I feel so ashamed of saying these things now, while he's locked up. I'm just making a bad thing worse. I don't mean to unload like this."

"Mom, stop. It's me you're talking to. You can say anything. I get it. We understand each other." She leaned over and gave her mom a kiss on the cheek.

"We do, don't we? I love you, Missy."

"I love you, Mommy." They smiled at each other and held hands as they prayed for the strength to face whatever chaos they were flying home to.

Chapter Twenty-Nine

After settling in at the Airbnb in Gulf Shores, the girls and I met Det. Knotts and Capt. Marshall at the station.

"Do you girls want to come in here and do some drawing and coloring while we talk to Miss Braydee?" Everyone nodded, but I knew they were uncomfortable leaving me.

"I'll be right back. I promise." Again, they nodded.

I was led to a private area. I began to describe in detail everything that had transpired, from seeing Lucy and chasing the car, to being transported to Texas and destroying the security cameras at the property at "the farm". The officers recorded me and took notes.

"Did you know there was drone footage of you and the girls at the house where you were being held?"

"Seriously? No, I didn't know."

"We received a tip that a boy spotted the words 'Help Us' formed out of clothes near the house. The clothes that were used to form those letters were taken in for DNA testing. The sad thing is that only one child was listed as missing. We had DNA submitted by the parents from Marlea, but no one else has reached out anywhere to report one of those kids missing. We've reached out to social services in Texas to locate the families they were staying with."

"I believe it. It makes me sick to my stomach, but I believe it. Those are the kind of kids that get taken. The ones who are already on the streets. Even the foster care system is a problem."

"Especially runaways."

"Yes. I had no idea the drone saw our call for help. That's unbelievable. This has all been such a whirlwind. I haven't been able to process everything yet."

"I understand completely. You've experienced the worst of humanity and survived it! We hate for you to have to conjure up such awful memories, but we have some people in custody here that we need you to take a look at."

"Okay. Will they see me?"

"No. They can't see you. They'll be in a lineup of men, and you just point if you see anyone that had anything to do with your disappearance or your captivity."

"Okay."

"Are you ready?"

"Yes. I think so."

"Follow me then, Miss Braydee."

I stepped into a room with a large, mirrored window. In front of me were two of the faces that had changed my life forever.

"Him. That's the guy who called me into his office at Braxton. He told me if I didn't do what I was brought there to do that he would chop up the girls and send them to the four corners of the world. He knocked me to the ground at one point for being disrespectful. I think his name is John."

"Thank you."

"Do you know him?"

"Yes. He's a local judge. His name is John Sands."

"Him." I pointed at another man Infront of me. "That's the guy who helped put the zip ties on me and put me in the van. He was in a police car with the number 428 on the side.

"That's a pretty good memory. That's his squad car number."

"I have repeated that number over and over in my head. I was trying to remember everything I could in case I survived."

"You did well. I'm going to take your statement, and you'll be free to go."

"You're not going to let them get out on bail, are you?" The thought of them walking the streets was terrifying.

"No. This is too high profile, and the judge is too powerful in this county. We'll keep him until he goes to trial."

"Thank God, and when do you think that could be?"

"We're in the process of building our case, but it could easily be a year from now. He'll lawyer up with the best he can find, but we have a solid case against him."

"Thank God."

"We appreciate you coming all this way. I think that's it for us. If there's anything else, we'll give you a call.

"The girls and I are going to get busy building sandcastles." I wasn't going to let this monster steal one more day of my joy.

"Enjoy your time here. Be blessed."

As I stood up, I felt physically weak from reliving everything that had happened. My heart ached to think that none of the girls had been missed by their families, but truthfully, it was a relief. There would be no one I needed to fight for them.

Melissa and her mom passed Braydee in the hallway as she left. Braydee had no idea who the women were, but they both knew exactly who she was. John Sands sat handcuffed at the table waiting for his family. No one had shared any information about why and how John had been arrested. All they knew was that Capt. Marshall said he had been taken into custody.

"Hey, Daddy."

"Hey, Baby. Don't believe a word you hear. It's all lies."

"Hey, John."

"I'm so sorry you two are being put through this."

"What do they have on you?"

"Nothing. It's that damned husband of yours in the next cell, Melissa. He's trying to bring me down with him!"

"The next cell? Duke is here?"

"What? You didn't know he turned himself in?"

"Are you serious right now?"

Melissa left her dad and went to ask the guard about it.

"Yeah, he's here. I thought you were coming to see him, then remembered your dad was here. Aw, man. Sorry I didn't mean to sound brash."

"It's fine. I had no idea Duke was here. Can you take me to him?"

"Sure. This way. Wait right here. I'll bring him to you."

Duke couldn't believe his eyes when he saw Melissa standing there. Tears fell and he wiped his eyes with handcuffed wrists.

"You're here," he said.

"So are you," she replied.

"Yep. I swear on my life I didn't know what your dad was up to. Please believe me."

"What was he up to?"

"He was organizing the kidnapping of girls and women."

"And how do you know this?"

"He pulled me into a "secret operation" and that was to shred the tires of the woman, Braydee Quinn. I thought she was some high-stakes criminal. That's not all. His hitman was sent to kill me, but luckily, I overpowered him and zip-tied him. I took him out on your dad's boat, and he confessed to all kinds of crazy things that your dad had him doing."

"Where's this hitman?"

"Dead."

"That's convenient."

"I know how this all sounds. He told me where some things were hidden on the boat and when I went to find them, he jumped overboard. I swear on my life. Crazy. You've got to believe me."

Melissa felt numb once again. She knew Duke, and she could tell he was telling the truth. Her knees buckled, and she took a seat.

"Duke. My heart is so broken right now. I can't even comprehend half of what you just said."

"I know. I just need you to believe me when I say I know I did wrong by taking that girl's ring."

"And by giving one to me."

"I'm so ashamed. I got caught up in being the one who helped in a secret operation. I thought those girls were some awful people I had just caught. The guy handed me the rings and, well, I can't even believe it myself. Stupid."

He shook his head and stared at the floor.

"It was so stupid. But honestly, I'm glad you did because it led us to this moment. If what you're saying is true, then you taking the rings exposed something in our own backyard."

"Literally," said Duke.

"I want to believe you didn't know you were helping kidnap the girls, because if that's true, there's hope for me and you."

"It's true. We can survive this. Do you still love me?"

"Of course, I do, with all my heart."

"Then we can make it. That's all I needed to hear from you."

"But, if it's true, I can't face my dad. I'm so lost right now. I don't think I can even look at him again knowing this."

"He's not who we thought he was. He's a very bad man, Melissa."

"If this is true, he's an evil creep, and I'm ashamed he's, my dad!"

"I wish I could hold you. I'm so sorry, Melissa."

"I wish you could, too." They sat in silence not knowing what to say. "I've got to go, Duke. I'm feeling so and I think I'm going to throw up. I love you."

"I love you. I swear if you will just keep the faith, I won't let you down again. You'll see."

"You'll have to prove it and that takes time."

"I'll prove it to you. I swear. Just don't give up on me."

She walked back into the room where her mom was visiting with her dad.

"Mom. I feel sick. We need to go. I'm about to throw up."

John growled at her. "Did you go see that rat down the hall?"

"Can you just shut up, Dad? Just shut the hell up! There I said it. Sit on your hands and shut up for a change." Melissa didn't say goodbye to her dad. She just stepped outside the room and waited for her mom.

Once they were in the car, Melissa told her mom everything Duke had told her. Rhonda listened without interrupting.

"I'm sorry I lost it like that. I'm just so tired of hearing Dad put Duke down. He's done it throughout our entire marriage, even before. After hearing what Duke said, I couldn't stop myself."

"Melissa, you're taking the words of your husband over the words of your dad. He said they are all lies, and I believe him."

"Seriously Mom?"

"Until it can be proven, I believe him."

"The truth will come out eventually. I don't want this to come between us. We have no idea what they have on him."

"Then let's not discuss it anymore."

"I'm sorry, Mom. So very sorry."

"I'm sorry for you."

"We'll get through this," said Melissa.

"We always do. I love you."

Rhonda patted her daughter's leg. "I love you."

Chapter Thirty

I asked Mom and Dad to come meet the girls and help me out on our vacation. They arrived in Orange Beach just a few days after we did. Everyone was busy playing and watching TV in the living room of the Airbnb when they walked in.

As I ran into my mom and dad's arms, a rush of emotion washed over me, and I felt as if I could barely stand. My tears flowed for the first time uncontrollably, and I sobbed like a baby on her shoulder.

Mom's hand rubbed circles on my back, and I could feel peace coursing through my veins. I have no idea how long we stood there all holding each other... Maybe it was a few seconds or maybe a few minutes. I had left my body completely, and time was meaningless.

Feeling their arms around me was euphoric. At times I thought I would never see them again, and here they were surrounded by six children that were about to become family to us. I had already told my parents my plans to adopt the girls before they arrived, and they were ecstatic!

"Mom, Dad, meet everyone." I smiled and nodded to the girls.

One by one, the girls introduced themselves. I had them lined up by age. Nikki, thirteen. Baily, eleven. Clara, eight. Jill and Lexi, seven, and Katrina, five.

"I'm so glad to meet you!" Katrina did a curtsey and there were a few giggles.

"What do you want us to call you?" asked Lexi.

"What would you like to call me?"

"Can we call you granny?"

"Of course! And you can call him Paw Paw." She giggled.

My dad laughed so hard at Mom being called granny.

My mom couldn't get enough of them, and they couldn't get enough of her. My heart ached at the thought of any of them being reclaimed by a parent or guardian and being separated from us.

Our ten days at the beach were beyond anything I could have dreamed of. I had enjoyed so many fun girls' trips and vacations but listening to the laughter of the children and watching them play together, and building sandcastles for the first time, was something on another level. I could feel a sense of fullness in my heart. It filled a deep empty space that I didn't even realize was there.

There was only one thing that would make it all so much better. Chandler. I couldn't stop thinking about him. I woke up, wondering if he was thinking about me. I went to bed, wishing he were lying next to me. He was the other missing part of my life.

It had been over a week since we had said our goodbyes at the hospital, and then ... he called.

"Braydee?"

"Hey, Chandler! I was just thinking about you."

It rolled off my tongue so easily. I didn't want to say I had never stopped thinking about him.

"Really? Well, that makes me happy." He smiled. "They released me today. I'm headed home now. I had you on my mind and just wanted to make sure you were okay."

"Everything is going well my way. I can't even believe I'm saying that."

"I'm sure it'll take a while to soak in. Are you still coming back to Texas?"

"Of course, I am. My home is there, I still have a job at Baylor, I hope." I chuckled nervously.

"Okay, good. Don't forget I'm still here as well!"

I could tell he was grinning and oh, how I loved that grin.

"Let me start over. Of course, I'm coming back. I need to see you."

"That's much better. I like that."

Flirting with him felt so natural and perfect.

"Are the girls loving the beach?"

"So much! My parents came in and I quickly became second fiddle. They're having the best time together. To see them now, you would never imagine what they've been through."

"Do you believe in destiny? I mean, like divine intervention and fate?"

"With all my heart. The dots that had to be connected for me to find these girls and for me to find..." I stopped just short of saying 'you'.

"And for me to find you?" He finished the sentence for me and laughed. It's okay to feel some kind of way right now. It's happening for me too."

"I still can't believe the way I lost my words when you spoke to me for the first time. That was crazy So embarrassing."

"You have an excuse though. Those were some pretty unusual circumstances to be meeting someone."

"True."

"You were adorable though. I think that's when I knew I was smitten." When was the last time he had used the word adorable?

"You're smitten? Really?"

"Um, pretty much. I just risked my life for you."

"I can truly say I owe you, my life."

"You don't owe me anything."

"This is going to sound crazy, Chandler, but I need to ask you something."

"Nothing is going to sound crazy. I swear. After what we just went through, bring it on."

"Okay. I'm not the kind of woman that plays games or hooks up. I was married before, and I loved being married. I just want to be upfront with you so that we don't waste time with each other or disappoint one another later."

"I get it. I was married before as well, and I loved my wife completely. She and my daughter were everything to me."

"You have a daughter?"

"I had a daughter. I had no intention of this phone conversation getting too heavy. I was hoping to really get to know you before opening up this way."

"Same. But if we're both feeling something special, let's just put it all on the line."

He took a deep breath and began. "My wife committed suicide after she had a car wreck that killed our daughter."

I wasn't expecting that.

"Oh, Chandler. I'm so sorry."

"I'll never completely recover from that, but for the first time since losing them, you came along and have made me feel something so great, it's surpassing everything sad inside me."

There was a long pause. I felt overwhelmed with emotion. Happy, sad, excitement, wonderment. Everything at once.

"I get it. From the first day I met you, it was like our souls were meant to collide."

"Exactly and when I didn't see you for a few days, I felt incomplete. Is this too much for a first phone call?" He laughed. "I swear I was just calling to check in with you."

"You don't have to apologize. I wanted to know how you felt. But since you're feeling the same way, I am, I wanted to tell you something. I can't have children."

"I'm sorry. I know that's so hard for you."

"It's been hard. My ex-husband left me because he didn't want to adopt. I'm okay though. I recovered from the divorce, but I never recovered from the pain of not having kids. That's one of the many reasons I'm going to try to adopt these children. All of them. This is a whole new start for me. I feel like I've been born again into a new life. One that I could have never dreamed of. I didn't want us to put in time together and not be on the same page. I've done nothing but think of taking care of these girls for the last sixty days."

I waited briefly for his response.

"And I would support you and help you take care of them for the rest of our lives if that's where our relationship leads. I promise you," he said. "My heart is so full. I've gone through the worst of times to get to the best of times. I've heard so many people talk about how they believed God had ordered their steps but never truly felt that until now."

"Exactly. I began to really seek God in the years after my divorce. I have prayed for direction every single day since my ex walked out. Every step I have taken from planning my vacation to stopping in at The Undertow, has led me to this moment. You have no idea how happy I am right now."

"I think I have an idea of how happy you are. I feel alive for the first time in many years."

I blushed. I didn't want to get off the phone, but two little girls ran in the room with buckets and sand shovels in hand bouncing around with excitement. I knew it was time to head to the beach.

"We have so much to talk about, and I'll see you in a few days. I need to go because I have some excited little girls jumping on me right now. Tell Mr. Chandler hello." The girls yelled out to him.

"Can't wait to see you all! When will you be home?"

"We're heading to Texas in three days, and it will take us another two days to get there at the speed we travel. Lots of bathroom and snack breaks with six girls."

"OK, be careful. I'll see you soon but call me when you get free. Anytime is a good time. I'll be off work for a few more weeks."

"I can't wait to see you, Chandler. Truly. I can hardly wait."

"Be safe and come home!"

Come home. Come home. The words rang in my ears, and I felt more comfort and love than I could ever put into words.

The day before we were scheduled to leave Gulf Shores, I asked my mom to watch the girls. There was something I needed to do. I pulled my hair back in a ponytail, put on a large brim brown hat and thick sunglasses and headed to the jail where John Sands was being held. I had made an appointment for twelve-thirty to visit him.

Pulling up to the jail, my body trembled. I didn't have anything to say to the man. I just wanted to look him in the eyes and let him see me walking free. I was afraid that if I got too close to him, I would spit in his face. I didn't want that visual image to haunt me and I was sure that seeing him would awaken a rage monster inside me.

I walked into the station.

"Hello, ma'am. How can I help you?"

"I was coming to visit an inmate, but I've changed my mind. Do you have a piece of paper and a pen? I'd like to just leave a letter for him if that's possible."

"Absolutely. Here you go."

Hello, John,

As you read this letter, you're locked behind bars, and I am walking free. Oh, the irony. I'll never forget your greasy, red, ruddy face, your nasty breath, and the half-cocked eye that looked past me as you slapped my face at Braxton.

That's right, it's me. Braydee Quinn. Were you wondering what they had on you? Well, let's see. Maybe you don't remember what you said to me, but I remember it perfectly.

I remember the phone call you took from your wife. I heard your name that day, John. The girls you had locked up are with me. They're safe now. You aren't safe though, but I guess you know that now.

The tides have turned, John. Lady Justice is coming for you. I don't think you're going to like what she looks like. She's strong, mighty, and ready to chop you into tiny pieces and ship you to the four corners of the earth. I hope you're an organ donor; I don't foresee prison being too kind to someone like you.

Oh, to be a fly on the wall as you read this. As your heart races and the desire to put me in my place rages, I hope you will visualize me spitting in your face every day for the rest of your life. However long short that may be.

See you in court.

Braydee

My hands wrote the words without my mind even realizing exactly what I was saying. I folded the paper and handed it to the clerk.

"Can you give this to John Sands, please?"

"I certainly will."

It was my little form of revenge.

It didn't feel good to write a note like that.

IT FELT GREAT!

Six Months Later

Chandler sat on the park bench with all the girls waiting for Braydee to arrive. Nikki held a picnic basket full of sandwiches and chips. Baily had a box of cheese and crackers. Lexi had the desserts. Clara sat on an ice chest full of water bottles and champagne.

Braydee approached the group of smiling faces.

"Hello, my people! This is certainly a surprise."

"It was all Chandler's idea," said Katrina.

"Yep, all my idea. Let's go over here under this big tree."

Briefly, ever so briefly, my mind shifted to the park where I had helped take Marlea. I shook it from my thoughts. I wouldn't let this beautiful day be marred with a bad memory like that. I prayed for God to clear my head and keep me focused. It was a daily prayer.

We opened the blanket and started to lay out the picnic.

"Hey, Braydee! The girls and I have a question."

"What is it?"

Everyone jumped down on one knee, and Chandler pulled out a ring. In unison, everyone yelled, "Will you marry me?"

My mouth fell open and stayed that way.

"Yes, yes, yes!! I'll marry you!!"

Everyone jumped and cheered. We all held hands and began to spontaneously walk in a circle. I started to cry. I was so happy, but I wondered if, at that moment, anyone else was having a flashback to "the secret circle."

I saw tears in Nikki's eyes, and I didn't think they were happy tears. I was afraid to ask. I didn't want to ruin the moment but one of the other girls didn't mind asking her what was wrong.

"Are you ok Nikki?" Katrina grabbed her hand and gently caressed it.

"I'm happy but afraid of us not staying together."

"Nikki," I held her face in my hands. "We're a family and we always will be. You're never going to be able to get rid of me. I'm yours for life." I kissed her on the forehead, and she smiled.

"You promise?"

"I promise!"

We sat on the blanket, giddy and happy and laughing. We all began discussing the wedding and planning what it would be like.

Chandler interrupted. "I want to get married today."

"Are you serious?" I was ready - I had been ready - but I didn't know he was.

"I know you're in the process of adopting the girls, and if we're going to get married one day, I don't want us having a bunch of different last names. I want this to be the Grey family."

"Oh, I love that so much!"

"We're going to be the Grey family!" exclaimed Jill.

"I love it, too," everyone chimed in.

We finished our picnic and immediately headed to the courthouse where we were married with six witnesses. Witnesses who would soon be our children with our last name.

Chapter Thirty-One

Duke's trial lasted for three days. Phone records showed multiple incoming calls from an unknown number. The location was traced to the courthouse where John worked.

Braydee testified that Duke made mention of her being a criminal "in custody" when he was securing her wrists with the zip-ties. Braydee told them that he took great care to make sure her arm was bandaged before the van took off. She also testified that he genuinely seemed to be unaware of his role in the plan and was handed the rings by one of the other guys.

The bartender, Jenn, who had seen Duke the night of the kidnapping, testified that Duke said he "thought something was off" with an assignment his father-in-law had him doing.

Melissa testified on Duke's behalf that she had seen her dad visibly angry and arguing with Duke at the BBQ and that she had never seen anything like it between her dad and Duke.

The post office had records showing that the post office box containing the cash and rings belonged to John, and it had only recently been used by Duke.

Whit testified that when Duke came by the night after the kidnappings, he said he had been on a secret mission and couldn't discuss it, and that was all he knew.

Altogether, the evidence convinced the jury that Duke was unaware of any nefarious activities and had acted out of respect for his father-in-law. The jury was convinced that Duke had no knowledge of any human trafficking activity.

He was sentenced to three years' probation and suspended from the police force for taking the rings and using the police car for activity outside of specific assignments.

As months turned into a year, John Sands sat in jail waiting for his day in court. With bail set so high, and everyone close to him afraid to let him free, he had no choice but to sit and wait.

As evidence against him mounted, a conviction was becoming increasingly inevitable. There were ten years of phone records between him and Gavin Mateo, the CEO of Braxton Therapeutics. The flight records of private airplanes to Waco for nearly a decade were incriminating, as well. In addition, there were videos of him with the missing officer, who he'd said he didn't personally know. There were records and pictures of the two of them eating together on a trip to Waco, and a bank account with several million dollars in it that couldn't be accounted for on a judge's salary.

There was DNA evidence of missing girls obtained from the boat, including the shoes of Kasey Kendall, who thankfully had been found.

John Sands watched smugly as Judge Diana Ogletree took her seat and called the court to order. Although the two of them weren't in the same circle of friends, they knew of each other. The judge glanced up at the defendant and he winked at her.

"Mr. Sands, I suggest you keep yourself in check throughout this entire process. I'm not your buddy or your friend, and I would appreciate you showing a little more respect for the situation you're in."

No one saw the wink, so everyone was confused about exactly where the judge was going with her commentary. John didn't respond.

"Do you understand?" bellowed the judge.

John gave a half nod.

"A nod is not an answer. I said do you understand?"

"Yes." It took everything for John to swallow his pride and respond politely to the judge.

Duke stepped onto the witness stand.

"Do you swear to tell the truth, the whole truth and nothing but the truth, so help you God?"

"I do."

The lawyer jumped right in.

"Why did you put tire shredders down the night Braydee was kidnapped?"

"My father-in-law, John Sands, called me one day and said he wanted to talk to me about something. He told me he had a special assignment that he needed me to do. No one was to know about it. He told me where and when to be there, and I did it."

"Why would you just show up and do something without having any details?"

"Because I loved and respected John. I wanted him to respect me as well. It was the first time he had ever asked me to do something for him."

"And you liked the way that felt?"

"Of course. Until then, the two of us had never even met for lunch."

"He asked you to meet him for lunch?"

"Yes."

"Where did you go to eat?"

"We had oysters at Acme."

"When was that?"

"May 23. I remember because my friend Janese Purves waited on us, and she said it was her birthday."

"And your friend Janese is here today to verify that. Is that correct?"

"Yes."

"Has your father-in-law ever asked you to do anything involving police work?"

"Never. We aren't close like that. John and I spoke only at family functions."

"So, for the first time in your life, you're suddenly going to be in the good ole boys club if you do this for him."

"Objection! Leading the witness."

"Sustained."

"Let me rephrase it. How did it make you feel when John came to you asking you to do this very secret thing for him that involved catching fugitives?"

"I was ecstatic. I was never his pick for his daughter. I always fell short of his expectations, and he made that clear on numerous occasions. I thought if I pulled this off, he would ask me to do more things for him, and I would gain his respect. Hopefully, it would make us closer."

"Makes complete sense to me. Did he pay you for this?"

"Yes. He gave me five thousand dollars two weeks before Ms. Quinn was kidnapped. I put it in a post office box that John had gotten for me."

"You left that much cash at the post office? That doesn't seem smart at all."

"Yes, I agree. I thought it was crazy. I had it wrapped up nicely. It wasn't going to be there long, and I was trying to keep it hidden from Melissa. I was going to move it as soon as I could."

"I'm confused. Why would you use the post office, when you could have hidden it somewhere in your house?"

"I didn't want to take a chance on Melissa finding it. John suggested the post office. Probably his arrogant way of hiding something in plain sight."

"Objection."

"Sustained. Stick to the questions you are asked."

"Why didn't you tell your wife that her dad wanted you to do something for him?" asked the lawyer.

"I didn't want to break the trust bond. I had made a promise to John."

"Tell me about the day you realized you had helped kidnap a woman."

"I was freaking out. I approached John at a cookout trying to get details. He wouldn't tell me what was going on. Things got heated between us."

"When they found your fingerprints on the car, what was the first thing you did?"

"I reached out to John. I hoped he would have an answer. Some words of advice."

"What did he say?"

"He asked me to meet him at an abandoned boat slip in Perdido Key. We had met there once before. He said no one was to know about it."

"What happened when you got there?"

"John's boat was sitting there, and I was attacked by someone he sent to kill me."

"What happened?"

"I overpowered him and stuck him with a sedative he was holding. I zip-tied him and took him out on the boat. That's where he told me about John."

"What did he say?"

"That John had helped him get out of prison in exchange for working for him and that John was running a massive human trafficking ring along the coast."

"Objection your honor. That's hearsay."

The questioning continued until finally it was Melissa's turn. Stepping into the witness stand was the hardest thing she would ever face.

"Have you ever seen any violence that would lead you to believe your husband could kidnap someone?"

"No. Never."

"What about your dad? Have you ever seen him get violent?" Just like that, she was forced to face the demons her family had hidden for so long.

Melissa sat quietly. She looked at her mom sitting there still wanting to believe it wasn't true but knowing in her heart it was. She looked at her dad. The only dad she had ever known. It was bad enough that he could possibly be going to prison for the rest of his life, but to say he had a history of beating his wife over the years, would only humiliate her mom and destroy what little bit of dignity they had left.

"Mrs. Davis? Can you answer the question? Did you ever see your dad get violent with your mom?"

"No." Her eyes darted towards Captain Marshall. He knew the truth, and he shook his head wondering why she would protect her dad after she had already told him her dad was abusive to her mom.

"No, you never saw him, or it never happened?"

"He loves my mom with all his heart, and she loves him."

Tears fell from her mom's eyes as she looked at the tissues in her hand, too weak to wipe her own eyes. The pain was unbearable. Rhonda clenched the back of the bench and slowly pulled herself up. Leaning on the bench for support so that she wouldn't fall, she began to speak.

"He beat me."

Everyone stared with mouths open as Rhonda spoke again. "He beat me!" she yelled louder.

"Shut up, Rhonda!" John Sands angrily shouted the words before he could stop himself.

"Order in this court!" Judge Ogletree banged her gavel repeatedly over the murmurs and sounds in the courtroom. "Mrs. Sands. Please take your seat. Your time will come."

Melissa and her mom locked eyes and through a beam only visible between mother and daughter a sense of relief was felt. No more hiding behind the curtain of shame. It was finally time for her mother to be seen.

"Melissa, why did you lie to this court?" asked the lawyer.

"I was protecting my mom, not my dad."

"How is allowing someone to beat your mom protecting her?" asked the judge.

The words rang in her ears and somehow made all those years of staying silent seem ludicrous.

Melissa looked at the jury.

"I'm sorry. I lied to you. My mom has spent her entire life hiding the bruises. I didn't want to be the one to make it public like this. I'm so very sorry." She choked back her desire just to lay her head down and cry. Instead, she glared at her dad and held her head high.

"I've seen the best in this man, and I've seen the worst. But if I can officially change my answer, yes, he has beaten my mom many times over the years."

Rhonda held her eyes on her daughter, but she saw John staring at her from her peripheral vision. It was finally out in the open. No more hiding the sins of her husband with makeup and scarves. No more canceling dinner dates with friends until she recovered. She was finally free from the bondage he had inflicted on her for decades.

The last person on the stand was Braydee. The questioning began.

"Do you see the man who was holding you hostage."

"Yes, I do."

"Will you point to him?"

Braydee stood up and began to step down from the witness stand.

"Miss Braydee, you can point to him from there. Take your seat. No need to... Miss Quinn!"

Within seconds Braydee had crossed the room and slapped his pudgy red face as hard as she could."

The fat on his face rippled and for a moment she thought his cock eye had straightened. He grunted and attempted to stand, but the guards had already made their way over to take control. An officer grabbed Braydee by both arms, and she didn't resist.

"That's him," she said.

The entire courtroom erupted with cheers, and the judge beat her gavel. "Order. Order! Settle down. Miss Braydee you're out of line!" She spoke loudly into her microphone over the unruly courtroom audience. When she finally made eye contact with Braydee, it didn't feel like the look was one of reprimand. Judge Ogletree had never seen anything like it in all her years of being on the bench.

"Miss Braydee. You will not disrupt this court again, or you will face a serious face or worse, jail time."

"I understand, judge, it won't happen again."

She was escorted back to the witness stand, and an officer stayed close by her.

In the back of the courtroom sat two heavy-set men in their mid-fifties. Braydee hadn't noticed them until she was on the stand looking out at the crowd. After the slap, one of them began to laugh loudly. Her mind raced back to The Undertow. To the place where it had all begun.

She could hear the laugh long after the cheers subsided; long after the judge had quieted the courtroom. It was the laugh she had heard from the kidnapper. The sound of a car with a dead battery. Her eyes went to the back of the courtroom. She breathed in deeply and slowly exhaled. She didn't want to give away her excitement.

"Judge Ogletree, I need to tell you something."

"Okay."

"I can't say it out loud."

The judge leaned in, and Braydee whispered in her ear.

"The two men in the ball caps sitting in the back of the courtroom, far right, are the two men I followed out of the bar the night I was kidnapped. They put Lucy in the trunk and they're the ones who transported me from Orange Beach to Texas."

"You're sure?"

"Yes. I'm one hundred percent sure. I'll never forget that look or that laugh. One of them has a tattoo on his arm."

"Draw it for me if you can." She handed her a piece of paper, and she did the best she could at drawing a mermaid drinking a beer. Underneath it, she wrote, "This is supposed to be a mermaid drinking a beer."

"Thank you."

Judge Ogletree made an announcement to the courtroom. "Everyone please remain seated. I need an officer at the back door, please." She made a phone call to get extra security in the courtroom and officers arrived within minutes.

Orders were given for the two men to be arrested. Cops quickly surrounded the men and handcuffed them. They were shocked. The loud murmuring of the crowd had reached an unacceptable level.

"Everyone, please remain calm."

Braydee spoke into the microphone. "I hope you two rot in hell!" It was louder than she expected, and she knew she was in trouble.

"Not another word, Miss Braydee. This is your last warning. I promise you."

Braydee nodded. John turned around to see who was being escorted out. There were his two hatchet men. He shook his head in disbelief. Why were they in the courtroom? Idiots.

As order was called back into the courtroom, the questioning continued.

"How do you know for certain that this defendant is the one who had you kidnapped?"

"We met one day at the facility where they had me working. He made it clear he was in charge and that if I didn't do what I was told, he would chop up the children and send them to the four corners of the world."

The courtroom gasped.

"He said those words to you?"

"Yes. He slapped me so hard it knocked me to the ground."

Rhonda Sands nodded in her seat. She knew it was all true. Even Melissa didn't know some of the worst things he had said to her over the years.

"How did you find out his name was John?"

"His wife called several times during our meeting."

"Dumb bitch!" John blurted out. He didn't care. He knew his fate.

"She was talking loudly and was upset. She was asking him questions, and she said his name, John."

Rhonda straightened her spine and raised her chin proudly for the first time since the trial had started. She was the one who had given Braydee the information needed to identify John by calling him at the exact moment he was meeting with Braydee. Such a twist of fate.

After further questioning, Braydee took her seat.

"Finally, Judge, we have a video from a former police officer who says John tried to recruit him less than eighteen months ago." The district attorney held the remote, ready to click the play button.

"Do you have the name of this officer? Has the defense seen this?"

"Yes, the defense has a copy. We have spoken to the officer, but we need to hide his identity for his safety."

"Go ahead."

The slideshow began.

John held his breath and gritted his teeth. His temples pulsed.

There were candid photos of girls in cages and John Sands could be seen in the background. There was a picture of John on his boat with two girls on his lap.

The courtroom was silent, other than a few noises of disgust and sobs as they watched the video of John giving orders at the very house where Braydee had been held.

John Sands's fear of this video leak is what kept the officer alive.

John looked at his lawyer and stood up. "Let's save everyone some time and money here. I never thought this day would come."

He never thought it would come, because he always thought he was smarter and more cunning than any human alive.

"Are you changing your plea?"

"I am."

"You're what? I need to hear you say it."

"I'm guilty."

There was a very long moment of disgust as Judge Ogletree read the sentencing.

"I hereby sentence you to life in prison without the possibility of parole. There will be no death penalty for you. You will die a slow death in prison being held captive as you have held others over the years."

John looked back at his wife who was sitting next to Melissa. Tears were streaming from the eyes of both women. Melissa wrapped her arm around her mother and squeezed her tightly. The pain of what they were experiencing can only be described as a gut-wrenching loss, shock, and sickness that would take therapy and years to overcome. They watched as he shuffled out and wondered what he was feeling. That would be the last day either of them ever laid eyes on John Sands, the husband, dad, provider, child molester, and overall fraud. He was headed into a true pit of despair. Prison would be unbearable for a former judge.

Chandler squeezed Braydee's hand three times. It meant "I love you." She squeezed his hand back three times.

"I love you, too. It's over. It's really over," she said.

"Let's go home."

As they stepped outside the courthouse into the open air, Braydee looked at Chandler.

"I would do it all over again if it meant getting you and the girls."

"I know you would, Braydee. So would I."

He leaned in and kissed her on the top steps of the courthouse as reporters with cameras overtook them.

Headlines on the evening news showed John Sands being escorted out of the courtroom in handcuffs, followed by a picture of Braydee and Chandler kissing on the steps of the courthouse with the words "Souls Unite Under Unusual Circumstances". In the article, Braydee was quoted as saying, "If it wasn't for Lucy, I wouldn't have Chandler and the girls. God bless you Lucy, wherever you are."

Justice was served.

Braydee Grey and her entire family continue to work with national agencies to help fight human trafficking, which continues to grow around the world.

Nikki is enrolled at the University of Alabama and volunteers for a nonprofit organization working to rehabilitate survivors of sex trafficking.

Chandler works to support the family while Braydee homeschools the other children with the help of friends and family.

If you would like to donate in order to physically help rescue human trafficking victims, please check out COVENANT RESCUE www.covenantrescue.org

I personally know the men involved in the rescue operations, and they are trusted, dedicated individuals.

Despite increased awareness, international attention, and resources from states and other non-governmental institutions, human trafficking around the world continues to rapidly grow.

Made in United States
North Haven, CT
09 August 2025